D0843969

BLOOD
STAINED

An unputdownable crime thriller with a breathtaking twist

REBECCA BRADLEY

DI Claudia Nunn Book 1

JOFFE
BOOKS

Joffe Books, London
www.joffebooks.com

First published in Great Britain in 2021

Cover design by Nick Castle

ISBN: 978-1-78931-731-2

PROLOGUE

Fear climbed Ruth's spine.

He was standing directly behind her.

She pulled her hands out of the sink and suds floated into the air. The scent of lavender drifted under her nose, the sweet relaxing smell at odds with the tension taking hold of her body.

No one spoke or moved for what felt like an age.

The fear clawed at the base of her neck, sure-footed and certain in its ascent, like some small creature with needles for nails.

She had the memory of hiding under the covers as a child; if she couldn't see the monster, the monster couldn't see her, no matter how large her own outline. She was applying the same logic here. If she didn't turn around she was still safe. After all, she was in her own home, standing at the sink, clearing up. A mundane task, not something that would put her in the sights of a monster in this way.

And yet, here they were.

Ruth took a deep breath in. The fear now gripping her scalp. It had nowhere else to go. She had to do something.

She had to move.

He wouldn't allow her to stand here indefinitely. That was not why he was behind her. He had patience. She knew that. He was confident in what was going to happen and how it would play out. He didn't need to rush.

She realised her mind had seized up. She had done nothing but think about the washing up and her childhood bedroom. There had been no thoughts of escape, or of fighting. Though she would. She wouldn't go down without a fight. But fear had gripped her so tight in its vice that her mind had fled and she had frozen herself to the spot.

She exhaled.

And that's when she heard it.

He exhaled.

She spun around with the glass still in her hand.

She had a weapon. She could fight. She had no choice. She had too much life ahead of her yet.

His face was impassive. That scared her more than anything.

She expected to see the monster her mind had conjured up, but his face, it was quiet.

He took a step towards her, his hand outstretched and open. She turned to her right and ran, a scream about to leave her lips as his hand closed on her hair jerking her back, pulling her feet up from under her. Pain shot through from the roots of her hair to her eyes and she blinked back tears.

The glass flew up into the air as she landed with a thud on the floor at his feet. Her hip twisted beneath her and she grimaced as the shock vibrated through to her spine. The glass shattered at the side of her head, the sound loud in her ears. Shards embedded themselves into her arm and face, spreading into her skin like it was warm butter. Ruth winced at the one that sliced below her right eye. It could have blinded her had it been a few millimetres higher. Her weapon was now gone and instead turned on her.

His hand was still tight in her hair. He twisted it, increasing his grip. She cried out, a low complaint in the circumstances. He turned, bent over and straddled her. Face to face, he was so close she could smell the coffee on his breath. There was no coming back from this.

The fear that had gripped her only moments earlier sank into the pit of her stomach. She reared up, fists and feet flying. She caught him between his legs. He sank down onto her. Knees coming together, a small grunt of air leaving his mouth. It brushed her face, warm and sweet.

She could do this. She would resist. She would have headbutted him, but he still had such a tight grip of her hair she couldn't move her head. She punched out again and straightened her hips and pulled her knees up with as much force as she could muster, her breath coming strong and ragged. He leaned down close onto her to protect and gather himself. She continued to punch out and kick and squirm.

And then it came.

A blinding blow to the side of her head from a fist she didn't see coming. The whole side of her vision went dark and a searing flash of red-hot pain slipped behind her eye. She lifted a hand to the spot where damp now trickled down the side of her cheek.

'Stop fighting,' he grunted, his voice hot on her face and raspy over his throat. The first words to be spoken.

It would not help her if she stopped fighting. She had known the minute she felt him behind her that this was a to-the-end confrontation. His weight was on her and she was pinned down, unable to do anything to save herself. But she would fight back the minute he gave her room to manoeuvre.

He raised himself up, pushing his elbow into her shoulder. 'Stop fighting,' he growled again.

'Never,' she said. And she wouldn't. She wouldn't give in. She would fight to the death.

Her death.

CHAPTER 1

Claudia

Nine hours since Ruth's attack

DI Claudia Nunn tapped her foot on the grey patch of ground at Snig Hill police station in Sheffield and tried not to show her frustration. Her DCI, Maddison Sharpe, was not the kind of woman who would take kindly to a show of . . . what? What was it exactly she was feeling following Sharpe's request? Frustration possibly.

They were standing outside in the roughly put together wooden smokers' hut. Sharpe inhaled deeply, slim fingers gently caressing the disgusting tube she insisted on keeping a habit. Claudia hated cigarettes and in turn, hated being in the smokers' hut, but Sharpe had wanted to speak to her urgently and was also in need of a smoke, so they had ended up here. The smell of the cigarette was burning a hole of annoyance in Claudia's brain.

The shed was not exactly private. Anyone could come along and join them, though Sharpe would give them a stare and they would soon scuttle away. Sharpe reminded her of Cruella de Vil.

It was early April and the sky was mirroring the grey concrete below her feet, the very concrete she was tapping her foot against as she tried to think of a response to the request Sharpe had made.

'Don't you have anything to say, Claudia?' Sharpe exhaled. The smoke drifted across Claudia's eyeline.

She had the urge to wave her hand in the air to clear it away but restrained herself, instead shoving her hands deeper into her pockets.

'I'm not sure I'm the best person for the job if I'm honest, ma'am.'

Sharpe flicked the cigarette and the ash dropped gently to the ground. Sharpe didn't care if there were cigarette bins at the side of the shed they were standing in, if she wanted to drop her ash where she was standing then she would.

'I wouldn't have proposed you do it if I didn't think you were the right person.'

Claudia tapped her foot again.

Sharpe looked at her.

'It's a sensitive job and there are those above me who are nervous about the whole thing. If anything goes wrong and they end up with mud on their faces they won't be very happy. They seem to think that you will be the person best suited to do this.'

She paused. Sucked on the cigarette, inhaled, looked up at the leaden sky, exhaled and peered at Claudia.

'I happen to agree with them. You're a brilliant interviewer, Claudia. Please don't sell yourself short.'

A short sharp laugh burst from Claudia's lips before she could stop it. Sharpe narrowed her eyes.

'I'm sorry,' Claudia said quickly. 'It's not that I don't think I'm qualified for the job. I'm well aware of my qualities.'

Sharpe lifted an eyebrow.

'I'm not going to be coy here. We both know I excel at my job, I'm not on the fast-track promotion scheme for nothing. That's not what this is about and well you know it.'

Sharpe exhaled one last time and flicked her cigarette onto the ground. She stepped forward and twisted the tip of her pointed shoe onto the stub to put it out, her perfectly made-up face impassive.

'That may well be,' she said, 'but qualifications aside, yes, we do think you are still the best person for the job. *I* think you're the best person for the job. You're close to him, you know him, if anything is amiss then you'll be the one to unsettle him. He'll not like being interviewed by you. But if nothing *is* amiss then it won't faze him and you have nothing to worry about.'

'You don't really think he could be guilty here, do you? This is Dominic we're talking about.'

'It's up to you to prove he's innocent. Would you rather it was someone else?'

Claudia looked at the flattened stub end on the ground. 'And if something is amiss, what then?'

'Then, my dear Claudia, you will be the one who will be leading the charge and I'd imagine that's where you would want to be.'

Sharpe let out a breath and paused before she spoke again. Claudia waited for her.

'You're a stickler for protocol and in an ideal situation you shouldn't be the one going in there to interview him, but this is far from ideal. Let me be brutally honest with you — we want to get to the bottom of this, you know that. We need to know what has happened and in this case we feel it's the best way to get results and fast.' Sharpe looked her in the face. 'And you want results, don't you?'

'Of course I do.'

'That's settled. He's waiting in the witness interview room for you.'

The air had a damp quality to it and Claudia shivered.

'You are up to this, aren't you, DI Nunn?'

'I'm up to this, ma'am. Don't worry about me. But promise me if this goes tits up there's going to be no blow-back on me. I want it on the record that I'm against this plan.

Yes, I'll go through with it, but I don't think it's the best way to deal with it. This could blow up in all our faces.'

Sharpe smoothed down her suit jacket before looking at Claudia again. 'Your sentiments on the case have been duly noted, Claudia. But, whatever you may feel about this, trust me when I say I really do think you can get under Detective Sergeant Dominic Harrison's skin and find out the truth of the matter, and that's what's important here.'

CHAPTER 2

Claudia

With one hand on the interview-room door handle, DI Claudia Nunn took a deep breath. She hadn't wanted to take this case. It wasn't one she should be dealing with, but Sharpe had been adamant.

She would have to put all her personal feelings aside. She would have to put on her most professional face, the one she pulled on in difficult circumstances like interview boards and big cases where the outcome was dependent on how she handled the person in front of her.

Like now.

But this was different.

She didn't currently work on the same team as this witness but she had a personal relationship with him and there was no way she should be involved. What, for instance, would happen if it all went pear-shaped?

She shuddered thinking about it and let out the breath she was holding.

She was a detective inspector in South Yorkshire police, she was up to the task. She could compartmentalise this and do the job she had been tasked with. It was important that she do so. She was pleased that the higher-ups were taking it seriously. She understood why they were. They were concerned about their own culpability in the matter. She'd figured that one out quickly enough. If they wanted her to do this then she'd do it properly.

Her fingers curled around the handle.

A young officer walked along the corridor behind her. 'Morning, ma'am.'

Claudia was surprised from her thoughts. 'Oh, sorry, morning, Simon.'

She turned her attention back to the door, pressed the handle down and walked into the interview room.

It was a sparse box of a room. A rectangle with dirty cream walls, a dark-blue tiled carpet with a table and four chairs taking up the centre. A window allowed light to leak into the room from high up on the longest wall, too high to see out of. And on one of the chairs facing her was DS Dominic Harrison.

Dominic was a tall man, greying hair at the sides, and dark eyes that widened as she stepped into the room.

It was the only indication he was surprised that she would be the one to interview him this morning.

'Morning, DS Harrison.'

Dominic stayed silent.

'Do you mind if I call you Dominic? I'd much rather that than call you DS Harrison throughout all of this.'

'Not at all.' His voice was low and gravelly. Claudia marked it as a sign that he was tired. He probably hadn't slept.

'Have you been offered a drink?' she asked. 'I could do with one myself to be honest. We've been thrown together, which is unusual — we may as well make ourselves comfortable.'

Harrison straightened himself in his chair.

'Look, Claudia . . .' He paused, let out a sigh. 'Can I call you Claudia? You're the higher rank here, but, you know . . .'

She inclined her head. Dominic hated that Claudia was a detective inspector and he was only a detective sergeant, and he'd deliberately brought that up She wouldn't rise to it though. It was meaningless right now. Let him have his jab if it made him feel better. She had a job to do.

He continued.

'I don't care who interviews me this morning. All I care about is finding Ruth and bringing her home safe.'

Claudia smiled. 'So, coffee?'

Harrison sighed. 'Okay, yes. Thank you.'

Claudia hadn't even sat down yet. She turned on her heel, left the room and made her way to the kitchen.

So far as first impressions went, she had broken the ice. She had shown him that it was her who would be doing this, that they were in this together. He hadn't seemed too put out by the prospect. His focus appeared to be on his wife.

They were all focused on his wife. Sharpe had made that clear. But Claudia didn't need Sharpe to outline the seriousness of the situation to her. If Ruth was missing then she was all in. Nothing would stop her from pursuing this and identifying where she was or what had happened to her. Ruth would do exactly the same for her and she had no intention of letting her down now it was Ruth in this position.

She filled up the kettle and pulled a couple of mugs out of the cupboard. As she waited for the water to boil, she remembered the last time she had seen Ruth, which had only been two days earlier. How could it have been that only a matter of days ago she was laughing and drinking a glass of wine with her and now she was the subject of a missing person investigation. Come to think of it, something had seemed kind of off with Ruth that evening. She hadn't talked about it, which was odd in itself. They usually talked to each other. Confided in each other. And yet Claudia had allowed it to slide. She could kick herself now. What if it had something to do with her disappearance?

Come on, Ruth, have you left some kind of trace for us to follow? Let us know what happened to you.

With a coffee and a tea made, she returned to the interview room. Harrison was as she left him — hunched in his chair, still in his jacket, his body screaming tension at her. His glasses that he used for driving were on the table in front of him. Claudia placed his coffee next to the spectacles.

'Thank you.'

She sat on the chair opposite. 'You know I'm only here to help, don't you?' How could he believe otherwise?

'That's what you think, is it?' He tipped his head to the side as he looked at her.

'What do you think?' she asked, genuinely interested in how he saw this. Surely her level of concern was obvious; she would do everything in her power to locate his wife.

He ran a hand through his hair. 'Like I said earlier, I don't care as long as we find Ruth.'

Claudia crossed her legs, started to make herself comfortable. 'But you don't think my being here means we're taking it seriously?'

'That's not what I said. I think it means they're taking it very seriously, but in what way, I'm not sure. Help certainly doesn't spring to mind.'

'Why wouldn't we help you, Dominic?'

'Look, instead of going around in circles and dissecting what's happening here, can we get to the meat of the matter, please? Can you start asking questions that are actually relevant?'

She could see that he was more worn out than she first thought. There was a hint of a salt-and-pepper, five o'clock shadow shading his cheeks and jawline and darkness smudged underneath his eyes.

'You don't think assessing our situation as you see it is relevant?'

'For fuck's sake, Claudia, do you have to answer everything with a question?'

'It's kind of why I'm here, and I'm interested in why you see me being here as such a threat.'

She was settling in now and was getting into her stride.

Harrison rubbed at his face, his large hands hiding his feelings from Claudia momentarily, before he spoke.

'I don't see you as a threat. Far from it. Why would I?'

She waited him out. It was one of the tools of interviewing; interviewees hated silence. They had a need to fill the void. But DS Dominic Harrison used this tactic as much as she did. He was good at his job, and he worked well when interviewing either witnesses, victims or offenders. She might not work with him now, but she'd worked with him in the past. She'd observed his techniques. She was here to help him but she was also here to get as much information out of him as possible and she would do her utmost to ensure that happened.

Harrison crossed his arms. 'You know it's likely to be something to do with the job, don't you? That's why they're so twitchy. They're afraid they've put her in a position where she's at risk. One of their own and now she's missing. It doesn't look good.'

This was sensitive; she didn't need telling. They wouldn't have let her anywhere near it unless they were worried. The fact that they had thrown the rule book out of the window proved just how worried they were. It didn't sit well with her. She liked the rules. Surely there could have been another way to do this without using her? She leaned forward, her voice quiet.

'Tell me about last night, the night Ruth went missing, Dominic.'

He scratched at his head. Waited before he spoke. Used his own silence. Claudia didn't know if he was even going to respond. Then, with a deep sigh, he began.

'You know the case we're working on, the one they're calling the Sheffield Strangler?'

Claudia did. Everyone in the force knew the Sheffield Strangler case as more and more staff had been seconded onto it with each subsequent murder. It had consumed South Yorkshire Police for the last six months. She knew Dominic was a part of the investigation team. 'You know I do.'

He continued. 'It had been a long day. Management were stressing. There were more meetings about the case than I could count on my fingers. All we wanted to do was catch the bastard. Yesterday we were looking at a potential new witness around the latest abduction site. I'm responsible for a small team of four DCs and Rhys Evans had taken a statement from a guy who, though he hadn't seen anything himself, said there was another man loitering on the street corner where the last victim was taken from. He was eating a bag of chips and trying to hold a conversation on his phone at the same time. It was the reason our witness remembered him. This is the closest we've come to the Strangler. We're so close we can taste it. We're exhausted after six months, but it feels like it's in grabbing distance now. We just have to track down this unidentified guy eating chips. Ask him what he saw.' The excitement and fatigue of the investigation lifted Dominic's voice. He was connected to the case. 'We were closing in on him but I told my team to go home in the end.' He let out a sigh.

Claudia had been in this situation often enough with her own teams. Cops got tunnel vision when information started to come in; sometimes they forgot they had homes to go to and needed to be sent away. For all the flack the police received in the media, they really were good men and women, working around the clock to help the people who needed it.

'It didn't take long for me to get home. When I did, the house was in darkness. That in itself wasn't unusual, we're both working hard at the moment, but Ruth's car was on the drive. I couldn't remember whether she'd driven to work or if she'd been picked up by a colleague that morning.

'I entered the house, flicked the lights on and closed the curtains. I quietly checked the bedroom to see if Ruth had gone to bed because it was late. She wasn't there so I rang her mobile to see how long she'd be and if she fancied takeaway as I was too tired to cook and realised I was actually hungry. The phone went straight to voicemail, which I found unusual, and that's when it started.'

Claudia raised an eyebrow.

'A small niggle. It wasn't like her. She could easily have turned it off because of a case she was working, but it seemed a little too late in the day to be doing something that would involve turning your phone off — and besides she would have texted me to let me know if she was going to be later than usual.

'Something didn't feel right but I couldn't put my finger on it. I tried Ruth again and her phone was still off.'

The fear that Dominic was describing started to knot in the pit of Claudia's stomach. They were talking about Ruth here and the fear nearly froze her, but she ground her teeth and nodded for him to carry on.

'We know the twenty-four-hour rule people tend to believe is a fallacy built up by television dramas. The reality is I could report Ruth missing as soon as I felt she was. But I needed to make some enquiries of my own first before I sent the balloon up.

'First, though, I tried to calm myself. Told myself I was being irrational. She was as much a workaholic as I was. She would laugh at me if she knew how paranoid I was being.

'I called Ruth's sister. Had she seen her, had she popped round to have a glass of wine and unwind, maybe to moan about my dirty socks on the floor. You know how it is. We all need to let off steam about our relationships somewhere. But she hadn't seen Ruth and my call only served to worry her.

'The next call I made was to Ruth's office. It was possible she was working and her phone had died. Which only served to concern me considering what she'd been dragged into. There was no answer. It appeared they'd all left for the night. I tried her phone again, and again it went straight to answerphone.

'I'd been home three hours. It was plenty of time for her to have either walked through the door or sent me a message to let me know where she was. After all, it was one in the morning. Yes, I'd worked that late before, we all had, and later, but not without a message home to say so.

'Something wasn't right. It was time to call it in.

'My wife was officially missing.'

CHAPTER 3

Claudia

Her tea was cold. She hadn't touched it. When she had offered to get drinks it had been more of a stalling tactic than a need for one. She had needed a minute to gather herself after seeing him in that interview room.

Sharpe had given her all the information they had before sending Claudia into the room. They were prepared for this.

An officer was missing. Ruth was missing.

'Have you slept at all?' she asked Harrison.

He let out a long sigh. 'Does it matter if I've slept or not?'

'I'm wondering how much help you can be if you're at breaking point.'

'Don't worry about me. You need to worry about Ruth. I've been told no one has seen her since she left work yesterday. That means she went missing between work and home.'

'Or from home.'

'What?'

'You said she went missing between—'

'I know what I said.' Harrison raised his voice. 'What I want to know is what you're implying?'

Claudia kept her own voice even.

'I'm not implying anything. I'm working with facts. The other option is she made it home and went missing from there.'

Harrison glared at her, his face rigid, locked tight, eyes hardened in Claudia's direction.

She waited him out, understanding that his emotions would be all over the place. She had a job to do and the best way to find Ruth was to work Dominic as she would work anyone else. Ruth was her priority here, not how Dominic was feeling.

'You know we've started the investigation, don't you?'

He broke the lock he had on her, looked towards the door, then back to her.

'Of course. I'd expect nothing less.'

'Is there anything you want to tell us before we find it out?' she asked.

'Like?'

'I don't know. You tell me.'

He sighed.

'There's nothing. I told you what happened. All I want is for you to find my wife. For you to do your job to the best of your ability—' he stared hard at her — 'which I know is particularly good. And for you to find her. Do you think you can do that?'

She picked up her cold tea and took a sip, then scowled at the cup as though she hadn't known it was going to taste disgusting.

'That's why I'm in here. They could have sent anyone in but they sent me. They think it will unsettle you and if there is anything to tell then you'll let it slip, whereas you would be a tighter drum with anyone else.'

He twisted his lips, thought for a second.

'It's not a bad plan. It would work if I had anything to tell you, but I don't. I told you how it is. I told you what happened.'

'Do you think there's a possibility she's simply left you?'

He shook his head.

'No, I don't. There's no reason to leave. We have a good marriage. Yes, we have our bad days, but doesn't everyone? It's the way marriages work.'

Claudia stood, lifted her arms over her head and stretched out her back. She hated sitting for long periods of time and yet interviewing was a part of the job that she loved. A contradiction if ever there was one.

'Are you sure about that?' she asked.

'What the hell are you getting at? First you suggest she may have gone missing from the house and then you query our marriage.'

'Why should it be dismissed that she went missing from the house? Maybe she got home before you and did go missing from there. We can't discount anything at this stage. And while we're talking about that, can I have your house key so officers can go and do a search?'

'You want to do a search of the house?'

'It's protocol, you know this.'

'Yeah, for little kids who may be hiding in the house and their parents haven't realised.'

Claudia raised an eyebrow at him.

'Oh yeah, and in case I've killed her and have her locked in a trunk in the bedroom.' He pulled a bunch of keys out of his pocket, unhooked one from the bundle and placed it on the table. He pushed it over towards Claudia. 'You won't find anything. It's a waste of your time.'

Claudia picked up the key.

'I won't be a minute.'

She left the room and went to the uniform sergeant on duty, asking him to send someone round to do a missing person search.

'Don't leave any stone unturned, this is for a missing cop. Pull out all the stops.'

Back in the interview room, Dominic was on his phone. As Claudia entered he put the phone down.

'I tried Ruth again. The phone's still off.'

Claudia sat opposite him again.

'Thanks for the key. You know we have to do it.'

He didn't comment.

'I have to ask you about something,' she said.

'Go ahead, I have nothing to hide.' He leaned back in his chair.

'We have a statement from your neighbour.'

'Okay. I'm a little surprised that you needed a statement. What exactly has she seen?' Harrison leaned forward. 'Do you have a lead? What's happened?'

'No, Dominic. We have a statement that says three weeks ago you and Ruth could be heard screaming at each other. Do you want to tell me what that was all about?'

Dominic rubbed both his hands through his hair and let out a sigh. 'Ruth told me the job had come into the office. I wasn't best pleased about it. That out of two females in an undercover unit she was the only one to fit the profile. I didn't want her to do it. The case I'm working, the Sheffield Strangler, he's dangerous.'

He rubbed at his hair again.

'Let's just say she was less than impressed I was trying to tell her what jobs she could and couldn't take on.'

'And how did the conversation play out?'

'Not in violence if that's what you're thinking.' Dominic bolted upright.

'I never said that.'

'You didn't need to.'

'Just tell me what happened.'

Another sigh.

'She put me in my place. You know what she's like. I had no choice but to back down. She laughed in my face and told me she couldn't go to her boss and tell him her husband told her she couldn't do it. I kind of got the message.'

'But you weren't happy?'

'Because it wasn't safe and now look where we are.' He waved his arm around the interview room. 'We're in the fucking police station because she's missing and you're asking about something that happened three weeks ago when I want to know what happened last night.'

'So it was an argument about work? About her joining the team on the case you're working?' Claudia leaned back in her chair.

'Yes. Like I said, we're both passionate about the job and if I try and get protective Ruth gets annoyed and gives me a piece of her mind. Tells me she's as much a copper as I am and to back off. Which is what she did that night. Only we might have been a bit loud about it. You'll have heard how bad this case has been. I was frustrated. I didn't want her to go undercover on my case. The Sheffield Strangler is a brutal killer and he scares the crap out of me. And look, I have good reason to have been scared. Ruth hasn't left me, Claudia. The Sheffield Strangler is responsible for this. She starts working my case and now she goes missing. It's not a coincidence.'

CHAPTER 4

Dominic

Six months ago

The call came in about half an hour before the shift was due to end. Dominic was working on the Richards file — a domestic murder case. The husband had lashed out for the first time in his life and with one slap around the face had knocked his wife's head into the door frame and killed her. It was one of those fluke impacts where any other time it would have been a simple assault, but a knock in the wrong place had resulted in her death and her husband was facing years in jail.

Though Dominic hated violence against women of any sort, he had a little sympathy for Richards. Prior to the assault he'd been made redundant, they had lost their son to drugs two years previously and he was a man struggling to hold his life together. His wife had physically pushed him out of the kitchen. Pushed him three times, laying her own hands on his chest with force. Their marriage was imploding with the stress. One dreadful mistake, for which, in his opinion, the deserved punishment would have been his wife walking out on him, saw the vestiges of his family destroyed. In totality.

CPS were asking for everything to keep their case together and Dominic's eyes were tired from looking at the screen. It was DC Paul Teague's case but, as his supervisor, he was supporting him in making sure it got through the process. CPS were playing hardball. Because of the sympathetic details they wanted to pin it down hard so he couldn't wriggle out of it. Every day they asked for something new. Paul was losing his shit with it and Dominic was trying to hold him and it all together.

Then the DI called him into his office, just as Dominic noted there was only half an hour until his shift ended. DI Adyant Kapoor was reading something on his computer monitor when Dominic walked in. His face was set, his jaw tense and his eyes dark. He waved Dominic into a seat as he finished reading what was in front of him.

Dominic liked Kapoor. He was a straight-laced officer but he was always fair. He'd worked hard to get to where he was — taken on the difficult jobs during his service. Dominic had crossed paths with him in the past when Kapoor had been a lowly DS himself. He had always volunteered for anything that came up. Anything to build up his portfolio ready for the promotion boards. There were rumours that he wasn't a real copper, that all he wanted was to be top brass. But that could be said of any of the bosses. Dominic had his own suspicions of why Kapoor was targeted with such rumours and it made his stomach churn.

It wasn't often that Dominic had seen his boss's face look so serious.

'A job has come in, Dom,' Kapoor said, leaning back in his chair. 'Uniform officers were called to the body of a woman found in Ecclesall Woods. A dog walker had stumbled upon it.' He flicked an invisible piece of rubbish off the top of his desk. 'Literally fallen over it, actually, likely damaging evidence. From what I'm being told it's a nasty one and is going to need our best efforts. Are you free to go to the scene and take control while I take command here?'

'There's something you're not telling me,' Dominic said. 'What have you missed out, boss?'

Kapoor let out a sigh. 'The violence, Dom. I've left out the bloody violence.' He rubbed his face with his hands. 'Do you ever feel as though you're too old for this job?'

Dominic thought about it. He was fifty-two and only had a few years left in the job; he could retire when he was fifty-five at the earliest or hold on until he was sixty. The fact that he could leave in three years seemed surreal; he didn't feel old enough. 'No, I don't feel old at all, boss.' He smiled.

Kapoor scratched at his cheek with the pen that was in his hand. 'Maybe it's sitting in this office that's aging me. Or maybe it's having a wife who is over ten years younger than you that keeps you young, Dom.'

Dom laughed. 'To be fair, Ruth tires me out. She has so much more energy than I do. A decade is a lot when it comes to aging. We don't feel the difference when we're sitting together talking, but when it comes to physical activities like bike riding and fell walks, then I notice. I'm glad she's over forty now. It means she's slowing down a little more herself, but she's definitely been hard work to keep up with.'

Kapoor tapped the sheet of paper in front of him. 'This is the incident report. It doesn't make for pleasant reading.' He picked it up and handed it to Dominic. 'Get yourself over there and get control of the scene. I've instructed uniform to keep a wide cordon, we want to preserve as much evidence as is possible. CSU are travelling. We want to keep this as quiet as we can for now until we know what we're dealing with. No press involvement. I don't want to scare the public. We need to be able to control the narrative, not have it running away with us, so keep your circle tight and remind uniform to do the same, will you?'

Dominic was reminded again of how the boss always had to think of the wider picture and not just the crime scene. He'd taken his inspectors exams in the past but hadn't got the required mark. He was happy as a DS though. He could get his feet dirty and still have some supervisory power. He had his own little team within the unit.

He rose from his chair.

'Keep me updated, Dom.' Kapoor looked up at him. 'And keep it contained.'

Dominic took the report off Kapoor. 'Yes, boss.'

With the incident report in his hand he left the office and started to read down the sheet. It was exactly as Kapoor had stated. The dog walker sounded pretty distressed on the original call. He read the text.

Caller states he was walking his dog in Ecclesall Woods when he stumbled and fell. He couldn't help but fall onto her, he said. His hands dropped straight onto her body as he put them down to lessen his fall. He was pretty incoherent but he fell into a woman's body and he says she is dead. He got off her as quickly as he could and has not touched her since. He knows she is a crime scene and that he has contaminated the scene and will wait for police to attend. He has blood on his clothes and has had to put his dog on the lead to prevent him from nosing around the woman.

Dominic would need to bring the walker back to the station so he could be forensically examined and have his clothes seized from him. He walked back into the incident room and grabbed his team. They had worked together for the past four years since DC Paul Teague had joined them.

'This is a dark one,' he said to them as they grabbed their radios and car keys. 'Make a quick phone call home if you need to, let your loved ones know you're going to be late.' They were due to be on rest days the day after next, but now this job had come in there was no way they would be having any days off. It regularly happened like this.

He sent a quick text to Ruth explaining a body had been found and they were being sent out to it. She said she'd leave him some food in the microwave in case he didn't manage to eat at work. She wouldn't be annoyed if he grabbed a bite on the job. She knew what it was like. Sometimes they had the opportunity and other times they were run off their feet and there was no chance. Not that he cared if she was annoyed or not. The job was more important than anything else for him right now. This was where his focus was.

He spun his car keys up in the air and caught them as they came down. 'Let's go and see what we have out there,' he said.

CHAPTER 5

Claudia

Ten hours since Ruth's attack

Claudia interlocked her fingers on the table. 'Okay. Look, I'm going to go out and do the search of your house myself, I—'

'Why? What have I said that has made you decide you need a look?' Harrison was practically leaning across the table.

Claudia kept her poise. 'As I was saying—' she eyed him straight on and he backed off a little — 'I think I owe it to you to do a proper job on this and that means doing every step myself and not fobbing the premises search off onto uniform officers. Yes, I'll take them with me but I want to have a look around. That way I'll also have more of a feel for things as we talk.'

Harrison pursed his lips.

Claudia ignored the look he had given her and ploughed on. 'You going to be okay here if I disappear for a short while?'

'What else am I going to do? I might go a little stir crazy, but as long as I know people are looking for her then I can wait.'

Claudia stood. 'I'd better go, before the sergeant I gave your key to disappears off to your house. And yes, people are looking for her. What do you imagine her team are doing right about now? You think they're twiddling their thumbs? Or continuing with the case as usual? No, they'll have split resources and they'll be focusing on Ruth.'

Harrison looked at her. 'What about my team? What happens to that job?'

Claudia was at the door. 'You're seriously still worrying about that case in the light of what's happening?'

'I am. Because he's responsible for what's happened to Ruth. Why aren't you listening? We're so close to catching him that he's decided to strike back.'

Claudia pursed her lips. 'There are still plenty of officers working on it and we'll consider your thoughts as we progress today. Let's see how things go.' And with that she was out the door leaving Harrison sitting at the table, in the room, with the too-high window, all alone.

It took Claudia about twenty minutes to drive to Dominic's home address at Green Lane, Wharncliffe Side, with the uniform officers. She had been many times before but it made her skin crawl to be there with cops to search the place for signs of wrongdoing in relation to Ruth and what may have happened to her. Claudia desperately hoped that she was safe and well. That she had walked away for some time out, even though she knew better than to go without leaving word of where she was going. Even if she had walked out on Dominic and didn't want to contact him, Ruth knew to let someone know where she was. Claudia would probably be that someone. Right now though, Ruth going walkabout would be better than the alternative.

Claudia thought once again of what was on Ruth's mind that last night she saw her. Could it have driven her away or caused her to come to some mortal harm? And if she was at the mercy of another, why hadn't she confided in Claudia if she was in trouble? Claudia wondered if it really had been job related. Maybe that was the reason for her distraction.

One of the cops carried a search bag in. He dumped it in the entrance hall and Claudia bent down and pulled out a pair of small gloves, snapping them onto her hands. They had to be careful in case they found something and needed to call a forensic team in.

She walked into the neat and welcoming living room, a room she was familiar with. There was no sign of a problem. Nothing looked out of place. All the cushions were positioned where they were supposed to be on the sofa. Prints and family photographs hung on the wall. Ruth smiling down at her, carefree and happy. A knot of worry caught in her chest. Come on Ruth, where are you? Give us a clue as to where you've gone, what has happened?

'I'll go upstairs,' said one of the uniform cops.

'Okay, I'll go check out the kitchen and utility room,' Claudia replied as she made her way through the door into the kitchen.

There was a dirty mug on the kitchen worktop. Everything else was away. Nothing seemed out of place here. She pushed the foot peddle on the kitchen bin and peered in. The container was filled with the usual kitchen rubbish. Food leftovers and non-recyclable containers. She was about to let the lid drop when something glinted. With a gloved finger she moved a piece of kitchen roll and found shards of broken glass. Yes, glassware was easily broken in homes, but what were the odds of her finding a broken glass in the kitchen the day after Ruth went missing? She would need to get a CSI team out to examine it.

'Don't anyone touch that bin,' she said to the cop entering the kitchen.

'No, ma'am.'

'Anything out of place anywhere else?' she asked.

'Not as far as we can tell, but it's a tidy home so if there was a struggle you'd think it would be easy to identify.'

'Mmm.' She agreed. Plus wouldn't Dominic have mentioned it?

26

She pushed on the door to the utility room where the washing machine and dryer were housed.

'What's through there?' asked the cop, eyeing up the closed door at the other side of the room.

'It leads to the garage. An internal way in.' Claudia flicked on a light switch as they walked through the utility room, pausing to check the washer for clothing that might be being dumped in it following an attack of some sort, but it was empty. As she'd known it would be. Then she pushed open the door to the garage. It was heavier set than the rest of the doors in the house. 'He doesn't keep his car in here, he parks on the drive like most people. I think it's filled with junk.'

She turned and stepped into the garage. A strip light fitted on the ceiling glowed down into the space. There were shelves on the walls filled with small and large boxes and other bits of stuff she could only describe as junk.

The cop who had walked into the kitchen was standing behind her. She stepped into the garage and walked further in. There was something on the floor towards the front. It looked like an oil spill, sleek and glossy. But she'd said to the cop behind her that Dominic didn't keep the car in here, and looking at the boxes along the walls it didn't seem as though he could drive the car in here to work on it either, there was not enough room. Maybe a canister behind one of the boxes had been knocked over and spilled.

She took a couple of steps closer. Her nose twitched.

That was not the smell of oil. Her stomach roiled.

She turned to the cop behind her. 'Get the CSU here.'

'What do we have?' he asked.

She took another step forward. 'There's a broken . . . a smashed . . .' She stumbled over her words as she focused on the ground in front of her. 'There's broken glass in the pedal bin in the kitchen that needs examining.' She struggled to believe what was in front of her.

She could see it now. She could see the colour of it closer to the edge of the puddle where the fluid was thinner. It was definitely not oil. It was not black.

It was red. Deep slick red.

'And I think we have a large patch of blood here in the garage.' She concluded as calmly as she could manage, though as her own blood rushed through her veins she was anything other than calm.

He peered around her. 'Jesus.'

Claudia reached out a hand towards the wall to the side of her, grasping for something to hold on to, clawing, needing something solid to hold her up. The understanding of what this meant for her friend sinking in. But the wall stayed where it was, solid, silent and elusive. Out of reach. Claudia bent over and put her hands on her knees. The blood swimming in front of her as her vision greyed out. An internal thermometer jacked up her heating system and a far-off bell started to ring in her ears.

'Can someone live with this much blood missing?' Claudia's colleague asked as she tried to stay upright.

'I don't know. I really don't. You only have eight pints of blood in your body. I'm not sure how many you can live without before you die.' There was a hell of a lot of blood on the floor in front of her. If this was Ruth's, she was missing a lot, and Claudia was sure as hell Ruth needed it.

'Well, whoever's this is, they're not going to be doing so well.'

Claudia turned and snapped at him, the bells fading out, her vision clicking back into place. 'Have you contacted the CSU yet?! It's all well and good standing around here chatting about it but we won't know anything until we get the professionals here. So stop trying to guess and get a move on.'

'Oh, erm, yes, ma'am.' He flustered then grabbed for the radio on his shoulder and called up the control room to request the crime scene unit.

Claudia turned on her heel and stalked out of the garage. 'No one comes in or out of here. It's for CSU only,' she said to him as she passed.

'Yes, ma'am.' He moved towards the door and away from the pool of blood that was glistening under the strip light.

Claudia walked through the house to the search bag that had been left near the front door, pulled out two plastic bags and climbed the stairs. Walking into the main bedroom, she searched until she found a hairbrush with long strands of hair trapped within the teeth. She pushed it into one of the bags and sealed it before writing on the exhibit label stamped on the outside of the bag, signing it with the date and time. Then she went into the bathroom, selected the pink toothbrush and bagged that up also, signing and sealing it. The CSIs would now have something to compare the DNA of the blood against when they got back to the lab. They would be able to tell if the pool of blood was indeed Ruth Harrison's or not.

CHAPTER 6

Claudia

Claudia decided she would climb the stairs to Sharpe's office rather than the easier option of taking the lift. She needed something to take this pent-up energy out of her before she spoke to the DCI. It was as though there was electricity running through her veins and she didn't know what to do with herself. Surely Sharpe would take her off this case. She couldn't keep her on it. She had texted Sharpe her findings so she had a heads-up as to what this conversation was to be about. Time enough to run it up the flagpole. Surely no one in their right mind would keep Claudia on this investigation now.

At the top of the stairs Claudia assessed herself. Her jaw was clenched and her heart was thudding hard in her chest. Walking up those few steps had not helped her in the least. She was most definitely not the best person to continue.

'Is she in?' Claudia asked Maxine, Sharpe's PA.

Maxine looked up from her computer, curls pulled back from her face, a few strands coming loose and tumbling down to her shoulders. 'She's in. She said to send you straight through as soon as you arrived.'

'Thanks.' She didn't have much capacity for small talk today.

She pushed open Sharpe's door to find her standing behind her desk with her landline phone to her ear. Finely polished fingernails twirled between the curls of the cord separating the phone and earpiece. With her free hand she waved Claudia in.

Claudia let out a breath, closed the door behind her and waited for Sharpe to finish her call.

'Yes, yes, I know. Yes, I know. Yes, of course. We're on it. Yes. Yes.' A deep sigh escaped Sharpe's lips and she rolled her eyes at Claudia. 'She's one of ours, of course we're pulling out all the stops. Yes, I'll get in touch as soon as I know anything.' She put the phone down with a crash.

'Bloody civilians,' she muttered.

Claudia raised her eyebrows.

'The police and crime commissioner. Doesn't think it looks good that one of our own has been abducted, potentially fatally injured. Thinks it will scare the public. We need to deal with it as quickly as possible.' Sharpe stopped talking. 'I'm sorry you were the one who had to find the crime scene, Claudia. How are you? And what a bloody idiot leaving it there for us.'

'I'm fine, ma'am.' She was far from fine. She wanted to be as far away from this job as she could get.

Sharpe pulled her chair back from her desk. 'Grab a seat, Claudia. Grab a seat. Don't stand there looking untidy.' Sharpe sat in her own chair and Claudia in the one opposite.

'So, you have to arrest Harrison then.' Sharpe picked up a mug and drank from it.

'I beg your pardon?' Claudia snapped back up to standing.

'Oh, do sit down, Claudia. Let's talk about this. We don't need hysterics.'

'Hysterics?' Claudia turned her back to Sharpe. Was she being hysterical by not wanting to carry on with this case? She didn't understand why she was even involved.

'Okay, I might have been a little harsh.' Sharpe's voice softened. 'But please, do sit.'

Claudia was caught off guard; Sharpe wasn't known for backing down. She slipped back into the chair and stared at her boss. 'Why do you want me to make the arrest and carry on with the case?' she asked.

'When I got your message I took it up with Connelly and between us we think, as you've already started the process with Harrison, it would serve to have you continue. He'll know what you've found and he'll not expect you to be the one to go in and make the arrest and to interview him from here on in. We can use this to our advantage. To knock him off his comfortable perch. The more unsettled we keep him the better. He won't be able to keep himself together and whatever plan he has in play, we can scupper and find Ruth sooner rather than later.' She looked at Claudia. 'Whatever state she may be in.'

Claudia understood where her boss was coming from but she didn't like it. Sharpe was making an assumption that Harrison was guilty of a crime before they had any evidence. Evidence was the cornerstone of a police investigation and evidence was the only way Claudia could even begin to get her head around the whole scenario. Today had her spinning. How was she supposed to hold herself together while Ruth was missing and Dominic was their immediate suspect? Sending Claudia in to interview him now the blood had been found wasn't playing by the rules. Though there was nothing actually written down that said she couldn't do this. And he *was* going to be arrested, because yes, there certainly was enough to make an arrest, with the blood having been found at his home, just not enough to jump to the conclusion he was guilty — he was, after all, still one of their own.

Claudia frowned. 'He might be innocent.' It was a possibility. Again with the evidence. They had none either way — other than a pool of Ruth's blood in his home.

Sharpe tapped on the mug she was holding, waited a beat to respond to the statement. 'Of course he may well be.

And obviously you're going to come at the investigation from that angle. But we trust you to follow the evidence. You'll unsettle him, but also be open to whatever comes out in the wash. Guilty or not.'

'And what about, if it turns out that way, when it gets to court? They'll try to throw it out because I interviewed him.'

Sharpe placed the mug back on her desk. 'They can try, but as long as you stick to all the rules they won't have a leg to stand on. You're a stickler for the rulebook, Claudia. If that rulebook is followed to the letter and nothing goes awry, they have nothing to get it thrown out on. There is nothing in writing that says you can't interview him.' Sharpe leaned forward in her chair. 'The question is, Claudia, can you do this? Can you stick to the rulebook on this one?'

Claudia was starting to feel resigned to the fact that she was stuck with this investigation. 'If there was ever a case where I had to, then this is it and I won't step away from it.'

Sharpe clapped her hands together, the sound loud in the sparse office. Like a crack in Claudia's ears. 'Good girl. So, you're on board? You're doing this?'

Claudia let out an audible sigh.

Sharpe smiled. It was more like a warning, Claudia thought, than a soft, friendly expression. Sharpe was all pointy corners, a little like her name if you wanted to put it that way. 'You won't regret it, Claudia. You'll be the reason we get Ruth Harrison home and Dominic Harrison locked up at the end of the day. That has to bring you some peace,' she paused, 'of some description.'

Again Sharpe was presuming guilt. 'I'll make the arrest,' Claudia said. 'I'll interview him and I'll go from there. I can't promise anything. This could lead anywhere. It could be a real shit show or it could all be nothing, we'll have to see.'

Sharpe stood. 'That's all I can ask of you. You'll have your team working on this with you. You know them, they're dedicated and they won't give you any trouble. Work them hard, get to the bottom of this. If you need any more resources you will get them as soon as you ask. All hands are on deck for this.'

Claudia stood. 'If it turns to shit ma'am, it's on your head, or Connelly's, I don't care who takes the blame. I'm doing this under protest, but yes, I'm doing it. I want to know where Ruth is.'

CHAPTER 7

Claudia

Claudia walked towards the incident room. A niggle of anxiety twisted in the pit of her stomach. This would be the first time she had seen her team since Sharpe asked her to deal with Ruth's missing persons case this morning.

Sharpe had tasked them with the background work, so they were aware of what was happening. A case had never been so personally close to any of them before. This was unusual and she hated that it was her that was linked to the investigation. Her they would all turn and stare at. Though she knew them better than that. They'd be more discreet. They were a great team and she was grateful for each and every one of them.

She reached the incident room doors and took a deep breath before pushing one open and striding in. 'Morning, rabble.' A hush fell over the room. She'd aimed for light and breezy but it landed flat. The team stopped what they were doing and looked to her.

Her DS, Russ Kane, rose from his chair. Claudia shook her head and he returned to his seat. The team kept a careful watch.

They needed something from her. She had to fill this silence, to address the elephant in the room, before they could move forward and get back to work.

'You know what we're dealing with.' Claudia moved towards the front of the room. 'I know you're probably wondering how I'm doing. I'm not going into detail though I will tell you that I'm fine.' She perched on the corner of a spare desk. 'I was tasked with leading this investigation and that's what I'm doing.' She looked around at her team. 'That's what *we're* doing. Yes, I'm upset that we're looking for Ruth but let's try and keep personal feelings out of the way, shall we.' It was more difficult than she'd imagined, trying to keep her feelings on a level and to deal with this as though it was any other case that had landed on her desk. She fought to keep control of her voice. 'We conducted a search of Ruth's home address and there was a pool of blood in the garage. CSIs are there now and we'll know later if it's a match for Ruth.'

Russ rose from his chair again. Claudia glared at him but he ignored her, moved to the desk she was sitting on and placed himself on the opposite corner. Close but not intimately so.

The silence in the room was deafening. Claudia's breath came fast in her chest, hot in her mouth. Her cheeks flaring up.

Russ addressed the team. 'Let's have a look at what we have so far.' He looked to DC Lisa James. 'House-to-house enquires next to Ruth and Dominic's address?'

Claudia was grateful to him and took the moment to calm her breathing, taking it slow and steady.

Lisa cleared her throat. 'It hasn't got us anywhere.' She checked her notes. 'No one had heard anything. It's a detached house so things have to be pretty loud for sound to travel or the neighbours need to be outside in the garden and no one was last night. Especially not at the time we're focusing on.'

This made Claudia realise how loud Dominic and Ruth must have been arguing the night they were heard by their neighbour. They really had to have been going at it.

'What about a CCTV trail for Ruth?' she asked.

Harry Harbor, another DC on the team, piped up next. 'We've identified the time Ruth left work and collected CCTV from along her route home. There's a lot of viewing to get through to see if she made it home or if she veered off at any point. Obviously there's no CCTV round where she lives but we got as close as we could.'

'Okay.' Claudia was on a more even keel now they were talking investigative procedures. 'Someone's checked the hospitals, I take it?'

Russ spoke again. 'She's not been admitted and there's no unidentified females matching her description either.'

Claudia didn't know if this was a good thing or not. 'Dominic believes the Sheffield Strangler had something to do with Ruth's disappearance. While it's a long shot, we can't discount it. I'm going to interview him and try to get to the bottom of it. I'll feed back to you as I do. But the upshot is, his team were closing in on an arrest as far as I can make out and Dominic feels Ruth was targeted because of this, to distract him.'

The room came alive as the team immediately started to talk to each other about this possibility. The rare time a killer might actually set his sights on a police officer.

'Okay,' Claudia raised her voice. 'I know it seems a bit far-fetched, but we follow every lead. I want you to split the team and investigate Ruth as a missing person and also check the work Dominic's team was doing on the Sheffield Strangler case.'

Graham Dunne, an ex-soldier turned DC, looked puzzled. 'You want us to investigate the work of another team?'

She waved a hand at him. 'It's fine. I've run it past Sharpe and it's anything goes as far as this investigation is concerned. Ruth is one of our own. If checking up on that case can bring us answers then that's what we're to do.'

Graham inclined his head. 'I'll get access to the file straight away.'

'Dominic told me earlier that they felt like they were getting close. His team should be trying to ID a potential witness. I want that witness found at all costs today. Do I make myself clear? If this is connected I don't want to find myself on the back foot.'

Her team had her back. They'd pull out all the stops for her. She was grateful for them. Now she had to gather her strength. She had to go and face Dominic again. This time things were different and Claudia had no idea what to believe or how she was going to get through this.

CHAPTER 8

Claudia

Claudia walked down the stairs and back to the room that held Dominic Harrison. Again she found herself hovering outside the door, wondering what entering the room would mean for her in the coming minutes and hours. Never in her wildest dreams had she imagined when she got to work this morning that she would be doing this. But Ruth Harrison was missing, possibly murdered if the pool of blood was anything to go by. So now she had to do anything in her power to find answers.

She pushed the door open. Dominic Harrison was slouched down in his chair, head in his folded arms on the table. Exhaustion and defeat overwhelming him. He must have known what she would find when she went to search his house. He must have expected this next part of the process. His despair was visible in the defeated slouch of his shoulders. What Claudia couldn't figure out was why he hadn't cleared up the mess in the garage before he had come into the police station this morning. Hadn't he seen it himself? It didn't make any sense.

Harrison jerked upright as the door opened. The shadows below his eyes were even darker than they had been when she left. He looked terrible and she found it difficult to muster up any sympathy for him. She wanted to throw herself at him and scream and shout and beg for him to tell her where Ruth was. It was inconceivable to her that a cop could walk into a police station and not expect every other cop in their vicinity to want to pull his eyes out of his sockets if they thought it would help locate a missing, potentially murdered, colleague.

'Get up,' she glared at him.

'What?' Confusion played across his face.

'I said, get up. On your feet.'

'What's wrong? What did you find? Have you found Ruth?' His eyes widened.

Claudia took a couple of steps closer to him. 'I said get up on your feet.' She couldn't help her anger with him even though she had not ten minutes ago defended him to Sharpe. The arrest was out of her hands and she was angry she was in this position. Angry at the pool of blood in the garage. Angry she didn't know where her friend was and angry Dominic Harrison possibly had the answers.

'Why?'

'So I can look you in the eye when I arrest you. Now. Stand. Up.'

Slowly Harrison pushed back in his chair, his eyes locked on Claudia. 'Arrest me? For what? Please, tell me what's happened.'

Claudia stayed where she was and Dominic unfolded himself out of the chair and came to stand in front of her. 'Please, Claudia.'

She stared at him, the familiar lines on his face now alien to her. She felt disjointed and disoriented.

'Dominic Harrison, I am arresting you on suspicion of the murder of Ruth Harrison last night at Green Lane. You do not have to say anything but it may—'

'Murder?' he whispered so quiet she had to strain over her own words to hear him.

'—harm your defence if you do not mention when questioned something—'

'Ruth is dead?' His eyes were wide, his voice more insistent, though still quiet.

'—you later rely on in court. Anything you do say may be given in evidence.'

'She's dead?' He asked again.

'Yes, Dominic, evidence suggests Ruth is dead.' To her ears her voice sounded dead too. Flat and lifeless. Why had she said she could do this? She couldn't do this. Any DI could have made the arrest, it didn't need to be her.

'I don't understand,' he said, stepping back again, arm outstretched behind him, searching for his chair. 'I don't understand. She wasn't there when I left this morning. Tell me what you found.' His hand caught the chair and he dropped into it with a thud, his eyes unfocused and glassy.

'Her blood, Dominic. We found her blood.'

'Ruth, no, oh my God, no.' His head shot up towards Claudia who hadn't moved. She was still standing in the middle of the room, still facing him, watching his reaction. 'You have to believe me. No. It's not me. I didn't do this. Why would I come here knowing there was blood at the house? I've been framed. Claudia?'

Her mind tumbled. She'd thought the same thing herself. It didn't make sense.

'We have to take you to the custody suite before we can talk about this, Dominic. Then you can tell me what you think has happened.'

'Tell me you believe me, Claudia. Please, you have to believe I didn't do this.'

Her bones were leaden, like she was glued to the spot. Or like something heavy was weighing her down. But she had to move. She had to transport him to custody. She had promised Sharpe she would work the case and she would. Now she was involved she would do this to the best of her ability and find out what had really happened.

Whether Dominic was guilty or not.

For Ruth.

'Claudia, you have to believe me. Of all people, you have to know I didn't do this.' His voice was so quiet she had to strain to hear him.

With leaden limbs she pulled her cuffs out of her back pocket where she had pushed them before entering the room. 'I need to put these on you to travel to the custody suite.' She clenched her jaw tight to hold back tears that threatened to tumble from her eyes. This case was just too emotional for her. She had to draw on some real reserves of strength to get through it.

Harrison's eyes were on the floor. He looked up at her and at the rigid cuffs in her hands. His eyes darkened and he placed his wrists out for her to cuff him, gaze locked on hers.

'Take your jacket off,' she instructed.

'My jacket?'

'Take it off.'

He slipped the jacket off and threw it over the back of the chair, then put his hands back in front of him so Claudia could cuff him.

She clipped the first cuff into place, the metal teeth grinding into the locked position around his wrist and then she pushed the second cuff over his other wrist and he was secured. She picked up his jacket and draped it over his hands, covering his cuffed wrists, so anyone who saw him walking out of the station with her would see him carrying his jacket rather than the handcuffs underneath. Though the rumour mill would be working overtime soon enough, she didn't want him to feel all eyes on him as he walked out of there. If he had done what it looked like he'd done, then he would pay for it.

'You ready?' she asked. As much for herself as it was for him.

He took a deep breath in. 'Claudia . . .'

'I asked if you were ready?' She had to steel herself, as much as she hated to do it. What if he was responsible? It was all such a goddamn mess.

'I'm as ready as I'll ever be.'

CHAPTER 9

Claudia

Shepcote Lane custody suite was a fairly new one for Sheffield and heralded the closure of the other suites scattered around the force area. The fifty-cell suite was state of the art and had dedicated rooms for drug and mental health teams.

Claudia walked Dominic up to the custody desk and in front of the custody sergeant. Claudia knew the sergeant, Kirsty Greene.

'Well, good morning, you two reprobates. What have you brought me in this morning?' she asked with a smile, a mug in hand, halfway up to her mouth.

Harrison looked down, all blood drained from his face.

Claudia's stomach plummeted to the floor. 'Kirsty, it's Dominic.' She kept her voice as low as she could while still getting the sergeant to hear her over the high desk.

'I can see it's Dominic. What's he done, brought me in an offender who's going to be vomiting all over my nice clean cell?'

'No . . . it's . . .'

Harrison lifted his hands up and rested them on the desk, jiggled them from side to side so the jacket slipped off slightly and the cuffs could be seen. Kirsty stared at him in disbelief. Her hand holding the mug sank down to the desktop and she let it go.

'Oh.'

Harrison pulled his arms down and shook his head apologetically at Kirsty. 'I didn't do it, Kirsty.'

She shook herself. 'You can't say that to me, Dominic. Whatever it is. You can't talk to me about it. You know that.' She tapped her computer awake. She turned to Claudia. 'You're the arresting officer?' She looked around the custody suite to see who was paying attention but so far no one had noticed what was happening at her section of the large desk.

Claudia let out a sigh. 'I am. Take it up with Sharpe and Connelly. It's their decision. I'm just following orders. You know me, a rule-follower to the end. Even with this.'

Dominic frowned. 'I'm sorry, Claudia.'

'Prove to me you didn't do this and that will be apology enough.' She was tired already and she had a long day ahead of her. Hours and hours in an interview room with Harrison as well as directing a team of officers who were working the investigation. It was one of the reasons she hated that so many of the custody suites had closed. You were never in the same station as your team when you were interviewing an offender. It made the process difficult to say the least. But costs had had to be cut and, in this case, custody suites were the victims.

'Okay,' said Kirsty. 'Reason and grounds for arrest, Claudia?'

Harrison looked back down to the floor. Claudia rubbed her face with her hands. She had to do this. The quicker she got through it the better. Once it was done she wouldn't have to do it again.

'He's been arrested for the murder of Ruth Harrison . . .'

There was a quick intake of breath from Kirsty. Harrison looked up at her and shook his head sharply. 'No, Kirsty, I didn't.'

'Be quiet, Dominic.' She glared at him as tears filled her eyes. She turned to Claudia. 'And grounds?' she asked quietly.

This was the part where she had to tell Kirsty why they thought Dominic was the one who had murdered Ruth. Claudia couldn't believe this was happening. 'There was a broken glass at his home indicative of a struggle and a pool of blood which we're having assessed to see if it is a match for Ruth, and also if someone could survive losing that much, but on first glance, we're saying, no, no they couldn't. Something bad happened at that address last night and we need to find out what that was.'

A tear slipped down Kirsty's cheek. She tapped in the details Claudia had given her into the custody system. 'You don't know where she is?' she asked.

'No, not at this moment in time.'

Seeing Kirsty become emotional made Claudia's own throat thicken. She tried to swallow past the pain and hurt inside her but she nearly choked on it. What had Ruth gone through? And where was she? Was she cold and shivering and bleeding out waiting for them to find her? The thought nearly brought Claudia to her knees. She grabbed hold of the custody desk and held on hard.

Kirsty continued to type into the system. Claudia could hear her giving Dominic his rights. It was vague and fuzzy, in the background. Words she had heard hundreds of times before. His rights to legal advice, his right to read the codes of practice, the book that said how cops had to work and also his right to have someone told that he was here. But who would he tell? The one person he might tell that didn't know was probably dead.

The acrid taste of vomit hit the back of her throat. She swallowed hard and winced at the taste in her mouth.

'I need a drink of water. Are you okay with him?' she asked Kirsty.

Kirsty waved her away. 'Yes, yes. Go. We'll finish getting him booked in and then get him fingerprinted, photographed and his DNA done etc.'

They both looked at her with sympathy written across their faces. Though she couldn't tell if Dominic's was for himself or for her.

She stumbled away in the direction of the toilets, walked into a cubicle and locked herself in, pushing her forehead against the door. She couldn't believe she had been the one to book him into custody. Sharpe had been cruel to put this on her. There were plenty of other people who could have done it. She turned around to the toilet basin. She wouldn't vomit.

Claudia could see why Sharpe had done what she'd done. If it was unsettling her then it would damn well be unsettling him. With a deep intake of breath she steadied herself and unlocked the cubicle. In front of the mirror she could see the day was already starting to take its toll on her. Dark shadows were starting to form under her eyes. She twisted the tap on and held her hands underneath the running water until it was cold, then scooped it onto her face. It was time to take Dominic Harrison into interview and see what he had to say for himself. Ruth was out there somewhere and she needed to be found. Whatever state she was in.

When she came out of the ladies her DS, Russell Kane, was waiting for her. Russ was a hulk of a man, with broad shoulders from his spare time playing rugby. He had a proper rugby player's nose that had been broken several times and was bent out of shape, but for all his bulk and threatening appearance, he was one of the most loved members of her team and she was glad she had him with her today.

'Hey, Russ.' She smiled up at him. 'Thanks for today.'

'No worries. How are you holding up?'

'Oh, you know. . . Sharpe said this was the best play to find Ruth. Bearing in mind it's the most important thing right now, I have to put my feelings aside and get on with the job. I hope we can find her before anything bad . . .' She paused a minute, rubbed at her face. 'Before anything worse happens to her.' She looked Russ in the eye. 'The blood needs to be tested. We don't know that it was hers yet. I've seized a toothbrush and hairbrush so they can look for a match, but until then, we hold out hope.' She didn't know if she was saying that for factual accuracy or to keep herself going.

'Got it.' He'd do anything for her and if she needed for him to hold it together and keep this day ticking over like any ordinary investigation then that's what he would do.

* * *

The offender interview room in the custody suite was not that different to the witness interview room they had left at Snig Hill — though this one held recording equipment and had a red emergency push bar running around the room.

Dominic had stated he did not want a solicitor. Neither did he want a Fed rep — a representative of the police federation, the police union, who could be present during the interview. He said he had done nothing wrong therefore he had no need of either of them. Those were for people who were guilty or had something to hide. He was neither.

Claudia and Kane grabbed their seats and lowered themselves down in front of him.

The room closed in on her. Small, suffocating and claustrophobic. Claudia wanted to claw at her throat but tried to focus on the job at hand. Kane unwrapped the discs the interview would be recorded on. The seconds dragged by as Kane loaded the disc into the machine, then they were ready.

Claudia made the introductions. When it was time for Harrison to talk for the recording and give his own name and address she gritted her teeth. Her body told her that Sharpe and Connelly were wrong. They were way out on a limb and she was not the best person to be doing this. She reminded Harrison that he was entitled to free and independent legal advice and cautioned him again, explaining the caution to him in plain speak, even though it was something he had done himself many a time, so understood the caution back to front.

Harrison never said a word throughout it all. He just looked at her as she walked through the initial procedures. Then it was time to remind him of his reason for arrest and she stumbled. Her words fell over themselves as they came

out of her mouth. 'You've been arrested on the murder of
— the suspicion of the murder of Ruth Harrison at some
point between yesterday afternoon, when she was last seen,
and today.'

A drop of sweat slid down her spine. She wriggled in her
seat in an attempt to get her clothing away from her skin.
Damp patches were an obvious sign she was struggling and
she would not give him the pleasure of seeing that from her.

Opposite her, Harrison was sitting back in his chair. He
could have been the interviewing officer for how calm he was.
Kane gave her the briefest half-smile. He was here for her and
had her back. She could do this.

'You've already explained about last night and how you
didn't see Ruth when you got home from work, Dominic.
Tell me what you think has happened to her,' she said, proud
that her voice came out calm and level.

Harrison scratched his head, his eyes dark. 'I've told you,
I think it's the Sheffield Strangler, the case I'm investigating.
I think he has something to do with this and in taking her he
might even have decided to set me up.'

'I'm not working that case. Why don't you tell us about
it?'

CHAPTER 10

Dominic

Six months ago

The team were parked a little away from the scene. It was the closest the car could get. They would have to make the rest of their way on foot.

Dominic had seen a couple of large lamps inside one of the CSU vans. These were in preparation for the darkness that was already threatening to descend. It was the start of October — it would be dark by seven and they needed to be organised. The sky was already overcast and gloomy, the wooded area adding to the feeling of being penned in. They had to work quickly to prepare the ground for where they wanted to place the equipment and make sure they weren't covering evidence with the base of the lights.

Further down the road was an ambulance with its rear doors open and sitting on the back step was a man holding onto his dog on a lead. His shoulders were slumped, his grip on the lead loose, but the spaniel lay quietly at his feet. 'Krish, go and talk to the caller, make sure he's okay and if the ambulance let him go, take him back to the station for a

CSI to do an examination and seize his clothing. If they take him to the hospital go with him and do everything you need to do there. I take it you brought a change of clothes in case he hasn't got anyone who can bring him a set?'

DC Krish Dhawan pulled his notebook from the car. 'Yes, all organised before we left. The fact that he'd fallen onto the body gave me a clue. I imagine he doesn't want to be in those clothes any longer than he has to be.'

'Let's hope he hasn't transferred too much evidence onto himself because until we take those clothes off him he will be shedding it as he moves. We need to get this done as quickly as possible. Maybe do it in the back of the ambulance if they'll allow. The change of clothes at least.'

Dominic was conscious of losing evidence. As there was no life to save, his priority was to preserve evidence so they could advance the inquiry and bring the case to a conclusion with a prosecution. And for that to happen they needed to be alert. They needed to take every step with careful precision and consider all scenarios.

Krish grabbed a bag out of the boot and headed towards the ambulance.

It was off one of the wooded footpaths that the body had been found and the uniformed officers guarding the crime scene had done as Kapoor had requested and kept the cordon wide. CSU had beat them there. Suited up, they were approaching the scene slowly and methodically under the canopy of the trees which was casting a dark gloom over proceedings.

There was no need for all of them to enter the scene so Dominic pulled on the white Tyvek suit, provided his details to the uniformed officer guarding the cordon, and followed the CSIs on the silver plates they were laying down.

It took them about five minutes to reach the woman's body. The officers had cordoned off the footpath to stop people coming to look. There was also a small cordon closer to the woman.

She was in a shallow grave with parts of her body above the soil. Dominic swallowed, not happy about what he was about to see, but he steadily approached the unsettled ground.

Her blonde hair was a matted tangled mess in the shrubbery and soil on the ground. She was somewhere in her forties. For some reason he had expected someone who was younger, but she had lines on her face that expressed her age.

Dominic stood over the woman and took in her state. There were ligature marks around her throat and yet it had also been cut. Had he tried to strangle her but failed, so cut her instead, or had the strangulation been part of an elaborate game? Her clothing was dyed red where the blood had run down from the slice in her neck. Her legs were still under the soil. She had been dragged partly out of the ground she had been placed in and Dominic surmised that it was probably animals that had disturbed the basic shallow grave, pulling on the woman in an attempt to better get at her, to see what she was. But he didn't think they had done much damage. It didn't look as though she had been in the ground long, though flies had already made themselves at home. He flicked his hand in front of his face to shift a stray fly that had moved too far away from his feeding ground.

A stain of bright red lipstick smeared around her mouth added a garish look to the poor woman.

Clicking sounded in Dominic's ear as one of the CSIs took photographs of the scene and of the woman in situ. Dominic stepped back out of the way and the CSI thanked him.

'Ah, Dominic, what do we have all the way out here, then?' The voice came from behind him. He turned. It was the Home Office registered forensic pathologist Nadira Azim. She was a petite woman with a softly spoken voice. He liked the way she worked. Her respect of the dead shone through in everything she did.

'It's not pleasant, Nadira,' he said as she approached.

'They seldom are,' she replied, lifting her face mask up to cover her mouth.

He moved to the side to allow her past and she stepped over to the woman in the ground and crouched down at the side of her. 'Good evening, what are you going to tell me today?' she said to the corpse in the ground, so quietly Dominic had to strain to hear her.

It seemed as though the only sound in the woods was the noise of the flies as they buzzed around the body. He hated death and what it did to people. He understood that it was natural. That this woman in front of him didn't feel any of this and that her energy was going back into the soil every minute that she rested here. But still, it irked him the lack of respect that was shown to her. She should be with her loved ones. Ideally alive, but if she was dead then she deserved to be laid to rest as she and her family had decided she would be. Not left like this for the wildlife to make the most of.

'She's not quite gone into bloat yet, Dominic,' Nadira said from her position on the ground. 'Which means she hasn't been dead long. I'd say a day or two but I can give you a better idea once I do the PM back at the morgue.'

'When will you be fitting that in?' Dominic asked.

She turned to him. 'I'll table her for first thing in the morning. How does that suit?'

'Suits fine. I'm hoping we'll have an ID by then. I hate when they lay unidentified. It seems so disrespectful.'

Nadira's fingers worked quickly as she took nail clippings from the woman before she bagged up her hands. 'I hope you do. I like to put a name to my patients.' She sat back on her heels. 'I'm not sure about bagging her head. It'll interfere with the cut mark around her neck.' She paused a moment and Dominic let her think. The flies continued their own work around her and Nadira ignored them, unperturbed. 'I think I'll leave it and make sure she's bagged properly as a whole so we don't lose anything. I don't want to risk that wound any more than those flies are damaging the evidence right now.'

Dominic peered over Nadira's shoulder at the wound across the woman's neck which was gently humming. His stomach twisted. 'Urgh. The natural process is disgusting. When I die you can burn me and make it quick.'

'You'd better have a conversation with Ruth then. Make sure she's aware of your wishes.' Nadira picked up one of the flies with a pair of tweezers — too stuffed with feeding to move out of her way — and unceremoniously dumped it into a clear glass vial before twisting a lid on.

'How do you want to go?' Dominic asked. 'Do you believe in all this green burial that's all the rage now? Where you're left in the ground without a casket to let the bugs eat you so you go back to the earth where you supposedly came from?'

Nadira continued with her tweezers, collecting flies and eggs and dropping them into vials. 'I do, Dom. It's a brave new world. As a Muslim woman I will be buried without a casket anyway.'

A couple of CSI clanged up behind them with the huge metal lights and suddenly they were bathed in fluorescent white light. The woman was illuminous in death in the white glow.

'That's better,' said Nadira. 'I was beginning to struggle. What with the tree cover and the time of day.' She turned to the CSIs. 'Thanks, guys. I appreciate it.'

The day was dragging on; they were losing the light. They needed a break in the case, some new evidence they could move on or the day would close on a new case with no leads.

CHAPTER 11

Dominic

They didn't have an identification for the woman as yet. There was nothing on her person that gave her away and most of her fingertips had been nibbled at by woodland creatures so fingerprints were out of the question.

The crime scene investigators did their thing around her body, sieving for evidence, slowly brushing away the soil around her. It wouldn't be a quick job to get her out of the ground. They couldn't just pick her up and take her away. The smallest piece of evidence in the damp woodland ground could prove to be the piece they needed to close the case.

'I'm going to talk to the witness,' Dominic said. 'We'll also search our missing person's database now I have some kind of description to go on. See if we can ID her before the PM tomorrow.'

He walked away from the burial site and the quiet efficient scene of people hard at work, tirelessly taking it step by tiny step. He admired the CSIs and how they could focus on such detailed work and in such difficult conditions.

Back on the road Krish was still at the ambulance and Paul was waiting by the car with DC Hayley Loftus. There wasn't much to do here as it wasn't a place you were going to get a collection of witnesses.

'What've we got, Sarge?' Hayley asked.

Dominic ran his hand through his hair. 'It's not pleasant. She's in a shallow grave and it looks as though animals have tried to drag her out. There are bruises around her neck but she's also had her throat cut. Nadira won't make a guess on which one killed her until she's done the PM, as you can imagine. The woman looks to be in her forties. We need to check our missing people to see if we have anyone of that age that matches her basic description. How's Krish getting on? Do we think the dog walker has anything to do with it?'

Paul shook his head. 'From what I can gather the guy is shaking like a leaf. He's either a really good actor or he's had nothing to do with this at all. We'll obviously look into him. Get his movements for however long this woman has been missing and around the time of death. Do what we can with him. But I think he's a witness and nothing else.'

'I'll go and check in with Krish and we'll go from there.' And with that Dominic turned his back and strode towards the ambulance where Krish, the paramedic and the dog walker were waiting.

The dog walker was an older gent. He had thick white hair with a bald patch at the top, and was pale and shaken, sitting on the steps of the ambulance with a blood pressure pump around his arm. He was wearing tracksuit bottoms and a plain white T-shirt. Krish had obviously managed to get him changed and seized his clothes.

Dominic hoped that a CSI had done his examination as well. It annoyed him when tasks were left half done.

Krish introduced the man. 'Sarge, this is Derek Fearns, he found our woman this afternoon. Derek, this is Detective Sergeant Dominic Harrison.'

Dominic held out his hand then withdrew it slightly, concerned that he would contaminate a crime scene — the other man's hand.

Derek frowned.

'It's okay, sarge, a CSI has been and Garry here—' he indicated the paramedic — 'allowed us to use his van, so the forensic examination has taken place. You're safe to shake hands.'

The puzzled look on Derek's face balanced out. 'Ah, yes, I've been prodded and poked and trimmed very comprehensively.' He held out his own hand and Dominic clasped it between both of his.

'I'm sorry you had to find her today. It must have been a shock. Thank you for staying around and helping us. We appreciate it. You don't realise how helpful it is when members of the public give us their support, so thank you.'

A little blood surfaced in Derek's face again and climbed up his cheeks. 'I would rather I hadn't needed to be quite so helpful if I'm honest, but I would never have dreamed of walking away. That poor woman . . .' His eyes drifted off for a moment.

The paramedic took the blood pressure cuff off his arm. 'It might be best if we get Derek checked out at the hospital.'

Dominic needed a quick account before they left. 'You've probably told this story a couple of times already today, Derek, and you're going to have to repeat it several more times before this investigation is through, but would you mind telling me what happened this afternoon?'

The dog, a shaggy-eared, liver-and-white spaniel, shifted at Dominic's feet, lifted his head from his paws and looked up as though aware of what they were talking about and wary of what they were putting his master through. Dominic leant down and rubbed his head. 'It's okay, boy.'

Derek let out a deep sigh. 'Oh, what a day. I so wish I had stayed at home.' He rubbed his arms as though he were cold. 'But Ralph here was desperate for a walk and he deserved a decent one so I brought him here. When he ran off the path I thought he was chasing a squirrel. I was so annoyed with him. I shouted and shouted at him. Remember that video of the man calling his dog that went viral? It was like that. He was ignoring me. I was furious. He's usually such a well-behaved boy.' They all looked down at Ralph who had now placed his head back on his paws looking for all the world like the best-behaved boy his owner was saying he was. Not the running wild animal he had previously been.

'And what happened?' asked Dominic.

'I chased after him. You know, like that video. I didn't want to lose him. He was turning a deaf ear and who knew how far he was going to run. I didn't want anything to happen to him. For all I was angry with him I still adore the old chap and had to keep track of him.' His voice faltered. There was real love between human and dog.

'And you found him . . .' prompted Dominic, eager to get to the pertinent part of the story.

Derek physically jolted. Like a small electric shock had been sent through his body. 'Yes,' he said. 'I found him. He was standing still, his nose down to the ground, but I was still running when I found him and didn't realise I had caught up with him. I had lost sight of him, you see, and when I suddenly came across him I was pulled up short and fell over him and right into what he had his nose in.' He went quiet, hugged his body and rubbed his hands up and down his arms.

The temperature was dropping as the clock was ticking on but Dominic knew that wasn't why Derek was rubbing his arms. It was the memory. He was back at the graveside. Stumbling and falling into the shallow grave of an unknown woman. A grave filled with flies. Dominic gave him a moment even though he was desperate to carry on and get all the information he could out of the man. But he would be a better witness if they handled him with kid gloves and they were compassionate rather than bull-headed.

Krish crouched down and rubbed the dogs head. Ralph lifted his nose and sniffed his hand before accepting the fuss and going back to his sleep. It broke Derek out of his reverie.

'It startled old Ralph. He jumped back away from the grave.' He barked out a laugh. 'I'd frightened him by falling but he hadn't been scared by the grave. That's the difference between us and animals.' The laugh died in his throat. 'I was terrified when I saw what it was I was lying in. I could feel something solid yet squishy under my hands and there was this sound that was freaking me out. It was persistent and loud. It was surrounding me and I thought it was going to invade me. I was terrified even if Ralph wasn't. I saw her face. My hand was on her stomach. I tried to push myself back, but didn't have my balance as I was still flat on the ground, so ended up falling back onto her.' He looked from Ralph up to Dominic. 'You should have heard me squealing. Not very manly, I'm afraid.'

'I can't say I blame you,' replied Dominic. 'It wasn't a pleasant sight and if you're not used to that kind of thing, well . . . it's not easy.'

Derek frowned. 'You find it easy, Detective Sergeant?'

Dominic took a step backwards. It was as though he had been physically punched. That wasn't what he had been saying. He wasn't used to this kind of thing either. It wasn't supposed to come out that way. He put his palm up. 'No. No, not at all. That's not what I was saying. I may have more of a coping mechanism in place to deal with death than you have because it's part of my job, is what I meant. Not that I have become desensitised to it. Especially difficult jobs like this.' He cleared his throat. He was making a mess of this. 'Any job. Any person who has been killed or has died in suspicious circumstances. None of it is pleasant, but we have to get on with it for the sake of the person we are investigating. To get the best result for them and for their family.' He stepped back up to Derek. 'You understand it's about putting something right that has originally been very, very wrong? Right in the best way we know how anyway.'

Derek nodded silently.

Dominic lowered his voice. 'I'm sorry you have had to go through this. No one should have to. It's wrong that people like myself and Krish are in a position where we have to make a place in our heads for this kind of stuff, but the world isn't all good and shiny. It's dark and sharp and people are hurt by it.'

Derek held up his hand. 'It's okay, Detective Sergeant. I'm sorry if I overstepped. It's been a long day as you can imagine.'

'I understand. We need to get you to the station when you've been to the hospital, as we have to get a statement from you covering what you've said.'

Derek scratched his head. 'But there's nothing there. Nothing I saw that would help you.'

'I know you feel that way, but as the person who found the body you are an integral part of the investigation and we have to get your account down as soon as we can. Is there anyone who can come and collect Ralph so you can go and get checked out at the hospital?'

Derek started, shaking his head. 'My wife, she'll be so upset by all of this. But she can take Ralph. I've already called her and she's on her way. I couldn't tell her everything as I wanted her to get here safely, but she's already worried by my cryptic message to come and get Ralph.' He peered sadly down at the dog. 'Wasn't she, boy?' He let out a sigh. Ralph swished his tail in response.

Dominic grabbed hold of Krish's arm and pulled him to one side. 'Follow him to the hospital, stay with him and as soon as he's ready to be released bring him back to the station and get his account down. For now we treat him as an unknown quantity. If he's going to trip himself up in any way I want it down officially and let's see him wriggle out of it then.'

Krish tapped his notebook. 'I've got his first account logged in here and I'll make sure to get him back to the station as soon as I can.'

Dominic turned back to Derek. 'I'll leave you in the capable hands of Krish. Again, I'm sorry you had to go through this today. We'll get you back home as quickly as we can.'

'Thank you,' Derek said, his voice shaking again. Dominic couldn't tell if he was stressed by the situation, or if he was lying. Maybe he was covered in the victim's bodily fluids because he had decided to move her and then changed his mind and called the cops instead. It was now his job to determine which one he was.

CHAPTER 12

Claudia

Fourteen hours since Ruth's attack

'So, you thought the dog walker had something to do with the first murder?' Claudia scribbled on paper.

'It was a line of inquiry as it would be for any investigation that is just up and running. The person who called it in is closest to the victim so we have to check them out. You know all this, why would you query me on ?' Dominic's tone was harsh. 'In fact, why are you questioning my actions on that case at all? What the hell does it have to do with Ruth going missing?'

'You tell me, Dominic. You're the one who is sitting here telling me that your case is the reason that Ruth is missing and potentially dead if the amount of blood we've found is any indication.'

'Yeah, I'm talking about the case. To let you know what it was about, so you'd understand how Ruth got involved and why I'm a target. Not so you can second guess my decision-making skills during the running of it. You might be a

DI but you're not my DI.' He was bolt upright in his chair now and completely rattled.

Claudia, on the other hand, was surprisingly calm. The louder Dominic became the calmer she found she was. She wanted answers and she would not apologise for doing her job. If he found that tough going then maybe he did have something to hide, though that thought terrified her. If he only wanted her to ask certain questions but not others maybe she was on the right track. His agitation seemed a little off. Like he was struggling to keep his thought processes in line. But his wife was missing and he'd been arrested for her murder so it was probably no surprise he was finding it difficult to focus on Claudia's questions. The problem was, going by the blood in the garage, if Ruth was not dead then she didn't have long to find her, and if Dominic could help with locating her then she would push as much as needed. Finding the truth, either way, was imperative.

'I might not be your supervisor but right now I am the person who is interviewing you and if we're being pedantic, Dominic, I do outrank you and I'm in control of you. Of when we talk, when you eat and when you sleep. I can put off this interview to follow other lines of inquiry if I want, but I thought you wanted to be involved? I thought you wanted to help the investigation into your missing wife? Yelling at me is getting you nowhere.'

Dominic slumped in his seat and dropped his arms onto the table, defeated. 'You know I want to do this. I don't want you to leave. I want to work with you to find her and I think I'm the best person to help you because I truly believe the case we were working is where you'll find your answers.' He looked from Kane to Claudia. 'I'm sorry, okay? We'll do it your way. Ask me anything you like. About the investigation, my decisions during the investigation. You might be right, it might be that one of my decisions has led us here.' He bowed his head.

Kane glanced at Claudia and she inclined her head to let him know that she was okay. He was ready to jump in and take the lead should she give him any indication that was what she wanted. This was going to be a long interview if they were going to work through the entire investigation of his current case. It had been running for the last six months.

She could keep Dominic here to question him for twenty-four hours before she had to make a decision on charging or releasing him, though she could apply for extensions. She'd need them because included in that twenty-four-hour time limit was allotted time for an eight-hour sleep, plus breaks for meals. There was no way she would work through what she needed — interviewing him and working through any evidence the interview threw up — in the basic twenty-four hours. She would be applying to a superintendent for a twelve-hour extension.

Claudia looked at her watch.

'You want to get on with it?' Dominic asked. 'I've said I will do anything to help you find Ruth and I mean that. I'm sorry for my outburst. I feel so helpless sitting here. I'd rather be a part of the investigation as you are, not in the way I'm being now.' He shrugged. 'But if it helps, then so be it. Promise me you are doing everything you can outside of this interview room, Claudia.'

She put the mug down with a bit of a slam. 'Do you think I want to be in here interviewing you? I'd also rather be out there following other lines of inquiry, but the powers that be have determined that I'm the best person for this task, so we're stuck with each other and with that, we'd better do the best job we can.'

Dominic rubbed a hand through his hair. A sigh escaped his lips.

'Why is it so important that you tell me about the start of the investigation, Dominic? Why not just tell me the pertinent parts? Wouldn't that be quicker?' Multiple questions were not the best way to interview a detainee but she had the feeling he was playing for time rather than trying to be helpful. What was the point of that, though?

'You haven't been involved in the case. You only know about it from the gossip that's been travelling round the force and from what you hear through the media like everyone else. It's important you know the savagery of who we're up against and how he works. If he's taken Ruth you might find something that piques your interest as I talk. You're a fresh pair of eyes and a very competent pair at that. It may be that you see something we missed and in doing so you find the way to Ruth.'

CHAPTER 13

Dominic

Six months ago

Nadira was ready to move the woman. They had spent hours at the site gathering as much evidence as they could. Outside scenes like this were difficult to process due to the amount of product that could potentially be part of the crime.

The woman's hands were bagged to prevent loss of forensic evidence and a body bag was laid out at the side of her. The crime scene unit would still have work to do once she had been removed from the shallow grave as they processed whatever lay beneath her. The offender could have left some microscopic evidence beneath her as he laid her down.

Very gently she was lifted and moved over to the body bag.

Nadira looked down into the empty space left behind. Dominic's eyes were trained on the same area.

'What's that?' She pointed to an area where the victim's torso had previously lain.

'Where?' Dominic couldn't see what she was pointing at.

'At the edge of the grave. Soil is covering half of it. Can you see, it seems to be reflective, shiny almost.'

Dominic spotted it and pointed it out to the nearest CSI who bent down and collected it, lifting it up for both Nadira and Dominic to see.

'What is it?' Dominic asked.

'Looks to me to be a . . .' Nadira tilted her head. 'Lipstick?'

The CSI tipped the item so he could see the bottom. 'Yep.'

'It looks pretty new,' Nadira said. 'Like he left it here for us.'

'Can we get DNA off it?' Dominic asked.

'We should be able to. I doubt he's used it on himself though and I'd not imagine he's left his prints on it, but of course it'll get tested for prints as well.'

'What do you think he's trying to say?'

'I don't know, but it smacks to me of organisation, of someone who has thought this through and who is playing a game. All things I tend not to like in a killing.'

* * *

'What do we have on the missing persons system?' Dominic asked of his team as they sat huddled around their desks, each of them with a bag of chips open, forks moving between bag and mouth as they talked. The sharp tang of vinegar permeated the room along with the slick of grease.

'We have it narrowed down to two possibles within the age range and ethnicity,' said Hayley. 'One of them, Vanessa Simpson, has been missing a little over three weeks and the other one, Julie Carver, has been missing—' she looked up at the team — 'four days.'

Dominic wiped his mouth on the back of his hand. Grease left a slick across his skin. 'It could be either, but the likely candidate is Julie, is that what you're saying?'

A chip was halfway to Hayley's mouth but she put it back down into the bag. 'I'd say she was the best bet with our woman only being dead about two days. If we were to ask family to ID the victim I'd go with Julie's family first.'

Dominic took a slurp from his mug and washed down the cheap and cheerful, but very-bad-for-him, meal they had grabbed while working. 'Okay then, let's visit Julie's husband, let him know what we have and see if he's willing to do an ID. It won't be pleasant for him but you're right, the likelihood is that this is Julie Carver. What was she wearing when she went missing?'

The phone on his desk rang and he held a finger up to hold the question before he answered the call.

'DS Harrison, it's Nadira Azim. I haven't caught you at a bad time, have I?'

'No, no, not at all. We were going through possible identification scenarios and think we have one. We have a little work to do on it first, of course, but I might be calling you back to do an ID procedure.'

'That's good. It's not easy when relatives don't know what's happened to loved ones.'

'It's not what you called for though.'

Nadira sighed down the phone. 'I've got the results for the lipstick on the victim's face and the tube left in the grave and they match.'

Dominic folded the paper over his chips and threw the bag of remains into his bin, then realised he would have to move it into the kitchen otherwise he would be haunted by the smell of greasy chips until the cleaners came in the morning and by then the whole room would be infused with the smell. He shook his head. He'd do it as soon as this call ended. 'You think he's starting a calling card?'

'It's the way it feels to me and I thought you'd want to know what you're dealing with sooner rather than later.'

Dominic checked his watch. 'What time are you doing the PM tomorrow?'

'I'm going to table her in first,' Nadira said, her voice had a faraway sound to it as though she was considering something else while she was talking to Dominic. 'So, I'll expect you about nine a.m.?' she asked.

'Can you get her prepared for identification tonight?' The smell of the chips was getting up his nose and annoying him.

'She's filthy, Dom. She's not in the best state to be viewed. It'll be better once she's been dealt with and we can wash her down. Better for the family, that is.'

Dominic agreed with her and said he would see her in the morning before hanging up the phone.

'Sarge?' Hayley turned to him.

'What is it?' They hadn't been on this job long and he already hated it. Hated the viciousness of it. Hated how it was making him feel deep down inside — hated the tone he had used with Hayley. He inclined his head in acquiescence of his sharpness and indicated she should continue.

Her eyes were narrowed at him but she relaxed them. 'We have a photograph on the missing person report for Julie Carver.'

He bolted upright. 'Let me see it.'

She spun her computer monitor around so he could see. Pressed a key on her keyboard and listened as the printer whirred into life. 'And it's not her husband who reported her missing, it was her brother. She was married but she's divorced.'

Dominic didn't know why he leapt to the conclusion she had been married — maybe it was something about her age. He stared at the screen. The face looking back was the same as the one he had seen not a couple of hours earlier. The hair was longer, the skin was pinker, her eyes sparkled, she was looking away from the camera, behind it and to the side slightly, a gentle laugh lighting her up. Something was amusing her beyond the person who was taking this image. Her blue eyes expressed her joy with the world. Her brother had given the police a photograph of Julie that showed her living, not merely as a statistic, which was what missing people were in the end. They were either found and returned home to those who had grieved for them before they needed to, or they never reappeared and became one of the huge number of missing people in the UK. People who disappeared and were never seen again with no rhyme, reason or explanation.

'This her?' Hayley asked.

'That's her.' Someone's life was about to be destroyed. As much as Julie's had been wiped out, her brother and any others who loved her were about to be decimated. 'We need to make contact with her brother. Contact details on the file?'

'Yes, I'm printing off the important things we need.' She stalked to the printer at the edge of the room and pulled off the hot documents — a photograph and a couple of text sheets with Julie's details and those of her brother, Jonathan.

Dominic sighed and looked at Hayley. 'Come with me.'

She grabbed her coat from the back of her chair.

'I suppose we'd better go and tell him we've found her.'

CHAPTER 14

Dominic

Dominic knocked on the door. It looked to be a nice two-up two-down in Mosborough. After a minute the door was opened by a young woman with her hair pulled back quite brutally into a ponytail on the back of her head. Her face was scrubbed clean of any make-up but she wore bright red nail varnish on her fingers which was chipped halfway down her nails. Light spilled out from the doorway onto the front step where Dominic and Hayley were standing.

Dominic waved his warrant card in front of her. 'Is Jonathan Butler at home, please?'

A hand flew to the woman's mouth and she stepped backwards, giving Dominic and Hayley room to enter. Dominic stepped through first. He laid a hand on the woman's arm as he passed. He had no idea who she was, but she was about to be affected by the events of the next few minutes and he felt for her. She looked to already have an inkling of what was to come.

She closed the door behind them and ushered them through to a living room where an adult male and a teenage lad were sitting in front of the television. The adult male turned as they walked in. His brows furrowed to see strangers enter, then comprehension dawned on him. He switched the television off with a remote control and stood to face them.

Dominic lifted his warrant card again. 'I'm DS Dominic Harrison and this is DC Hayley Loftus. Do you have a few minutes to talk to us?'

Jonathan turned to the teenage boy who was staring at the now blank television. 'Ed, go to your room for a few minutes, would you? We'll talk to you soon.' The boy stood, looked at Dominic and Hayley and then skulked off towards the stairs and his room. Jonathan gestured at the sofas and the young woman strode over to his side. He wrapped an arm around her shoulders and she enclosed his waist in one of hers.

Dominic and Hayley walked to the sofas and sat down. Without uttering a word Jonathan and the woman settled down opposite them, their hands clenched together.

'Your son?' asked Dominic, not knowing the Butler's family set-up.

Jonathan Butler shook his head. 'No, Ed is Julie's son. He's been staying with us since she went missing.'

A cold shudder ran through Dominic. He felt Hayley stiffen at the side of him. The boy was now motherless. It was something this couple would have to take in then convey to their nephew.

Dominic looked at the woman. 'Mrs Butler, is it?'

'Oh, yes, sorry, Helen.' Her hand tightened around Jonathan's.

The couple's eyes were wide, the question clear for all to see. They were desperate for answers.

'I'm sorry—' said Dominic. It was as far as he could get before Jonathan jumped to his feet, refusal to hear the rest of the sentence blazing from every cell.

'Get out! Get out of my house!' he screamed at them. Any colour he had in his face now drained from him and his eyes bulged as the stress exploded from him.

Dominic stayed seated where he was, there was no point in escalating the situation any further. If he could calm Jonathan down and get him to talk that would be the better outcome. Having a knock-down fight with the grieving sibling of a murder victim was not going to happen on his watch. He kept his voice low and soft, could see Hayley looking at him out of the corner of his eye. 'Jonathan, I need to talk to you.' He lifted his hands in a placatory manner. 'I know this is difficult and I'm sorry.'

Helen was standing now and had both her hands wrapped around one of Jonathan's arms. She was trying to pull him down, her voice quiet in his ear. Dominic could just make out a couple of words through the noise Jonathan was still screaming at them. Listen. Please. Ed. Help. Julie. And it was at the sound of his sister's name that he stopped shouting and the room dropped into silence.

There was a moment's standoff as Jonathan glared at Dominic and Hayley and Helen silently pleaded up at him, still clinging on to his arm, gently pulling him back down to the sofa he had not long evacuated.

Hayley gave a soft smile to Helen in appreciation. There was no response. She wasn't doing this for the police. She was doing this for her husband. She hated to see him in so much pain, Dominic understood this. Whatever the reasoning he was grateful of the help.

When breaking news of a death you never knew what reaction you were going to get. Some relatives took it in their stride and barely batted an eye. You would have thought you had just informed them that their favourite football team had lost the latest match. It was surreal, but the emotions were forming. They were tiny, a small bud. They needed a little time to grow and push their way to the surface, but in the meantime the family member could function and get on with the tasks that needed to be performed.

Other relatives broke down. Crumbled like sandcastles in a hurricane. Falling in on themselves. Needing the support of their nearest and dearest, or those that were left behind that could help. Dominic did his best to support as he interacted with them, but he had a job to do. His job was to find out the information they held and progress the investigation.

Then there were relatives like Jonathan Butler. These were among some of the most difficult. Those in denial. How he was supposed to wheedle information out of them when they couldn't even process what they were being told was always something he hated trying to figure out. He shot a quick glance at Hayley. She had fashioned her face into a neutral mask. There was no point involving yourself in the grief of others.

Tears were streaming down Helen's face. She knew the truth, at that point still unsaid, and could only watch on as her husband fought against it. She held up a hand to Dominic and Hayley and turned to Jonathan, put a hand on his chest, stared into his eyes. He shook his head.

'No, Helen. Just no. No. No. No.'

He turned to Dominic again. 'You have to leave. You have to go right now.'

Helen spoke. 'Listen to them, John. Hear what they have to say. Whatever it is, we need to hear them and deal with it.' Her voice was gentle.

It may have been his wife's voice or her hand on him — whatever it was, he suddenly collapsed onto the sofa and covered his face with his hands. 'I just can't.'

Helen sat down beside him. 'I know, love.' Her hand found his again.

Jonathan stared at Dominic and Hayley. The question was in his eyes. He had no way to ask them. All fight had gone out of him.

'I'm sorry,' Dominic said again.

Tears slipped down Jonathan's cheeks.

'We found a body in Ecclesall Woods today and—'

The heartbreaking sound came up from somewhere deep within Jonathan. It sounded like an animal in pain. He bent over and clutched himself.

'We believe it to be Julie,' Dominic finished, to make sure they knew the reality of what they were there to tell them and so that there was no confusion later.

'It's not Julie, she's missing. We just need to find her. She's missing, she's not dead,' Jonathan pleaded.

'I visited the site earlier and having seen a photograph I strongly believe it to be Julie, but we do need you to do an official identification to make sure.'

Jonathan rubbed his face where the tears were tracking down his cheeks. 'So, it might not be, you still need me to tell you if it is her or not? It still might not be her, this isn't a definitive.' He was clinging on to the last vestiges of hope.

'We do need you to do the official identification, but it will be for official purposes only, Jonathan. I'm sorry.'

Helen sobbed and Jonathan cradled her close to him as they united in their grief.

'When can I see her?' Jonathan asked, his voice broken and weak.

Dominic took in a deep breath. 'I can take you to see her tomorrow. She isn't currently in any state to be visited.'

Jonathan sagged against Helen. It was as though the air had gone out of him. All the fight had taken flight.

'My beautiful girl. What did he do to you?'

CHAPTER 15

Dominic

Dominic's ears pricked up. 'What do you mean, what did *he* do to you? Who is *he*?' Dominic leaned forward, eager to know what it was Jonathan was talking about.

'Julie was dating. It's on the notes, I presume they made notes, the cops that took her missing report, I said she was dating some guy she'd met online.'

Hayley had read the report and relayed it to him, but there wasn't a lot of detail. 'What can you tell us about him?' There never tended to be much information when an adult went missing. You expected them to come back. Return to their lives when they were good and ready. If there was no mental health issue, or any major health concern, which there wasn't with Julie, then it was often considered that they had gone somewhere of their own volition and would return in the same manner they had left, abruptly and without a word to anyone.

Dominic remembered Julie's report stated she was dating, that it had been an online relationship until recently and that she had last been seen . . . He looked to Hayley, she shrugged and pulled out the report from the folder she was holding and flicked through the pages until she found the one she was looking for and handed it to him.

'We never met him.' Helen wiped away the tears but more were falling as she admitted what must have keenly felt like a failure on their part. 'It was all quite new and Julie said we'd meet him when she was happy they were a definite thing. She wanted to know it was real first.'

A deep sob bubbled up from Jonathan.

The page Hayley handed to him stared up at him. Ed had been left at home while his mother went out. When she didn't come home he got in touch with his uncle who reported her missing. When Jonathan tried to get in touch with her and couldn't he had worried so had gone around to her house and collected Ed. It was weird being there without her.

Hayley looked up from what she was reading. 'Were there signs he had been in the house?'

Jonathan shook his head. 'Not that I could tell.'

Dominic peered over Hayley's shoulder at the pile of paper on her knee. 'Would you mind going over there and walking through the house with us? We're going to need to search it anyway, but I'd like your eye on the place. We don't know what's out of place and what isn't.'

Hayley gave him a dead-eyed stare. They were not supposed to go in before the CSU team.

'He'll be suited up. We won't contaminate anything, but he can offer us a unique insight.'

There was a sliver of light that cut into Jonathan's eyes. He looked a little more alive. He sat up straighter. 'I'll do it. I'll take you to her house and look at it with you. If I can help you then I'll do it.' His voice was like a child at Christmas, all eager to please and full of wishes that very probably wouldn't come true. Santa wasn't real and he didn't come down the chimney.

Dominic agreed to meet Jonathan and Helen at Julie's address after they had talked to Ed and told him they were popping out for half an hour. They would inform him of his mother's loss when they returned. When they could spend the time with him. Now they needed to do this for Julie.

In the car Dominic called the office and asked them to arrange for the CSI search team to meet them at the address, giving them fifteen minutes grace to walk around the house first.

'Do we even have suits in the boot?' Hayley asked.

'Sure we do.' Dominic indicated right.

'And you want to do this?'

'Uh huh.' He took the turning.

'What if it turns out that Jonathan killed her?'

'Then he deserves an Oscar and we are covering ourselves by making sure he's fully covered in a Tyvek suit. Look, he's already admitted he's been in there anyway and he's a regular visitor. He's her brother, whatever we find in there that belongs to him isn't going to work in our favour, he's going to say it got there long before we went in. He's family. Stop worrying.'

Hayley blew air out through her nose.

'He didn't do this, Hayley.' He turned right onto Daresbury Road.

'I know,' she mumbled. 'I hate that you're right all the time.'

'If it makes you feel any better I lost on the horses at the weekend.'

She snorted. 'How did I not know you gambled on the horses?'

He turned and laughed at her. 'Because I don't. I was trying to make you feel better. Did it work?'

She laughed and punched him in the arm. 'That's for being a dick.'

'That's Sergeant Dick, to you.'

The house was a tidy mid-terraced on Myrtle Road, Heeley. Jonathan and Helen were not here yet.

'What are you expecting to find?' Hayley asked.

'I don't know, but she was seeing someone. I'm wondering if that someone had access to the house, if he left any clues to his identity in there. If he did then Jonathan and Helen might be able to pick it out.'

And right on cue their Fiesta pulled up behind them. Jonathan was out like a shot. The house key in his hand, ready to charge up the path and enter his sister's house.

'Slow down.' Dominic held up a hand to placate him. 'We need to get into the lovely white suits first. Protocol,' he said as Jonathan gave him a look.

It was with a jerky frustration that Jonathan clambered into the suit he was given and as he waited for everyone else to get into theirs his fingers tapped at the side of his legs.

'Okay.' Dominic gathered everyone together. 'We stay close at all times. This isn't an opportunity to go off and look around on your own. There is going to be an official search of the premises shortly, we are here for a visual search only, no touching anything. We shouldn't even be here but I'm doing this to see if it can help us.' He stared into Jonathan's eyes. 'Are we clear?'

Jonathan scratched at his nose. 'We are.'

'I know this is difficult, but you're doing us a huge favour by being here today. If you see anything you don't recognise, let myself or Hayley know. Or if you see something out of place, let either one of us know. Whatever you do, do not touch, pick up or move anything inside that house. Clear again?'

Jonathan looked to Helen before answering. She grabbed his hand and offered him a weak smile which he reciprocated in kind. 'Yes.' It was as though they were trying the smile on for size and it didn't fit properly because it quickly slid off their faces. It would be a long time before either of them were comfortable with that feeling again. Their lives had been torn apart and here Dominic was pushing them into an emotional storm that was their sister's house. The place she called home. Her safe place. A place she would never be coming back to again.

They trooped up the narrow pathway down the side of the house to the small garden at the back, Dominic in the lead, with the key in his hand, Hayley bringing up the rear. He placed the key in the lock of the back door, the one Julie used, and heard a sharp intake of breath.

'Jonathan, are you sure you're okay to do this?'

Jonathan was bent over, hands on his knees. 'Yes, yes. I'm fine.' He straightened himself up. 'I'm sorry. It hit me as soon as you pushed the key in that she wouldn't be doing this again.' Helen again soothed him by holding onto his arm. It was probably as much for her own comfort as it was for his.

'We can leave it to the search team if you'd like?' Dominic said, though the reality was he didn't want to. He desperately wanted this couple to go through the house. They might be able to help. They might offer some insight that they might not otherwise get. But it had to be on their terms.

'I'm good, let's go.'

Dominic wanted him to be okay with this. 'You're sure?'

Jonathan took a deep breath. 'Yes. This is for Julie.' A tear slid down his face but Dominic could live with a tear, if it was going to get him a line of enquiry. They had to move forward and do it before the search team arrived at the premises.

He turned the key in the lock and pushed the door open.

It was dark inside. As it was outside. And there was a chill to the property. That chill that told you no one had lived there for a week or more. That feeling when you've been away on holiday and return.

'Oh Julie,' Jonathan stammered behind him.

They had walked into the kitchen. On the sink drainer was an upside-down glass. Long dry. On the kitchen sides were clean bowls not yet put away. Left for another time. A time that would no longer come.

'Notice anything out of place, or anything you don't recognise in here?' Dominic asked.

Jonathan shook his head. His face pale in the shadow of the Tyvek hood.

On the side of the fridge was a list, stuck with a magnetic red blob.

Tomatoes.
Bread.
Onions.
Tampax.
Oranges.

To the side of that was another piece of paper, ragged, torn from a bigger sheet. Taxi and a number.

Below another scruffy piece of her life jotted down and magnetised to the fridge. Keeping her life in order one jotted-down note at a time. *Christian 30 Sept.*

Four days ago.

'Who's Christian?' Dominic asked.

Jonathan stared at the side of the fridge. Lost in a memory of his sister.

'Jonathan,' Dominic prompted.

Jonathan shook himself. 'I think that was the name of the guy from the website she was seeing. I can't be sure. She didn't say a lot about him. She was very coy about it. Her love life left a lot to be desired. After her marriage broke down she thought she would never find love again and the dating sites confirmed that for her, so she kept most of it to herself. Said she'd tell us more when she was sure she had something to tell us. Said she was too old to be doing this. She wasn't some little kid who was easily swayed by a pretty boy picture, this was all too hard for her.'

'Why do it then?' Dominic asked.

Jonathan stared at him for a long time. 'Because she needed someone in her life. Have you never had that feeling? Where you feel so alone, no matter who you are with?'

He kept quiet. It wasn't the time to talk.

'Christian,' Jonathan continued, 'was the guy, I think.' He looked to Helen for confirmation.

She shook her head. 'I don't know, love. I really don't. It could be. All I saw was a photo.'

Dominic rounded on her. 'You saw a photograph of him?'

She took a step back. Her grip on Jonathan released.

Hayley stared at him. Her eyes telling him he had gone too far.

He lowered his voice. 'When did you see a photo?'

Helen looked to the floor. 'Before she went missing. She was at our house and Jonathan was upstairs in the shower. She whispered that she was seeing this new guy and did I want to see him. Of course I did. She showed me his website profile.' Her eyes lifted to Dominic. 'There was nothing there. He was blotted out by the sun which was streaming in from behind him and blurring out the camera lens. Of course I told her he looked nice. How she could even tell I have no idea. You couldn't make anything out from that photo. You would be lucky to even tell his ethnicity from it.'

'Could you?' His tone was blunt. He was tired of getting nowhere.

'What?' Her tone indicated fatigue. Grief was tiring and they had a long way to go yet.

'Tell his ethnicity at least. Do we at least know what ethnicity this man is she met up with?'

Helen shared a look with Jonathan. A look that pleaded with him to help her. He stepped forward partially blocking Dominic's view of her.

'Helen?' Dominic prompted.

'Yes, I could tell. He was white. The man you are looking for is white.'

'Thank you.' It wasn't much. It wasn't much at all, but he was grateful to this couple who were giving it all they could just to stay upright. Dominic moved towards the door. 'Is there anything else in here, guys?'

They both shook their heads. The day bearing down on them.

'Let's move on, then.'

The walk around the rest of the house was uneventful. For Dominic anyway. For Jonathan and Helen it was something else altogether. They had just found out Julie was dead and here they were walking around her house.

'Thank you for coming.' Dominic shook Jonathan's hand at the side of the road. They'd stripped out of their Tyvek suits and looked to be your average human again, rather than the Tellytubbies' rather odd cousins.

'I'm sorry I couldn't be of more help,' Jonathan said.

'If there was nothing there, then there was nothing there. We can't fabricate evidence,' Dominic reassured him. 'Much as we'd love to find something immediately and clear this right up for you, it often doesn't work that way. We're methodical and we'll do it right.' He looked at Helen. 'Do you know the dating site she used?'

Helen shook her head. 'It was one of the new ones. I don't know which one. I wasn't paying attention. I was looking at the photo of the guy she was meeting. I told her he looked nice. It's what she wanted to hear, wasn't it? I couldn't tell her anything else, could I?'

'You couldn't,' Hayley jumped in. 'It's what we do. Our friends, our loved ones, they want support and we offer it. Regardless of what we really think. You had no way of knowing if this guy was on the level or not. It may be that he was. We might all be jumping to conclusions. We need to speak to him to rule him out of our enquiry.'

'So, it might not even be him?' She clung on to the hope Hayley had offered her.

'We don't know anything at this point so there's nothing gained in getting ahead of ourselves. One step at a time.' It was Hayley's turn to reach out and grab an arm. She squeezed Helen's. Helen inclined her head in thanks.

'I'll meet you tomorrow?' Jonathan asked, about the identification procedure.

'Yes. At the hospital. I'll see you there.' Dominic gave him his card with contact details on. 'We'll allocate you a family liaison officer, but in the meantime if you have any questions don't hesitate to give me a call.' He was asking for trouble and it should all go through the FLO but he could see Julie in the ground and wanted to do what he could for her brother. To bring peace to her family and, in turn, to her. Whatever form that took, he would do it. 'We'll also need to inform Social Care that Ed is currently living with you. They'll be in touch with you relatively quickly. It's a process in situations like this.'

Helen's shoulders drooped like she had all the weight she could carry on them, but she gave a quick nod and ushered her bereft husband towards home.

They watched as Jonathan and Helen drove away.

'You think it's the dating guy?' asked Hayley once they were out of sight.

Dominic shook his head. 'I don't know. She could have seen him and then walked away into the arms of her killer. CSU will seize her laptop, maybe the dating site or app is on there and we can ID him that way. The sooner we can find him the sooner we can eliminate him from our enquiries.'

They were only standing in front of the house for a couple of minutes when they heard a gentle cough at their side.

Dominic turned. Approaching them from their left was an older woman with grey hair and a little dog on a lead. 'I'm sorry to disturb you,' she said, not looking in the least bit as though she was sorry. 'But I saw you enter Julie's house with Jonathan a while ago, and the thing is, I haven't seen Julie and Ed in what seems like an age. Can I ask who you are and where Julie and Ed are? I'm worried, you see, it's not that I'm nosey.'

Dominic imagined the truth was she was probably a little of both. She desperately wanted to know who had entered her neighbour's address but she was also worried about her younger friend who she hadn't seen for a while. He could always fudge the truth, be the cagey police officer, but she was about to see the CSU van and that would set tongues wagging. Maybe the neighbour could help?

'Jonathan is worried about his sister. He hasn't seen her for a while and doesn't know where she is. Have you seen her about lately?' He already knew the answer to this one. The answer was in a refrigerator at the morgue. But it would lead on to the other questions.

The woman put her free hand up to her chest. 'Oh, no. I haven't seen her. I did wonder. Poor girl, I do hope she is all right. Do you think she will be okay?'

'We need to find out what's happened to her.' Dominic skirted the issue. 'Have you seen anyone around the house that you don't recognise? With Julie perhaps?' His hopes raised. She was obviously nosey enough to be paying some attention. If this guy, Christian maybe, came to the house to pick her up, he may have been seen and they might be able to obtain a description.

'I'm sorry, I didn't see anyone with Julie. She's a lovely woman but kind of keeps to herself, if you know what I mean. Comes and goes but doesn't talk to the neighbours much. I'm not sure anyone knows much about Julie. Even I only know her name, that she has that great boy and that Jonathan is her brother — and that was because I was in the garden one summer morning as he was visiting. Lovely chap he is — and his wife as well. Seem a close family.' She stopped for a minute then realised she had missed something. 'What about Ed? Where's Ed?'

'He's fine. He's with his uncle and aunt at the minute being looked after.'

She sighed, her relief obvious. She wasn't any help but wanted to stay and get the inside track on what the police were doing.

'I'll get someone to come around and get a quick statement from you at some point, maybe tomorrow. Just to say when you last saw Julie, if you don't mind?' Dominic said.

The dog tugged on the lead — he was bored standing on the pavement. Dominic couldn't say he blamed him. Headlights appeared behind the woman and started to slow down as they got closer. It was the CSU. Dominic pulled out his notebook. 'It's Mrs . . . ?'

'Hughes, from next door.'

Dominic scribbled it down and closed his book. 'Thank you for your time, Mrs Hughes. We appreciate it. I have to go and talk to these officers now. But we'll be in touch.'

Her lips pursed but she smiled tightly and turned around back the way she had come from. 'Come along, Walter, we can finish listening to that book.'

'DS Harrison?' A tall slender man climbed out of the CSU van.

Dominic held out his hand. 'Dominic.'

The man took his hand, his grip firm and strong. 'Andrew Greaves. I'll be in charge of processing the house this evening. Is there anything you are looking for in particular?'

Dominic let out a breath. 'I'm sorry, no. She went missing and was found in a shallow grave earlier today. Any signs of struggle, the usual electronic equipment to be seized. We don't have her phone. I don't know if it's in the house. It wasn't with the body.'

Greaves acknowledged Dominic's needs then turned away; they had a job to do and it was getting late. He wanted to get on. Dominic walked to the car with Hayley in tow behind him.

'Time to send everyone home. We can pick up where we left off tomorrow,' he said as he climbed into the driver's seat. 'This doesn't feel like it's going to be one of those cases where we close it in a day or two. You know the odds. The longer the killer is left out there, the more likely it is he stays out there, free.'

CHAPTER 16

Dominic

The drive home was one of those where Dominic couldn't remember the specifics of the journey. That was until the woman ran in front of his car, her hands waving for Dominic to stop. There was no need to wave, the fact that there was suddenly a human in front of him pretty much assured the woman that the brakes would be applied.

Dominic hadn't been travelling at any speed and easily glided to a halt, then climbed out the car.

The woman was on him immediately, her voice high-pitched and panicky. 'Quick. Help. Help me. She's inside. It's burning.'

It was at the mention of burning that Dominic turned in the direction the woman had run from. The semi-detached house was mostly in darkness, other than a light in an upstairs window. It was the blackened smoke that was twisting out of the open doorway that made his heart stop.

The woman grabbed his jacket in her fists, balling the cloth under his chin. 'Help her.'

Under the street light Dominic could see the woman's eyes were wild, her pupils dilated, filling her irises. Her face was streaked with soot.

'Someone's in there?' He gently took hold of her wrists, ready to pull them away.

'My daughter. My daughter . . . her bedroom.' Tears streaked through the ash on her face. 'Please . . .'

People were starting to gather on the pavement. Staring alternatively between the burning house and the stricken woman in front of Dominic.

'Call the fire brigade,' Dominic shouted at them. Hoping it had already been done and he hadn't needed to actually remind the people watching to do the simplest of jobs. 'Which bedroom?' he asked the woman.

The woman paused. Stumped by the question.

'Front, back?' He tried to clarify.

'Front.' She leapt away from him, urging him forward.

Dominic ran towards the house, pushed his way through a group of neighbours, nearly tripped over a pair of huge feet, but steadied himself and headed towards the door.

He could feel the heat as soon as he approached. The fire was well under way. A primal urge stopped him in his tracks as the blaze bore down on him. No one was heading into the death trap that was the house in front of him. What was he thinking pushing his way to the front like this?

He looked behind him at the neighbours. All of them safe on the street. The searing inferno reflected in wide eyes. He could stay here. Safe. Heated only by the flames in front of him, not by the fires burning around him.

Common sense told him to do as everyone else was doing and to wait for the fire department, but how could he when there was a child in the building who was losing her life with every second he wavered outside? The people watching wanted him to go in, to risk his life for that child. He could feel the weight of their expectation on him and it spurred him on.

Dominic pulled his jacket off and draped it over his head.

He took a step forward onto the doorstep, scanned the inside of the house. The fire was downstairs. It looked to have taken hold at the back of the house, where the kitchen appeared to be situated. Fire was licking its way up the doorframe between the kitchen and living room. Smoke was billowing from the flames and winding its way across the ceiling out past Dominic towards the oxygen rich air outdoors.

Dominic took one last look at the woman in the street behind him. If the fire was downstairs how had she not managed to save her own daughter who was upstairs? He didn't have time to consider that now. The only way the girl was going to get out of there was if he entered the property.

With head bent he stepped inside.

The stairs were directly in front of him. They were dark and wafts of smoke were following him up each step. Time was not on his side and he took the stairs two at a time. Once he reached the landing he turned right, towards the front of the house, facing two doors.

The heat was incredible up here. Burning through the floor. He didn't have much time. He needed to get into each room and find the child and bring her out as quickly as he could.

He thought back to the image in his mind of the house when he saw it from outside. One bedroom had a light on. Was this the room with the child in? Which side of the house was it? Dominic closed his eyes for a brief second, brought the image up, then rapidly opened the door on the left.

The light was on.

There was a bed in the corner and under the covers a lump. Dominic rushed over to it and pulled the quilt back. Curled underneath was a young girl who looked no more than five years of age. He scooped both arms underneath her and pulled her to him. Her eyelids fluttered but she kept them closed.

'It's okay, sweetie. Keep your eyes tightly closed until we get out of here. I've got you now.' He murmured into her ear. Her eyelids scrunched up and stayed scrunched. Her hands were in little fists by her shoulders. Her whole body was the same, curled tight and rigid. She'd been hiding from the fire, hoping it wouldn't find her under her covers, probably the same way monsters never find you when you're under your bedding.

The room was filling with smoke. Dominic coughed out the dirty air and turned towards the door. Out the corner of his eye a blue light spun through the thin fabric of the little girl's curtains.

Help was here.

The landing was darker than he recalled it. The smoke was thicker, making visibility more difficult. Dominic found the bannister and clung to it with one hand while his other hand hugged the child tightly to him.

He couldn't see anything now but relied on the hand-rail to guide his descent. As he reached the bottom the heat pushed him back a step. The fire moving further into the room and towards the door.

From under his coat he tried to see in front of him. The fire wasn't blocking his route out yet. He had to force himself to push forward regardless of the heat. It was the only way they were going to make it out of here.

Dominic took another step forward and the heat grazed his face. The child yelped in his arms. He pulled the coat from his head and draped it over the girl. He could see the spiralling blue lights of emergency vehicles through the open doorway. He had to make it through to them and they'd be free.

The fire roared and Dominic took another step backwards.

The girl whimpered. He could hear her mother screaming for her through the open doorway. The fire crew would be kitting up. They'd come and get them. But he couldn't bear to stand in here any longer than necessary. He was feeling claustrophobic and needed to get out. He needed to find a way through.

Dominic turned, keeping his hand on the bannister he ran up the stairs, turned into the bathroom, threw two towels into the bath and ran the cold tap onto them. Then he took the jacket from the child and enveloped the girl with a dripping towel and placed the second one over his head.

It was cool and welcome in the heat and smog of the house.

They were going to get out of here. Following the same handrail he made his way back down the stairs. They only had seconds to spare now as the fire was moving quickly.

'Take a deep breath in and hold it,' he shouted to the girl over the roar of the fire. He took his own deep breath and stumbled down the last two steps and forced himself towards the door. His free hand fumbling for the doorframe to guide him out.

A pair of hands grabbed his arms and guided him through. Then the girl was lifted from his grasp and he was pushed down onto an ambulance trolley to be examined and an oxygen mask placed over his face. The mask cool on his skin.

Dominic didn't see the mother again. The ambulance containing the little girl left for the hospital before his did. He was taken to be checked out but released a few hours later and told sleeping in a more upright position might help if he found it uncomfortable lying flat and to return should he feel he had any problems with his breathing.

He asked after the little girl and was informed she was being kept in overnight for observation but that his actions had very likely saved her life.

CHAPTER 17

Dominic

The team were in the office bright and early the next morning. It didn't matter that it had been a late finish the night before. This was the start of a new job. Morale was still high and his team were raring to go, determined to bring a killer to justice. Dominic hoped they could do this. The killer was a brutal man and Dominic had a feeling after seeing Julie's body that hers would not be the last. In fact he'd be surprised if she was the first. It was a dark way to start off if it was. He imagined that there would be a stack of smaller offences behind him and even a killing that was less dramatic, less savage.

They'd all heard about Dominic's trip into the burning building as Ruth had sent a message to Kapoor, much to Dominic's annoyance. But Ruth had wanted to make sure Kapoor was aware in case Dominic got into any difficulties with his breathing. Kapoor had informed the team.

Dominic hadn't made a decision on whether he was going to talk about last night and now the choice had been taken out of his hands.

Rhys pushed a mug of coffee into his hand. Steam spiralled its way up to his nose and he was grateful for the drink and for the wake-up call. 'Thanks, Rhys.'

'You deserve more than a coffee, Dom, but unfortunately we're at work, so it's the least I can do.' Rhys pushed another mug into Paul's hands. He'd made drinks for their team this morning. Must have drawn the short straw.

'Bit of a local hero this morning,' said Paul. 'Are we going to be seeing you in the paper this week?'

'God, I hope not.' Dominic was pleased his team were encouraging of his actions last night. His reputation meant a lot to him. 'No one wants to see this ugly mug peering out at them.'

'And how's the little girl?' asked Hayley.

Dominic scowled at them good-naturedly. 'I notice none of you contradicted me about my devilishly handsome good looks.'

'Of course we think you're press-worthy.' Hayley grinned at him.

'We always need something to wrap our chips in,' quipped Paul.

'Just how old are you?' Rhys played horrified. 'You'll have health and safety on your back if you wrap your chips in newspaper. Especially if it's got the sarge's mug printed on it.'

There was a howl of laughter round the room.

Hayley looked at Dominic again.

'I called this morning. They won't tell me much as I'm not family. But because I'm a police officer and the one who pulled her out of the building they were willing to tell me she was stable.'

Hayley smiled. 'That must be a relief.'

'Like you wouldn't believe.'

At that point DI Adyant Kapoor walked into the incident room and they stopped talking immediately.

'Morning, guys.' Kapoor was bright regardless of the pressure he must have been under to resolve this case. No one wanted a murder on their patch, never mind a vicious stranger murder like this. Domestic murders were usually the kind they worked. The offender was picked up immediately and the case was worked and put to bed at a reasonable clip. This was different. Everyone knew it. No one had to say it.

There were murmurings of 'morning' in response.

Kapoor turned to Dominic. 'How are you feeling this morning? Good to keep going?'

'I'm fine. I'm quite annoyed at Ruth for contacting you, but that's another story.'

Kapoor didn't need telling twice. 'Yesterday Julie Carver was found in Ecclesall Woods having been brutalised and her life taken from her.' Kapoor had their attention. 'We have no immediate leads and very soon the press will be breathing down our necks. I can't hold them off indefinitely. You have a little leeway today, but after that be prepared for questions.' He stared at them. 'But I expect no one to talk. Do I make myself clear?'

Everyone nodded. They were a good team, not just his small part of the team, but the bigger murder inquiry team as a whole. They were good people and he would trust them with his life.

'Okay,' said Kapoor, 'on that note, let's look at what we have, shall we?' He propped himself against a desk, one leg on the floor and one leg swinging as the corner of the desk held his weight.

'First of all, for your information, this investigation is filed under the name Operation Halo. And yesterday afternoon a call came in that a dog walker had fallen over a body, and in doing so had contaminated the scene because he had literally fallen into the grave. CSU are assessing if he caused any damage.'

There was a light titter around the room at the thought of the clichéd dog walker finding the body, but it was a cliché for a reason. Bodies were left in the ground or out in the open in fields and woodland areas which was where dog walkers and joggers tended to frequent. They'd had more than their fair share of dead found by this group of people, but never before had they actually fallen into the scene and contaminated it.

'DS Dominic Harrison and his team went out to the scene. What can you tell us about it, Dom?'

Dominic put his mug down, a tightness gripping his chest. He took a deep breath in and was rewarded with a fit of public coughing. 'I'm so sorry about that,' he said when he'd finished.

Kapoor was concerned. 'Don't worry about that. The important thing is, are you okay?'

Dominic hammered on his chest with his fist. 'I'm fine. Just leftovers from last night, I'm afraid. Nothing to worry about. A bit of a cough. I'm fine to be here though.'

Kapoor frowned. 'You're sure? We can cope if you need to go home.'

Dominic didn't like the sound of this. 'I'm absolutely fine.' He sat straighter in his chair. 'Shall we carry on?'

Kapoor didn't look convinced but indicated that Dominic could continue.

Dominic cleared his throat once more and got on with the task at hand. 'It wasn't pretty and that had nothing to do with someone falling on top of her, or how long she'd been left in the ground. In fact, the pathologist, Nadira Azim, said it looked as though she had only been there a couple of days. Whoever killed her did a nasty job on her. There was strangulation but, bizarrely, after that he decided to cut her throat and smeared her face with lipstick, leaving the used lipstick at the scene with the body. We have no idea what any of this means, but it seems as though for him, it holds significance. There is too much to this killing for it to just be a murder. It means something to him. And in scenarios like that we have to be concerned about escalation. Unless of course he knew the victim and the mode of killing was specific to her.'

The room was silent, there was no place for laughter when you listened to details like that.

Dominic carried on. 'We identified her reasonably quickly as Julie Carver as she'd been reported missing by her brother. He's going to do an official ID this afternoon after the PM. We spoke to him and his wife and they said Julie had been dating online and had met someone new recently. They couldn't give us any more details on him or tell us what the app was she used. She leaves behind a fourteen-year-old son who is being cared for by the uncle and aunt.'

Kapoor clapped his hands together. 'Thanks, Dom. So we need to identify the app she was using, dig into the background of the dog walker, see if anything suspicious pops up for him and I'd suggest that this guy she was dating has become our number one priority. Anyone disagree?' He waited to see if anyone else had any information to add to the discussion, perhaps a different viewpoint to look at.

The briefings were a fluid affair where every team member got their say and everyone was heard. Kapoor didn't believe in dismissing anyone. Any so-called silly observation or consideration could be the one idea that could break an entire case. Dominic wondered if Kapoor had learned this the hard way on another team, another case, another time. Whatever the circumstances, he liked the way his boss did the briefing and was inclusive.

'Okay, good. CCTV has been collected around the dump site. Because we believe it is a dump site and not the place she was killed. It's not bloody enough to be the kill site.' Kapoor looked at Dominic. 'Dom and one of his team are going to the PM this morning and will be doing the ID this afternoon. Lizzy Fields is to be the FLO on this case and will pick up with the family as soon as the ID is done.'

Lizzy raised her hand in the corner of the room. FLOs were not a part of Major Crime teams but were brought in off their own teams when a case was up and running. There was a list of FLOs who could be used so one single FLO didn't burn out being given every case that came up. Dominic liked Lizzy, she was calm and practical and the families tended to get on well with her. This was important because much as people thought FLOs were there to soothe the family through their nightmare, they were actually a conduit between the

SIO — Kapoor — and the family. A way for information to flow between the two and mostly from the family back to the investigation. It was the little things that could potentially be important that families let slip when they were comfortable in their own homes, things that they might not otherwise say when being questioned by police in a more official capacity. They relaxed more with a FLO, even though the FLO was always upfront that they were there to gather information. Lizzy was great at keeping families onside about this.

'What time is the post-mortem?' Kapoor asked.

Dominic looked at his watch. 'It's in an hour, boss.'

'Okay. Anyone have anything else they want to add at this point? Your team leaders will sort you out with actions from HOLMES. Let's pull together on this one. I'm afraid it's going to be long hours and maybe a long job, so get ready for that. Let your families know. I'll give you some time off as and when I can, but you know the routine, the first days matter. Let's make them count.'

CHAPTER 18

Dominic

Nadira Azim was already in the mortuary at the Medico-legal centre on Watery Lane with Julie Carver, who was laid out on a steel table. Julie was still in her clothes waiting for the police to seize and exhibit them as they were removed one item at a time. Dominic had brought Krish to the morgue with him. He was one of the more steel-stomached of his team and this was not going to be an easy post-mortem.

'This isn't a pleasant one, Krish,' Dominic said as they both changed into spare scrubs.

'No worries, sarge. I ate a while ago, there's no concern about me bringing my breakfast up. Besides, I'm a professional guy. You never have to worry about me.'

'I know that.' Dominic put his clothes and mobile phone in a locker. 'I want you to be prepared for what you're going to see. I imagine I'm going to be shocked again as it'll be more visible now she's out of her grave. It always is. The bright lights bring everything to life.'

Krish locked his own stuff away and the pair of them walked into the morgue.

There was an overwhelming smell of disinfectant and an underlying smell of Julie. Her body was starting to break down. Dominic recognised the scent of decomposition.

'Morning, Nadira.' Dominic gave her a smile and she turned around from the notepad she had been scribbling in and gave him a wide smile in response.

'Morning, you two. It's good to see you, even if it is under these circumstances.' She stared hard at Dominic. 'How are you feeling today?'

Dominic groaned. 'I don't believe it.'

Nadira raised an eyebrow.

'That you've heard about last night here.'

'We have,' she said. 'It was a very heroic thing you did going into that house.' She narrowed her eyes. 'And very dangerous. Really, how are you?'

This wasn't a good time but Dominic had a huge urge to cough and couldn't stop it. He covered his mouth and coughed as lightly as he could. Then he smiled at Nadira. 'I'm fine, honestly. A little residual cough, but other than that, I'm fine.'

Her look was serious. 'You have to be careful. If you find it difficult to breathe then you need to get checked out again. Are you listening to me?'

Dominic couldn't help himself, he saluted her.

Nadira rolled her eyes. 'For your own good.'

He realised this and thanked her for her concern and advice.

'Are we ready to go ahead?' she asked, looking at the woman in the centre of the room.

'We are,' Dominic agreed.

Smithy, the morgue tech, took each item of clothing off Julie one at a time and Krish bagged them up meticulously, sealing each bag and signing the exhibit label with his signature and the item details, date and time. One item per brown paper bag. Items sweated if you placed them in plastic bags. A photographer was there recording every move they made and recording the process Julie went through. He took shots of her whole body, then closer shots with a ruler at the side of all the marks and injuries so they could be logged correctly.

She was still wearing the clownish looking lipstick that had been smeared around her lips, overlapping the edges. The bruising around her throat was dark and vivid against her now chalky skin.

'While the last of the photographs are taken shall we have a look at the X-rays we took before you got here?' Nadira walked over to her computer monitor in the corner of the room. She moved the mouse and woke the screen up, bringing the X-rays into view; she had obviously prepared them before their arrival.

'Anything interesting?' asked Dominic.

'Actually . . .' Nadira scrolled through the images until she found the one she wanted. 'If you look at this one here—' she pointed with a pen — 'you can see a couple of breaks, here and here.'

Dominic peered at the monitor and could see black lines cutting across the white of the bone, and white bone sticking out past the sleek line of the external edge. 'What are we looking at?'

'Her right arm, and—' Nadira clicked the slide to another image and pointed again — 'see again here.'

'What a bastard,' Krish breathed behind them.

Nadira clicked through to another screen.

'What, more?' Dominic clenched his fists.

'These are her ribs. There are two breaks in here as well.'

'And strength needed to cause these injuries?' he asked, his fingers dug into his palms.

'She's only a petite woman, an average sized man who was angry enough could cause these injuries, and looking at the state of her I'd go so far to say he was pretty angry, wouldn't you?'

Krish huffed behind them both again.

Nadira and Dominic turned around to face him and Dominic unfurled his fists and placed a hand on his shoulder. 'Come on, mate. This is going to be a tough morning. We can do it, for her.' Krish lifted his chin and they all made their way back to the table.

Nadira logged each injury by drawing it on a body map, even though photographs had been taken. Next she took more swabs, even though she had taken some at the scene. She swabbed Julie's neck where the bruising was. There was utter silence in the room as Nadira worked. All samples were logged and signed so the evidence could be forensically examined and to ensure it would be allowed should a case go to court. Then she swabbed the victim's lips and the lipstick.

The rest of the post-mortem went by without a hitch. Julie was a healthy woman who had no sign of illness and was reasonably fit and was capable of putting up a fight. Her muscle tone was good and her internal organs healthy. Cause of death was exsanguination from the cut across her throat.

Having finished up, Krish leaned on the counter writing up the exhibits list with all the items they had seized. It was important the continuity be kept for all items so nothing could jeopardise a court case.

'I have the lipstick here for you.' Nadira walked to a drawer under one of the counters. It was locked. Nadira pulled a key from a pocket and unlocked the drawer, pulled out a bag and held it up so Dominic could see inside. There was a single lipstick container. It was dirty from being buried with Julie.

Dominic reached out and took the bag from Nadira. 'What's his thing with the lipstick?'

'I don't know, it's obviously important to him. It has some meaning, I imagine.'

Dominic stalked over to Krish and took the pen out of his hand. Krish glared at him. Dominic signed the exhibit label then handed the bag over to Krish to add to the exhibit list.

'Pen.' Krish held out his hand.

Dominic dropped the pen into his palm. 'Thanks, mate.' He stared at the lipstick in the clear bag. If they were lucky the killer had been sloppy, and they could get some fingerprints from the outside casing. But Dominic knew they'd need more than luck to catch this guy.

CHAPTER 19

Dominic

They returned to the station and booked all the exhibits into the secure area ready to be submitted for forensic examination.

A couple of hours later they were back at the hospital.

Jonathan and Helen were already waiting for them. It didn't look as though they had slept at all. Their eyes were sunken. Dark shadows were smudged underneath, making their pallid complexions look even more sallow.

Dominic held out his hand to Jonathan. 'Thank you for coming.'

Jonathan took his hand, his grip weak and limp. 'I need to see my sister.'

'Of course. This way.' Dominic led them down the corridor and took the elevator down to the viewing room. 'I'm afraid you can't be in there with her. There may need to be another post-mortem at a later date should we arrest her killer, so we have to be really careful not to contaminate any evidence. I'm sorry.'

'You're going to do this to her all over again?' A sob escaped from deep inside Jonathan.

Something quivered inside Dominic's guts. He hated dealing with the grief of the loved ones. He rolled back his shoulders and steeled himself. 'It's part of the process. When we catch them, they're entitled to a defence post-mortem. Much as you might hate it. She will still be treated with dignity.' He opened the door to the viewing room. A small room, carpeted, with a couple of sofas pushed against two of the walls. Floral wallpaper and a potted plant in the corner gave the sense of being somewhere else other than a hospital.

The wall opposite the door had a large window and on the other side of the glass were a set of curtains which were drawn across so that they were unable to see through to whatever was beyond.

Dominic ushered everyone into the room and they stood silently in the wallpapered room a moment, the reality of where they were sinking in.

'Let me know when you're ready to see her,' Dominic said. 'And once the curtain is drawn back you need to verbally let us know if this is Julie or not.'

Jonathan's lips drew back into a thin line. Helen clung to his hand. She hadn't uttered a word yet. Jonathan turned to her. Helen squeezed his hand a little tighter. A sign that they were ready for this. They were in this together and they could do this. He'd seen this many times in the past. Words were rarely used — it was usually a squeeze, a look, something intimate that one loved one gave to another to say they were ready for the worst moment in their lives.

And he was a part of that moment.

'You're ready?' Dominic clarified.

'As I can be,' Jonathan said.

Dominic pressed the button on the wall at the side of the window and spoke into the intercom, informing whoever was beyond the wall that they were ready for the viewing.

Slowly the curtain moved. Helen sucked in air. The hand grasp tightened even more, both of them clutching the other.

Hayley stood silently behind the couple, ready if one of them needed to escape the room at speed.

The room beyond was gradually revealed. There was a trolley with a body covered in a white sheet being exposed as the curtains drew back. The Butlers leaned forward to get a closer look, to see if it was Julie, but the curtains were still blocking the view.

Their faces were practically pushed up against the glass. The curtains finished their slow painful journey across the window and the trolley and its occupant were in full view. Jonathon's chest was heaving up and down.

Behind the trolley stood a short male in scrubs and with a raised finger from Dominic he stepped forward and gently lifted the sheet from the head of the person on the trolley and laid it down over their chest.

'No!' Jonathan's hands went up to the window and tears streamed down his face. 'No. No. No. Julie. No. Oh God. Julie. Oh God. No. Julie.' His forehead tipped forward and also touched the glass. It looked as though he wanted to push himself through the glass and be with his sister.

Quietly Dominic asked, 'Is this Julie Carver?'

'Yes,' whispered Helen. 'It's Julie.'

CHAPTER 20

Dominic

It was Friday and it had been a couple of days since Julie Carver's body had been found in the woods. When Dominic walked into the incident room, the atmosphere was still upbeat. No one was feeling like this was a slog yet. People were raring for the day ahead even though it was early and they'd had another late shift the previous evening.

Dominic sat in his chair, shifted the paperwork he'd left in a puddle in the middle of his desk to the side and switched on his computer. He needed to sort out this paperwork and file it today. He had been exhausted when he walked out of the office last night.

'How's the chest today?' asked Hayley.

Dominic patted his chest with his hand as though you could feel from tapping what was going on inside. 'All good now. Healthiest human there is.'

'So you're now in better shape than before you ran into a burning building?' Rhys laughed at him and Hayley smirked at the joke.

'Glad you're doing better,' she said.

'You're a funny guy, Rhys. I'm surprised you don't cut yourself with that tongue.' Dominic threw a paperclip at him. It landed wide on the floor somewhere.

He turned back to his work. His emails, when he checked them, included a couple of thoughts from Kapoor late in the evening. He must have messaged him from home. Rubbish from HR about the new online payment system. There had been a glitch with the software and IT would repair it as soon as possible. Dominic didn't care so long as the money went in his bank every month. And an email from someone on the incident team requesting money because one of the civilian staff had delivered a bouncing baby boy. The funds would buy her a basket of baby goodies and a pamper gift for herself. He had no issue with this and put his hand in his pocket and found his wallet, fished out a twenty-pound note and put it on his desk ready to give to the collector in a minute.

The last unread email was from Jonathan Butler. Sent at one thirty-seven this morning. He was asking if they had identified the dating app that Julie had used. Dominic shook his head.

'What is it, Sarge?' Hayley was behind him. 'That shake of the head doesn't look like a good start to the day.'

'It's Jonathan Butler. He wants to know if we've tracked down the dating app his sister used. This is what his FLO is for. To provide him updates. For him to talk to about the things he's anxious about.' He looked back down at his email. 'But this came in the early hours of the morning when, I imagine, he will have been brooding about the case and Lizzy isn't due there until this morning.'

Hayley stepped closer. She was right behind his left shoulder peering at the email he was reading. She was so close he could smell the perfume she was wearing, soft and floral. It tickled his nose and he found he liked it.

'You're right,' she said. 'He'll know you won't respond, but it probably helps him to send it anyway. Makes him feel like he's taking some kind of action.'

Kapoor walked into the incident room and Hayley moved back to her own desk. Dominic closed down his screen. He would reply to Jonathan as soon as the briefing was over. They hadn't identified the app. They didn't have her phone and the computer tech guys were still examining her laptop. It wasn't an overnight job as often indicated on television shows.

Kapoor clapped his hands together. He was the epitome of smart preparedness. 'Morning, team, glad to see everyone here and in good spirits still. Let's have a look at what we have so far and where we're going from here, shall we?'

Dominic picked up the twenty pound note off his desk and waved it at Sofie who put her thumb up and smiled. He would make sure he handed it to her straight after the briefing.

'So,' said Kapoor. 'We're at that stage in the investigation where there's a lot of waiting around. The exhibits have been sent to forensics so we have to wait on those. As we know, different item results will come in at different times so let's hope we can get something from them. Christie is on CCTV viewing. That's another slow and tedious job, but one that needs to be done. Every car that passed near the woods within the timeframe we've set is going to be tracked down and the owner spoken to and a statement obtained. If you get anything hinky from any of those visits — which will keep many of you occupied for a good couple of weeks — then let your supervisor know straight away.

'Tim, how's your team going on the house-to-house around Julie's address?'

Tim Eaton pulled a sheet of paper closer to his eyeline and peered down at it. 'We've got some statements providing last sightings of Julie, but nothing of note for who she might have been seeing. We've still got a couple of addresses to do but they don't seem the nosiest people I've come across.'

Kapoor looked at Dominic. 'How has the dog walker fared?'

'Everything is coming back clean for him so far. He's a family man, seems to go to work, go home, walks his dog and returns to his family. Not much time for extracurricular activity like brutally murdering women.'

'And anything on the dating app yet?'

Dominic scratched his head. There was so much to do but so little reward coming in at the moment. 'Not yet, sir. We still don't have her phone and her laptop is being examined. We've searched her house for paper bills for her phone provider but no luck. It appears she either shreds them or she's paperless. Because if we know who her provider is we can put in a request for her data and see if it comes up on that. But I'm not sure app use does.'

Kapoor shook his head and let out a sigh. 'We won't let that slow us down, even if it is one of the biggest lines of enquiry. Fingers crossed forensics pull something out of the bag. I'm doing a press conference later today and I want you to be there, Dom, as you're the one who has had first contact with the family. They know you and are used to you. It will be good for them to see a friendly face.'

'Are you getting them up on the table as well?' Dominic asked, knowing full well that if he did it was to see how they reacted to the situation. Close relatives were never ruled out of a murder enquiry and because Julie had died at night and Jonathan only had Helen as his alibi — they had been at home together — there was nothing to say they hadn't been in this together. You only had to look at history to see couples who worked in pairs to murder strangers or even family members. It was not out of the realms of possibility.

'Yes, I asked through Lizzy last night if both the Butlers can be present. They're anxious about doing it but they've agreed. They said that if it has any possibility of bringing Julie's killer closer to justice then they'll do anything to help.'

Dominic rolled his eyes but made sure he had turned away from Kapoor. He felt for the Butlers, he did, but his copper's instinct told him not to rule them out. So any mention of catching the killer made him that little bit twitchy. The team had an open mind. They couldn't have anything else. If they closed up and made a mental decision about something then any evidence they found would be forced to fit the narrative they had decided upon. It had been seen to happen time and again. So for this reason, they didn't rule anything out or rule any set decision in until all avenues had been checked and double checked.

'You've all got a lot to be getting on with. We'll gather again later towards the end of the day and debrief the press conference, see what has come out of it. If someone can set up a tip line and get it manned sufficiently, please, that would be a real help.' And with that he strode out of the room.

The phone on Dominic's desk rang. He picked it up.

It was the front counter — there was someone here to see him. Said he wanted to talk about the investigation.

Dominic probed a little more — you didn't engage with anyone who just wandered in off the street and decided they wanted to talk to one of the team members involved in the investigation. It could be press wanting an exclusive, or a member of the public wanting to insert themselves into the investigation. But this guy wanted to talk to the officer who had dealt with Julie Carver's family at the start of the investigation. He was adamant.

This specific request needled Dominic's curiosity and he wandered through the station to the front desk and met the man, who introduced himself as Samuel Tyler.

Samuel shook Dominic's hand, his grasp firm and strong, his eyes bright and piercing. His face shielded by a pepper pot, dark-grey beard. He looked to be about thirty-four, but the beard was off-putting, as it was for many people who chose to go that route nowadays. It made aging a person more difficult.

'How can I help?' asked Dominic.

'I'm sorry, did the receptionist not explain?' Samuel looked back towards the front counter confused. 'I'm a victim support officer and I've been assigned to the Butler family.'

While the FLO was the family's main point of contact during the investigation, the victim support officer was an extra resource for them. The FLO was there for the investigation team, whereas he would be there for the Butlers.

'I'd like to get some information on the family before I make the approach so I don't go putting my foot in any sensitive areas.'

That made sense. Dominic checked his ID and led him through the secure double doors, pressing the pin code that allowed access, to an interview room. 'Grab a seat, let's see what we can do for you.'

Dominic pulled out one of the chairs and sat. He had a lot of time for the civilian staff of Victim Support. They gave their time to victims of crime when they needed someone to talk to, to lean on.

Samuel pulled out the opposite chair and fished out a notepad from a satchel he was carrying. He laid it out with a pen on the table in front of him, burn scars covering the entirety of his left hand, bright and livid.

'An accident when I was a child.'

'I'm so sorry, I didn't mean to stare.' Dominic shook his head, ashamed of himself for looking and for being caught so obviously staring.

Samuel laughed. 'I was expecting it. When you live with disfigurement as long as I have you learn to get used to people and their reactions. I tried to fry bacon in a lot of oil as a child and ended up tipping it all over myself. My mum had left me alone and this was the result.' He lifted his hand up and showed the pink rippled skin that stretched over the skeleton of his left hand.

'Must have been painful.' Dominic winced.

'I'll admit that it's the most painful thing I've ever experienced. I wouldn't like to go through it again in a hurry.' He laughed again. 'I soon learned how not to cook bacon.'

Dominic leaned back in his chair. 'I'm sorry you had to go through that. Let me know how I can help you today.'

Samuel opened his notepad, pressed down onto the middle creasing and clicked his pen on. 'Like I said, I don't want to put my foot in it with the family. Anything you can tell me that isn't on the crime report that I should take note of, or should avoid, would be a real help.'

Dominic thought of Jonathan and Helen Butler. 'I'm not sure what to tell you, to be honest. They are, as you'd expect, devastated by Julie's murder. Julie had a son and they've taken him in as there's no dad in the picture.'

'They're a good family for him?' Samuel asked as he scribbled in his pad.

'Yes. Yes, they seem to be. They offer him stability and comfort and love at a difficult time.'

Samuel gave a small smile. 'They're the basics a child needs. It's good to hear he's in good hands.'

Dominic rubbed his forehead. 'He should be getting the love he needs from his mother though, not from other members of his family.'

'Of course he should. But in the circumstances he finds himself in, is what I was talking about, DS Harrison. It would be awful to lose one's mother and then be left out in the cold. I'm glad he has the support he has.' Samuel made another note. 'They've engaged well with the investigation?'

Dominic relaxed a little and leaned back in his chair. 'It's still early days but everything we've asked of them they've provided no matter how difficult it's been for them. We couldn't have asked for more. Her brother gets a little upset from time to time, he's impatient for an arrest. I think he presumes that will help him come to terms with her loss.'

Samuel stopped writing. 'I'm not sure anything will help them come to terms with their loss. Not as much as they think it will.'

'You're right, but they have a perception and because the case is not following that perception it's causing some issues.'

'I'll bear that in mind when I speak with them. That's really helpful. Thank you.' Samuel closed his notepad, clicked his pen off and packed them both away into his satchel. 'And thank you again for seeing me today. I know you're busy.'

Dominic rose. 'Anything I can do to help.' He held out his hand again and Samuel shook it.

'You have a difficult task ahead of you, Detective, I wish you all the best with it.' He pulled a small card from his pocket. 'If you need to get in touch.' He handed the card to Dominic who took it.

Back in the incident room Dominic returned to his desk. He was glad the Butlers were going to get the support they needed.

His computer monitor gave a quiet ping as another email slipped into his inbox. He hated his email inbox. He could never get on top of it. He tried to prioritise it and dealt with the important stuff, but there was so much crap that came through. Mundane stuff from different departments providing updates on this and that. Stuff he didn't care about.

He was about to ignore this latest email when something niggled at the back of his mind. Like a whisper in a dark room. He clicked into his emails and saw it was from forensics. His excitement grew at reading the subject of the email.

Results were in on the lipstick seized from the dump site Julie Carver had been found at. There were no fingerprints on the casing. The killer had likely worn gloves of some description. He was forensically aware.

The make of lipstick was a common brand called Velvet Berry by House of Maven. You could buy this colour and make at any store that sold make-up. It was a popular country-wide brand. There was no way to identify where the killer had bought his lipstick from. They were sorry they didn't have better news for him.

Dominic slammed his hand down on the top of his desk.

'Sarge?' Paul spoke from his desk opposite.

Dominic told him what the email said.

'That's shit. We'd hoped he'd left us some prints on the case. It was a nice shiny surface. Bloody wanker.'

'It has to mean something to him though,' said Dominic. 'You don't go to the trouble of buying women's make-up if it doesn't mean something. Not if you're going to kill the woman you're meeting up with and—' he made air quotes with his fingers — 'giving it to.'

'That's one way to put it.' Paul grimaced. 'But yeah. He's sick in the head and only he knows what this lipstick means to him.'

'And that has to change, Paul. We have to figure it out. We have to know what it means to him. It could help us get that step closer to him.'

CHAPTER 21

Claudia

Fifteen hours after Ruth's attack

'You ruled the dog walker out?' Claudia sat back in her chair.

'You're going all the way back there?' Dominic's eyelid twitched.

'You know the way interviews work, Dominic. Don't play coy. We go through everything you've said; we don't just pick out the interesting things or the parts you want us to focus on. Doing that might lead us in the wrong direction and that's the whole reason they have me in here, to prevent this investigation going off on a tangent.'

'They really think that having you arrest and interview me will get them what they want?'

Claudia bit at her lip a minute while she thought through what he had said. Kane allowed her the time. He kept his laid-back position in his chair, mug in his hand.

'What is it you think they want?' Her brows creased over her eyes.

'To trip me up. To get me into a tangled mess and to admit to killing Ruth.' A flush crept up Dominic's face.

'You mean they didn't send me in here to find out the truth?'

Dominic leapt up from his chair. The force of his legs pushing him to his feet shot the chair out from under him and it toppled backwards, the metal frame clanging loudly as it hit the ground in the small room.

Claudia and Kane stayed where they were. Dominic pressed his palms on the table and leaned towards them.

'Stop trying to trip me up. I'm here because I want to find my wife. I want Ruth and I want your help in finding her. You're cops, do your jobs and help me find her.'

Claudia stared up at him, then stood, walked around the table and picked up the toppled chair, righting it behind Dominic. 'Please sit back down. You're here because you're under arrest on suspicion of her murder. We've moved way past you being here asking for help.' His temper had flared when he thought they were trying to trip him up. Why would he be worried about that if he had nothing to hide? Claudia had never seen him so volatile. It created more questions in her mind and she didn't like it. What she needed to do now was get him back under control.

He stared down at her as she sat back in her own chair.

'However, there is still an entire team working behind me on trying to locate Ruth and bring her home.' She indicated the chair. 'I won't tell you again. Sit in the chair or I will end this interview and put you in a cell until you can calm down and that won't get us anywhere, will it? You claim to want to find Ruth. Then get your arse down and do as you're told.'

Dominic's fingers closed into a fist on the tabletop. Kane shifted in his seat and put the mug down. Claudia gave a slight shake of her head. Dominic sank down into the chair she had placed behind him. His fingers relaxed.

'I'm sorry,' he said. 'I'm frustrated being locked up in here when I feel I could be doing more out there to find her.'

'If you believe your investigation is the crux of the problem then don't you think you're in the best place? Talking through it and letting us find lines of enquiry from within your investigation, from things you tell us?'

Dominic put his head in his hands. 'You're right. And I shouldn't worry about my current predicament because it's only temporary. I didn't do it and I trust in you guys to find out the truth so I'll be out of here at some point, but you have to see how it feels to be tangled up in this.'

Claudia stared across the table at him. 'If what you're saying is the truth, then yes, you will be out of here in no time. You do have to trust the process. I'm here because I want to know what happened to Ruth and nothing else. I'm not here for any other reason. You can trust that I'm not trying to screw you over and tie you up for this.'

Dominic leaned back and closed his eyes for a brief moment.

'Thanks for going through the start of the case with us. I'm going to leave you for now, give you a break — we've been going at it a few hours — while I go and see if the CSU have finished at your address. There's a question I need answering.'

'What is it?' Dominic asked.

'I'll let you know when I have my answer. But don't worry. I'll keep you updated.'

And with that she ended the interview and walked Dominic to his cell. He shuffled through the door into the small square space and turned and looked at her. Kane stood behind her like a personal guard refusing to allow her pain of any description.

'I'm sorry,' Dominic said as Claudia gripped the handle and stared into the cell at him.

'Promise me you didn't do this.'

'I promise, Claudia. But do as you are, follow the information. It'll lead you to the truth.'

She inclined her head and pushed on the solid heavy metal door, feeling the click as the locking mechanism slotted into place securing Dominic in his cell.

Her eyes were damp. She steeled herself and pulled back her shoulders.

'You need anything?' asked Kane. His bald head shining under the strip lights.

Claudia placed a hand on his arm. 'You being here is enough, Russ. Thank you.' She turned her back on the cell door and walked away. She had some enquiries she needed to make before she could talk to Dominic again.

CHAPTER 22

Claudia

They were miles away from their home station here in the custody suite, but Claudia needed to access her emails and she also needed a conversation with Sharpe for what she had in mind. She didn't dare do it without first discussing it with a supervising officer. Not considering the complexities of this case. She didn't want to be accused of favouritism further down the line.

There was a report-writing room in the custody block with computer terminals for officers to complete their paperwork. Claudia logged on while Kane went for a bathroom break. What she was looking for wasn't there so she made a phone call. The forensics team had finished at Dominic's house. They'd cleared out about ten minutes ago.

'What about the blood?' she asked, her stomach twisting in on itself as she formed the question in her mind. 'Can a person live with that amount of blood loss?'

The forensic tech on the other end of the line was quiet a moment. Claudia could hear paper shuffling. It sounded as though he was checking his notes. 'There was approximately three pints on the floor. You're on the borderline of whether they survived. A person can't live if they lose forty percent of their blood volume. You're looking at over four pints. If this person is alive then they are in dire need of medical attention. I'd suggest you need to find them as soon as possible.'

Claudia's stomach stopped twisting and it dropped. She felt sick. This was Ruth they were talking about. 'You're sure?' she said. Yes, they'd arrested Dominic on suspicion of her murder, but she'd secretly held out hope that the forensic team would come back with news that the blood on the floor was not enough to cause serious harm. Even though it was obvious from looking at it. To have all her fears confirmed was like a gut punch.

He sighed down the phone.

Kane walked in behind her. She turned and gave him a weak smile. He placed a hand on her shoulder.

'I'm sorry,' she said to the tech. 'Of course you're sure. You know many of us investigating this are close to her.'

'Yeah. I'm sorry about that. Look, she could be alive. You just need to get to her. Don't give up hope.'

'But we need to find her quickly.'

'The quicker the better. I hate to say this but she's going to be running out of time if she isn't getting medical help right now and I'd suggest whoever has done this to her doesn't have medical help high on their list of priorities.'

'You're testing the blood against the DNA I submitted to make sure it's Ruth Harrison's, aren't you?'

'Yes, we should have it back with you in a couple of hours. It's coming down from above that this is high priority and we're to do it straight away.'

'I'm interviewing a suspect, will you let me know as soon as you have the results, please?' She gave him her mobile number as well as her email and the extension of the custody block she was in.

'I got your half of that conversation.' Kane sank into the chair beside her.

'We have to find her quickly, she's running out of time, Russ. The blood loss. It's too much. She needs to get to a hospital.'

Kane tapped at the desk. 'I'm sorry, Claudia.'

She shook her head. 'No. Don't go there. We haven't lost her yet. I have an idea. I just need to run it past Sharpe. They seem to be in the mood for the unusual today, so I'm hoping it's a streak that will continue.'

Claudia picked up the phone and dialled DCI Maddison Sharpe. She answered on the second ring. 'Sharpe.' It was a quiet bark into the handset.

'Ma'am,' Claudia spoke. 'It's Claudia Nunn. I have a bit of an update and want to run something past you.'

'I've spoken to Forensics,' Sharpe said. 'I'm sorry the news isn't better. How's the interview going?'

Claudia let out a small breath of air. 'It's slow going. I'm starting at the beginning of his investigation. He's claiming it's connected and as Ruth's also connected to the case I thought I may as well start there.'

'Okay, and?' Sharpe was to the point.

'I don't know what you're going to make of this suggestion, but I want to take Dominic to the house.'

'What house?'

'His house. Forensics have finished. I want to go through the house with him. See if he can see anything out of place. He knows the house better than anyone. It's not something we'd usually do, but . . .'

There was silence down the line.

'Ma'am?'

'You think it'll help?'

'We're on the clock to find Ruth. I don't think it can hurt, do you? Kane and I will take him. I'm not concerned that he won't play ball. He's sticking to his story that he didn't do this and wants to find Ruth before anything worse happens. The news that she could still be alive goes in his favour as far as his arrest is concerned as well. You can't have a murder charge if she's still alive. If he's on the up and up he'll be no trouble. Plus he's a cop when all is said and done.'

'Exactly, he knows this isn't supposed to happen.'

'I got the idea from him actually. Not that he took a suspect to a crime scene exactly. But he did enter a potential crime scene with family members, hoping they'd see something Forensics wouldn't pick up because they didn't know the victim. A more personal touch. It might just help. We have to try everything.' She was rambling now but she was determined. Anything to find Ruth. 'He'll also know how much we're trying to find Ruth.'

'You can promise me this won't leave me with egg on my face, Claudia?'

Claudia nearly laughed but let out a small cough instead. 'As much as you can promise me that being the interviewer for this investigation won't come back to haunt me, ma'am.'

Another sigh. 'You have your permission, DI Nunn. Do not let him run from you.'

'He's not going to do that.'

'I trust you, Claudia. I trust Kane. Be careful.'

'You dragged me into this, I should hope you trust me.'

CHAPTER 23

Claudia

The drive over to the house was tense. Dominic's hands were in front of him, encased in rigid metal cuffs fastened around his wrists.

'You know we have to do this,' Claudia had said as Kane secured them at the cell door after she'd explained what they were going to do.

'You've really got permission for this?' Dominic asked again from the rear seat.

'Do you think we'd be on the way over if we hadn't?' Claudia turned around to face him from her position in the passenger seat.

'What does this mean? They think I did it or they don't?' he asked.

'There's no they in this. It is entirely my suggestion and *they're* letting me run with it. So please don't let me regret it.'

'So?'

'What?'

'You think I did it or you don't?' Dominic's voice was quiet, like he was scared of the answer.

Claudia let out a sigh. 'I want to find Ruth. I want to know where she is and I want to find her in time to save her. She's lost a lot of blood if that blood in your garage was hers. She's running out of time. If having you look around the house can bring us any closer to that aim, then that's what we're going to do. Other than that I'm trying not to think about it. It's too difficult to get my head around. I'm going where the evidence takes me. It's the only way for me to work this.'

Claudia turned back around to look out of the windscreen.

Five minutes later they were pulling up outside Dominic and Ruth's address. There was a uniformed officer on the front door guarding it from any unwarranted access. Claudia flashed him her identification and he scribbled all their names in his pad. He flinched slightly when Dominic's name was given. He had obviously been pre-warned about this little excursion.

Claudia unlocked the door and the three of them trooped in.

There were obvious signs of the CSU having been here. Dust from fingerprinting lay on the shiny surfaces, door handles and edges of doors. The narrow table in the entryway.

There wasn't much in here. A pair of trainers and some letters on the table. A mirror over the table and a charger with its cord wrapped around it. 'Notice anything out of place in here?' Claudia asked.

Dominic shook his head. 'I don't understand what you think I'll find that CSU didn't.'

She turned and snapped at him, her patience wearing thin. 'We've nothing to go on. Your neighbours haven't seen anything, this is the only thing I can think of to try. If you can't be bothered we can always take you back to your cell.'

Dominic grunted. 'No, it's fine. I get it. I'm here, aren't I?'

Claudia pushed a hand through her hair. 'Well damn well behave as though you have as much to lose as the rest of us then.'

His shoulders sunk under her glare. 'You're right. I'm sorry. Shall we go through the rest of the house?'

They moved upstairs and quietly walked through each and every room. Dominic paused as they stood at the threshold of their bedroom. Claudia waited, not forcing him to step into the space. With a deep breath he crossed into it. He stared at the bed. A bed he had shared with his wife, the woman they were searching for with a fear in their hearts they could not express. He looked away and turned to the rest of the room.

'Anything?' asked Claudia.

He shook his head, opened up the wardrobe doors, peered into the drawers and rummaged through the contents. It was difficult with his handcuffs on. He didn't say anything. Nothing was out of place and no item was there that shouldn't have been.

They trailed downstairs, first Kane, then Dominic and bringing up the rear was Claudia.

The living room was warm and welcoming. Cushions thrown all over the sofa, a couple of thick woollen throws for cooler evenings when snuggles were called for rather than the oppressiveness of central heating. Photographs dotted the walls. Claudia looked at them and swallowed. The smiles. Bright, happy.

'My mug is gone. I left it down at the side of the sofa.' Dominic pointed with both hands as they were tethered to each other.

'I presume CSU have probably taken it. We have to expect things will have been removed, but let me know if you can see any others and we will check with CSU when we get back. Make sure they all marry up with them and that nothing has gone walkabout by other means. When did you last see it?'

Dominic lifted his eyes to the ceiling. 'This morning.'

'Not likely it was taken by anyone else then, is it?' she snapped at him again. This was getting harder than she had imagined it would be. She'd told Shape she could do this,

122

but for all she tried to control them, she was a living breathing human and her emotions were leaking out.

Dominic didn't respond.

'Anything else in here?' she asked.

He walked around the room. Moved cushions and throws, a newspaper that was on the table. He shook his head. 'I can't see anything that is making me anxious.'

'Kitchen,' she spat.

The pedal bin had been emptied. The kitchen looked like anyone else's kitchen. Items lined the worktops. A toaster, a kettle, a knife block — that had been dusted for prints. There was a knife missing. The block was bound to have Dominic and Ruth's prints on it. That was only to be expected. This was their house. It was if there were other prints they would get excited. But what if it was Dominic? How would they prove it? These items belonged to him. She needed to ask him about the glass in the pedal bin when they were back in an interview room.

Dominic scratched at his head. 'I can't see anything. I don't know what you're expecting here. I don't get it. I don't know what I can offer you.' He was defeated and Claudia wanted to punch him.

'Ruth is out there, you fucking moron. She's relying on us not to give up. Stop whining like a baby and being defeatist and get your head in the game. You're a cop. Act like a cop. I don't give a shit if you're in handcuffs. Pull it together.'

The words were harsh, her tone even more brittle.

Dominic stared at Claudia, his complexion pale, allowing her words to sink in. 'I want to find my wife.'

'Okay then. We have one last place to check and this one is the hardest, this is the place we found her blood, we need to go into the garage.'

Dominic's shoulders slumped. 'You keep saying it's her blood, but the results haven't come back yet, have they?'

Claudia's hand was on the door handle. 'No, they haven't come back yet. I'll let you know as soon as they do. Are you ready for this?' She wasn't sure what she expected from him as she had no idea what had gone down in this house. If he'd killed her, would he leave the blood to be found like that? It was unlikely. And the garage was a place you didn't go into every day. It would be easy enough for him not to have seen it and walked into the police station oblivious to its being there.

Dominic bent over double, placed his hands on his knees — as best he could considering they were still bound together in the cuffs.

Claudia waited for him. 'You sure you want to do this?'

'I'll do anything that could potentially lead to us finding Ruth.'

She understood his anxiety. Claudia steeled herself to go back into the garage. This had been her idea, she couldn't blame Sharpe for this. Much as she'd love to. Sharpe knew she would do everything in her power to get to the bottom of the case and to find the truth. To find Ruth and to know Dominic's part in it. Even if it was difficult for her.

Back at the door she pushed down on the handle. 'No putting this off any longer. The quicker we go in here the quicker we get out again. I'm not expecting anything. I imagine it's going to be the same as the rest of the house. Especially as CSU have paid particular attention in here.'

The garage was cooler as they entered. It hadn't changed from this morning. Claudia clenched her jaw. This was a crime scene, she told herself, walk through it like you would any other. You're a professional, act like one.

Dominic walked in behind her and the door clicked shut as Kane brought up the rear. The sound was loud in the dusty, cold, grey, concrete space.

Claudia swallowed. Tension running through her. The hairs on the top of her arms prickled. The blood pooled in front of them where she had last seen it. It would be cleaned up later. All CSU had needed was a swab of the blood to test it.

Dominic was standing stiff at the side of her, staring forward at the dark red puddle between the walls.

Claudia laid a hand on his arm. 'Are you okay?' Her voice was soft. Quiet.

He didn't move.

She waited him out. Let him get his bearings. Like she had earlier that morning. She'd needed time to bring her head back around, she would give him a minute. She took her hand away and stepped back a little. Kane stepped close to her.

'What about you?' he asked.

She nodded. Mute. Her emotions wavering. She had no idea what she was supposed to be feeling never mind what she was actually feeling. No amount of training prepared you for this.

'All this . . .' said Dominic. 'They're saying all this might be Ruth's?'

'Like you said,' Claudia responded from behind him. 'They don't know yet. It might not be.'

'How could I not know it was here in my house?'

It was a good question but one she had already answered in her own head. How many people entered their garages every single day? Even if it was attached to the house via an internal door. If there was no reason to go inside, you just didn't.

'You tell me,' she said instead. It was her job to get the answers from him, not make them up for him.

He shook his head in disbelief. 'I don't . . . I didn't . . .' He turned to her. 'Claudia?'

She couldn't do anything to take the pain away.

'I didn't do this.'

He'd been saying this all morning. It's what Sharpe wanted her to find out.

Dominic took a step forward and then another. He was searching the garage space with his eyes. The CSU hadn't taken much. The boxes that had been there before this were still present. The usual crap that was stored in garages remained. But this was where it had happened.

Claudia watched him. Kane watched them both.

125

'I see something.' Dominic turned back to them.

'What is it?' Kane spoke up.

Dominic pointed forward with both arms. The finger of his right hand directing their gaze. Down and forward of the pool of blood.

'I don't see what you're looking at,' said Kane. 'This place is full of crap.' He looked from the garage floor to Dominic. 'Sorry, mate. You know what I mean. All garages look like this.'

Dominic shook the remark off. 'Over there. In front of the garage door, but pushed half under it, you could miss it if you weren't paying attention. What is it?'

Claudia stepped forward, straining her eyes. Whatever Dominic was looking at was black in colour which was why it was not standing out in the shadow of the door. She gingerly stepped around the blood. Dominic stayed where he was knowing this was not his time to move. Kane stepped forward to monitor him while Claudia went to check out the item that was getting Dominic wound up.

'You're sure it doesn't belong to you, or in here?' she asked, trying to figure out what it was.

'No. It might look like the garage is full of shit, but it's my shit and I know what everything is and where it is. It's tidy shit. Look at the plastic boxes on the walls. I put things away.'

Claudia looked at the boxes. She didn't need to. She'd seen them. But just mentioning them created the need to look again. She really needed to concentrate, though, on the item on the floor, pushed half under the garage door, barely visible. It was no wonder the CSU missed it. Or maybe they believed it belonged in the garage and bore no relation to what they were investigating. After all, they hadn't emptied the garage of its contents. They didn't need to remove everything that lived in there naturally. If they believed it was a part of the room then they'd leave it.

She stepped closer and bent down. She could make it out now. A shiny black cylinder. She turned to Dominic again. 'It's definitely not yours? It could be Ruth's?' She had to be sure.

'It's not ours.' He was adamant.

Claudia dragged a pair of gloves from her pocket and slipped her hands into them. 'Do you have a bag, Russ?'

Russ handed her a plastic evidence bag.

She bent down and picked up the item Dominic had been pointing to and showed it to the two men. 'Have you seen this before?' This question was directed at Dominic.

'No,' he answered, his voice taking on urgency. 'What colour is it, Claudia?'

It was a House of Maven lipstick. She turned it upside down and read the colour from the base, squinting to see the tiny writing. 'It's Velvet Berry.' Her head spun and her mind tried to place where she had heard that before.

'Oh God, no.' Dominic was backing away from the blood and the garage door and from Claudia. He bumped into Russ who would not let him move further.

'What is it, Dom?' he asked.

'That's the same lipstick that the Sheffield Strangler used on his victims and left at the crime scenes. He has Ruth.'

Of course. She'd heard the lipstick name in the interview with Dominic.

He was trying to get out of the garage. Russ had hold of him by his arm trying to keep him calm. But Dominic was on the verge of losing it. 'He has Ruth, we have to do something.'

Claudia indicated to Russ that they could move out of the garage. She bagged the lipstick and followed them into the kitchen. Dominic was wound up tight.

'If he left the lipstick with the bodies, why leave it here in your garage when there isn't a body?' she asked him. 'Have you known him to do that before?'

Dominic shook his head, his focus scattered. 'I don't know. And no, though we haven't always known the site where the women have been abducted from so maybe the lipstick is left at the scenes and we haven't known about it. Maybe he wants to play with me. Let me know he has her.' He spun on the spot. 'Jesus, Claudia, what the fuck am I going to do?'

He was distraught as he contemplated who could have his wife. Claudia couldn't bear to see him like this. Discomfort clawed in the pit of her stomach as a cold chill shrouded her shoulders and down her arms. Could the Sheffield Strangler really have Ruth? It didn't bear thinking about.

Claudia moved closer to him. It was against protocol but nothing could stop her now. He was breaking right in front of her and she had to comfort him. She couldn't stand by and watch him crumble. The lipstick implied so much. So much that they both feared. They both loved Ruth. Regardless of what Claudia's role in all this was she had to help him. She reached out and took hold of one of his hands. Held him still. He was shaking and was cool to the touch. She tightened her grip on his hand. She had never seen him like this, in all the years she had known him. It unnerved her a little to see him so fragile. He was always strong, always someone she would look up to, turn to for advice. He had never looked away and now she wouldn't look away from him.

She handed the exhibit, the House of Maven Velvet Berry lipstick, to Russ and fished in her pocket for the handcuff keys, pulling them out with her fingertips. Dominic stared at her but didn't say a word. Their eyes locked. The grief they endured was raw and palpable between them. It was shared and personal.

Tears filled Dominic's eyes as he moved his gaze to the keys as Claudia pushed the key into the first lock and the bar came away and his hand dropped free and then did the same with the other hand.

He stared down at her, bewildered. 'Claudia . . . I didn't.'

Tears filled Claudia's eyes now. She couldn't take this anymore. It was too much. She was so scared for Ruth and didn't know what was happening but how could she believe this man was responsible? How had they got into this position? She should have refused. She should never have had anything to do with this from the start. She should have walked away. No one would have blamed her. But it wasn't just Dominic, it was Ruth, and she loved Ruth as much as she loved the man in front of her. She made him a promise. One she never issued to anyone else. But this was different. She owed them both so much. 'We'll sort it out, I promise. We'll find Ruth and we'll get to the bottom of it. We'll find out the truth. I don't know what's happening, Dad.'

CHAPTER 24

Dominic

Five months ago

It was only three weeks until another body turned up. Dominic had been in the office an hour; they had been getting nowhere with the Julie Carver case but the team were still working hard on it. Talking to people, viewing CCTV, running press conferences to jog people's memories. It was full steam ahead.

Kapoor walked up behind him, placed a hand on his shoulder. Dominic turned. Kapoor stepped back. This wasn't good.

'What is it?' Dominic presumed something was wrong with the case. That maybe Jonathan had put a complaint in because it was going so slow. Jonathan and Helen wanted answers. Answers they hadn't been able to provide. They had never been able to locate Julie's phone, never identified the dating app she had been on and no amount of asking the public identified the male she had been on a date with. No one knew where she met him or what he may have looked like. All they had was that he was a Caucasian male. Gender and race. In three weeks. And that had been obtained on the first day.

Kapoor was starting to look tired. He was getting pressure from above, but right now he looked like he wanted to be anywhere but here. It was as though he was shrivelling in on himself. 'There's another one.'

Dominic heard him but couldn't take in what he was saying. 'What?'

'Another body's been found, this time in woods at the side of Hathersage Road. From initial reports it looks to be the same MO as Julie Carver.'

It hit him. 'Fuck.'

'You went out to Julie, I want you to go out to this one, see if there are any similarities or differences.'

'Fuck. Are we sure?'

'No. That's why I want you to go, Dom. It's not great news either way. If it is then we're on the verge of having a serial killer loose on our streets. If it isn't then we have two lunatics running free in the city. I'm not sure which of those scenarios is worse.'

Dominic's team were great cops and would handle this but no one wanted a serial killer. No one wanted the women of the city to be afraid to go out of their homes.

He remembered back to the last serial killer. He had only been a young lad, not yet in the police, but he remembered the Yorkshire Ripper. Women being told not to go out at night on their own. His mum holding onto her cross around her neck as she soaked up the news at tea time, clutching it like it would ward off all the badness that was coming through the set. The reporter talking about hammers and violent injuries. Fear had been something once removed for him as a young man, but he remembered the reporting and the general sense of shock in the city. That this could happen so close to them. It hadn't hit them in Sheffield but it wasn't far enough away for people to feel like it was just another TV report that they could watch and move on from. This was real to them. They were Yorkshire people. There was a

131

kinship to the women in the cities he was stalking. This felt like their lives. After all, he was the Yorkshire Ripper and they were Yorkshire folk.

Dominic couldn't bear to think that they could go through that again. The fear that seeped through the whole city, petrified that the violence and death would be visited upon them.

And this time, it was. Or it looked like it was heading that way.

He ran a hand through his hair. 'I take it everyone else needed has already been alerted?'

'Yes, CSU and the pathologist are on their way.'

Dominic alerted the team and within five minutes they were out the door and headed to the second crime scene.

* * *

It was November now and the day was chilly. There was a slight mist in the air in the woods and it added an eerie feel to the proceedings. Leaves crumpled beneath Dominic's feet as he approached the scene, some sticking to his shoes as he moved. Once at the perimeter, he placed the shoe guards on and approached the rest of the way on the metal plates placed down by the CSIs, stepping carefully on the damp woodland floor.

Nadira Azim was already there, standing beside a CSI over the grave. They were deep in discussion as Dominic approached.

'Morning. Please tell me it's not another of the same?' He came parallel with the two professionals and looked down at the soil, where a woman was on her side with her face in the dirt. Dominic had no idea of her age.

Again it was a shallow grave. It didn't appear that the killer was interested in hiding his victims well. It was as though he wanted to be caught, or at least wanted his kills to be found. Was he making a statement? The fact that he didn't bury the women deeper would indicate he had something to say with their bodies. They were a message. But who to and what was he saying? If only Dominic could answer these questions maybe he would be a step closer to finding out who was behind it.

'Morning, Dom.' Nadira smiled at him. 'We can't say for sure, we haven't been here long ourselves. But on first look there are a couple of indicators that this could be the same male offender. First, you can see some bruising that goes around her neck.'

Dominic let out a sigh.

'It's not what any of us wanted.' She pointed into the grave the woman had been dragged out of. 'In there you have a lipstick. It looks to be the same make as last time as well. I don't know the significance, but that's not my area of expertise.'

It was his and he was no further forward with it.

'That says a lot more than the rest of her body, doesn't it,' he muttered.

'It does say rather a lot. It's not something you've ever released to the press either so you couldn't imagine a copycat picking up on this and committing a similar murder. First things first though, this mist is going to tamper with our evidence so we need to get a tent erected as quickly as we can, preserve as much as possible.'

Just then a couple of CSIs strode up behind him carrying the white contraption that would protect the woman from the damp in the air. Dominic, Nadira and the CSI stood back out of their way and let them get on with their task.

As the tent was erected Dominic realised he could hear the birds in the trees, their song light and cheerful. The sound of life continuing beautifully around them so at odds with the scene in front of him. The dark damp leaves mulched down on the ground, the livid marks around the woman's neck giving voice to her violent ending.

'How long do you think she's been buried here? How long do you think she's been dead?' he asked.

'You know I can't give you a time of death at the side of the body like this. I do wish you wouldn't ask.' She wasn't annoyed but it was a familiar discussion.

'A rough estimate?'

'Can you wait until the PM? I'll be able to give you all the details then. Right now we have to process her. We have to take the conditions into account as well as the average body breakdown process.'

Dominic scratched at his neck, the Tyvek suit rustling under his fingers. The paper suit chafing at his skin.

'Look,' said Nadira. 'I know it's frustrating, you want to ID her and start your investigation, but it's important that we do things properly, especially at this early stage. If we don't then everything falls down here and you don't want that. Not if we do have a multiple killer on our hands.'

He let out a breath. 'You're right. I'm sorry.' She was right. They had to take it step by step and get each stage right. They couldn't afford for there to be any more women murdered by this guy. He was brutal. They had to stop him and that meant being meticulous.

The removal of the body was slow going. Dominic stayed for the whole period. For some reason he didn't want to leave her. The cold in the woods seeped into his bones the whole time he stood there, making him ache for a warm room and a glass of whiskey. But he stayed and gave the woman the respect she deserved.

His team was busy getting statements from the witnesses who had found the woman and starting to collect CCTV from around the area. But again, as with the last victim, Julie Carver, there was none in the immediate vicinity.

As soil was brushed away from the body and as the woman was moved her injuries became more visible. She had the necklace of bruises around her throat and the remains of a smear of lipstick across her mouth. Her abdomen was a mess after spending time in the soil and with animals having got to her. Dominic swallowed his fury and clenched his fists at his side. How was he supposed to tell her family what had happened to their loved one? It was too horrific. These women had suffered. He would channel his anger into the investigation and work to bring the killer to justice.

Eventually she was loaded into a body bag and taken away. Some of the wildlife that had used her as a temporary home had now been housed in tubs and tubes to dissect later.

The lipstick was excavated and examined. It was House of Maven, Velvet Berry.

They were definitely looking for the same man. And it looked as though he had a definitive MO.

CHAPTER 25

Dominic

The couple who had found the victim admitted they'd been looking for a remote spot for a bit of outdoor sex and had got a lot more than they'd expected. Dominic informed his team that the couple would need investigating but he didn't expect anything to come of it. Nothing had come of the old guy who had walked his dog and found Julie Carver. He figured again that this would be the same scenario. These were an innocent pair who had unfortunately stumbled upon a scene that they would now have to live with for the rest of their lives. It wasn't something you could easily forget and throw off as one of those things that happened. She was a dead body. A real person who had once been living and breathing and having sex herself.

The next line of inquiry would be to identify the woman. Someone was at home wondering where she was, hoping she would walk through the door again. She would be loved and cared for. Or she could be a single woman with no family. No one to report her missing. But if she had a job Dominic hoped someone somewhere had put a report in. No one deserved to die in this way and not have anyone notice.

Back at the station he trawled through the missing persons files himself as his team were busy on other tasks. Normally one of the other Major Crime teams would have gone out to the body this morning as their team already had a case running. Because she resembled their case so closely Kapoor had decided they would pick it up. That meant the workload had doubled and they were stretched. Kapoor would have to make an application for more staff, secondments from uniform and other departments.

He didn't have a timeframe for the woman's death yet so trawling through the missing persons files was slow going. He had no idea how long she had been in the ground. She could even have been murdered before Julie.

That was something they hadn't considered.

Approximately 200,000 people went missing every year. That was a lot of people. They took a huge amount of resources. Many of those returned. You got your regular teenage runaways. Those that left for the night, a couple of nights. Those in care homes that hated it and rebelled. They were all counted. They all had to be searched for even if the likelihood was they'd be found or come back of their own accord.

But some people, they simply disappeared and never returned. How many of those were buried, dumped out at sea, destroyed somehow? Dominic hated to think about it. The families who were left at home with no answers. Always wondering if their loved one would one day walk back through the door with a bunch of flowers and an apology for being away so long and worrying them. All would be forgiven because they were so pleased to see them back. But that day would never come because a stranger, or even someone close to the family, had destroyed their hope and hidden the evidence and it was never to be found.

Today one family had an answer. It wasn't one they wanted, but in comparison to years of unanswered hope it was . . . the better option? Dominic clicked through to the next missing person file. Could this be the one? She was forty-five-year-old Madeleine Chapman. Something about the photograph looked familiar. He checked the file. A toothbrush had been seized by uniformed officers attending the scene. They could do a DNA match to see if she was Chapman. She was reported missing by her mother a week and a half ago.

Dominic picked up the phone and made the request to get the toothbrush sent to Forensics and to get the DNA matched up to the body recovered. This could be done in a matter of hours if it was expedited as urgent.

This whole case was urgent.

It made Dominic's stomach crawl. Especially now they had two bodies. Someone was getting a taste for murder and Dominic didn't like it.

Kapoor walked into the incident room. His mood sombre. 'How are you, Dom?'

'About as you'd expect after visiting that scene, sir.' He leaned back in his chair.

Kapoor crossed his arms over his chest. 'Are we dealing with the same killer?'

'It looks like it. I'll know more this afternoon after the PM.'

'Dammit.'

'Sorry, boss.'

Kapoor shook his head. 'It's not your fault, is it? We need to do a press conference as soon as possible. Get in front of this before they start printing whatever they want to.'

'What are we going to say?'

Kapoor let out a deep sigh. 'I'm not sure I've got that far, Dom. That we've found another body and at this time it's too early to say if it's linked to the one we're investigating from three weeks ago. We're cautiously using the same investigating team and will let them know as soon as we have anything more definitive.'

'I think you're telling them it's linked by using the same team.'

'I know. But they're going to know. No matter how much I tell people to not talk to the press there's always a leak. They always find out. We have to be as open as we can be. It saves embarrassment further down the line.'

Dominic tapped his pen on the desk. 'Do you want me there for the press conference?'

'Ideally. You're the one who's been to both scenes. If they ask any questions you're going to be best suited to answer.'

'The answer will be no comment. Even you can give that response, boss.'

Kapoor laughed. 'You're right, I can. But there might be one or two in there we're willing to answer. You never know. I'd feel better if you were there.'

'I have the PM today, what time are you scheduling it for?'

'What time are you back?'

This time it was Dominic's turn to laugh. 'Okay. I get it. I'm definitely doing this press conference. I'll get on to Nadira and see how soon she can set up the PM.'

'I'm grateful, Dom. Go and get a bite to eat. You have a busy day ahead of you.'

The PM was grim and evidence gathered indicated that it was the same offender who had killed Julie Carver. Nadira put her time of death at seven days which meant he had kept her for a few days before killing her. She'd been missing a week and a half. Cause of death was exsanguination from the knife wound to her neck. It appeared he had had some fun with his hands before he finished the job with a knife. She would have bled out quickly. Death, Dominic thought, might even have been a release for her. He couldn't imagine the fear she would have gone through at the hands of this guy.

By the time he made it back to the station the DNA test had come back from the lab and it was confirmed that the body they had examined belonged to Madeleine Chapman. He let out a long sigh. He had to go and break the news to her mother. A task he hated with a passion. Parents should never lose their children under any circumstances. Murder was particularly horrific.

He walked to Kapoor's office, knocked on the door. 'Boss.'

Kapoor waved him in. 'What is it, Dom? How did the PM go? Anything out of the ordinary?'

Dominic barked out a laugh. 'It was all out of the ordinary. He's one sick bastard.'

Kapoor leaned back in his chair. 'You know what I mean.'

'It looks to be the same offender. He has his own rituals and we need to get to the bottom of them.'

'None of this goes out to the press, are we clear on this?' Kapoor opened a notebook on his desk and started to scribble in it.

'About that . . .'

'You're not backing out. No way. Not now we know they're connected. This is something you need to be present for, Dominic. No excuses.'

'The DNA has come back on the toothbrush I submitted. We have a result, an ID on the woman. I need to go and speak to her family. Give them the death message.' He paused. 'Before the press tell them we've found another body of a middle-aged woman and they jump to conclusions.'

Kapoor let out a sigh. 'Okay, you get some time to inform the family, but I'm delaying the press conference, I'm not cancelling it and I'm not doing it without you.'

'Yeah, okay.' Dominic stood. 'I'll get on that home visit and catch up with you when I'm back.'

'Don't be too long, Dom. I can't keep the baying crowd back for long.'

Dominic walked towards the door. 'Beers are on you, boss, when we catch this bastard. The team are working their arses off on this case.'

'I'll take them all out and thank them when the time is right. But let's make sure we have something to celebrate, shall we?'

CHAPTER 26

Dominic

The house was a small terraced property with a ramp at the door. Dominic had come alone. The team were tied up with their own enquiries. He couldn't pull them away. He'd allocated an FLO who was currently tying up all their loose ends on their own workload and preparing to visit the family after Dominic had broken the news, which involved getting a personal briefing from Kapoor. They needed to be up to date with the investigation as it was.

The door was opened by a woman in a wheelchair. Her left leg was amputated from above the knee. She appeared to be in her sixties, but still young considering what she struggled with in her life. Dom brought himself up. Maybe she coped perfectly fine. Why shouldn't she still look young because she was in a chair and was an amputee?

'Mrs Grady?' He hadn't phoned and warned her he was coming because if he had she would have jumped to conclusions and would have had to wait for the answers. Instead it was better to give her the news and the answers she needed all at once.

'Yes, can I help you?'

He had his warrant card clasped in his hand and opened his palm out to her to show her the identification. 'I'm DS Dominic Harrison. I'm here to talk about your daughter, Madeleine.'

Her hand went to her mouth. Not a sound escaped, but it was that moment when the news passes silently between people without a word having to be said. Dominic hated it. He would rather form the words and have an actual say in how the news was imparted but this freaky sense that some people had of taking the information from you without you having any choice in the matter rattled his cage.

He stepped over the threshold and into the house. They were still on the doorstep. 'Can we go inside?'

She moved back allowing him to enter.

'Shall we go into the living room and I can explain why I'm here.'

She agreed and pushed the door closed behind him.

'Is there anyone else here with you?' Dominic asked.

'No. I'm here alone. Madeleine used to visit me every day. That's how I knew she was missing. My grandson is currently staying with me since she went missing but he's out at college at the moment.' She wheeled herself into the living room.

It was comfortable with a large cream sofa facing the small television in the corner and plenty of room for her chair to move around. Dominic paid attention to the size of the television because nowadays most people had the largest TVs they could fit into the house. This was small and neat and fitted well with the décor of the room. It was comfortable. Homey.

He indicated the sofa. 'Mind if I sit?'

Mrs Grady shook her head and Dominic sank into the deep cushions, feeling at odds with Mrs Grady in her hard looking chair. He tried to straighten himself and stiffened his back in the process but ended up collapsing further into the softness of the fabric. He wriggled to gain control but was losing so gave up and hardened his posture as much as he could.

'I'm sorry to tell you, Mrs Grady—'

'Gwen.'

'Sorry?' The uncomfortable position he was lodged in was affecting his brain.

'My name,' said Mrs Grady. 'It's Gwen.'

He had to lean forward to hear her. A feat of its own.

'I'm sorry, Gwen. We think we've found Madeleine.'

'You're not talking about safe and sound, are you?' Her hands were tight in her lap.

'No, I'm sorry, I'm not. We found her body early this morning. A young couple happened upon her.' He left out the reason they were out and about. No need to add details like that.

Gwen Grady talked down to the floor. 'What happened to my baby?'

'She was killed. We've launched a full murder inquiry and no stone will be left unturned in order to identify who did this.' He climbed out of the soft fabric that held him and crouched in front of her. 'You're going to hear on the news that her murder may be linked to another murder we had a few weeks ago.'

'You could have stopped this?' Tears were streaming from her eyes.

Dominic hated this question. He shook his head. 'Not with the evidence we have so far. And on that basis I need to ask you some questions about Madeleine, if that's okay? We need to learn more about her. About her life and her last movements. Shall I make us a drink first? Is there anyone I can call to come and sit with you?'

Gwen let out a quiet sigh, like the world was now too heavy for her. 'The kitchen is through there. I'll call my sister while you do that. She thought the world of Maddy. She'll be devastated.'

Dominic stood and walked through to the kitchen. Everything had been lowered so that Gwen could do the tasks herself. He could see she was an independent woman even if her daughter did come to visit her every day. At first he had presumed it had been to come and take care of her, but looking at the layout of the kitchen, the units and the utensils, he realised it was probably because she loved her mother and wanted to see her. Some parents had such a relationship with their children.

He walked back into the room with two mugs of coffee and placed them on coasters on the small square table at the end of one of the sofas.

'How's your sister?' he asked.

'She's on her way, but it'll take her a while to get here. We can talk.' Gwen was shaking, tears silently slicing their way down her face.

This time Dominic perched on the edge of the sofa and managed not to collapse into it. 'When did you see Maddy last?'

Gwen took in a deep breath. 'It was about two weeks ago. Like I said, she comes to see me every day. She doesn't live far away. She didn't want to move too far from me. I told her I didn't need her but her whole life she's been the same. She married and stayed close by and when they divorced I thought she might take the opportunity to move and get away from those memories, but she didn't.'

'How did she seem?'

'She was good. She said she'd met someone.' Gwen's hand fluttered over her chest as a gasp of grief escaped.

Dominic's ears pricked at the mention of the similarity to their current case. 'She was dating? Do you have his details?'

'I'm afraid I don't. She'd only just met him. She joined a dating app for women over forty. Said she was too old to date otherwise and was thrilled when she matched with someone. She showed me his photograph though.'

Dominic leaned forward. 'We need to talk to anyone who saw Maddy in her last days. Can you describe him, or sit with an artist to do a composite?'

She shook her head. 'The photograph was awful. I laughed at her.' Gwen's hand went up to her mouth. 'I actually laughed at her. That she had chosen to go on a date with someone she couldn't see from the photo. She in turn scolded me for being so shallow. Oh, I don't mean we had a falling out or anything, it was more relaxed than that. After the divorce she was the shell of the woman I knew her to be. It had taken her a while to start dating again. Her husband wasn't a good man and had made her feel less than human. It was so good to see her excited about going out.' She sobbed again and Dominic comforted her until her sister arrived.

CHAPTER 27

Dominic

Dominic gathered the team. Kapoor was waiting for him so they could do the press conference, but Dominic wanted to pass on the details of the meeting with Gwen Grady before he moved on to the next step.

Paul had stopped at the bakers and they all had a sandwich or pasty in their hands, chewing as they listened.

Dominic tried to make a start on the chicken sandwich Paul had brought him but it was difficult to talk and eat at the same time. He swallowed what he had in his mouth. His stomach gurgled. He hadn't realised how hungry he was. 'We have the husband's details so I'll pay him a visit tomorrow. Get a timeline of activity from him. Paying particular attention to when Maddy went missing.'

'Does Mum think the ex-husband could have something to do with it? Do we think he did the first one to cover up this one?' Rhys wiped grease away from his chin.

'Mum didn't specifically lay blame at the ex-husband's door but was critical of him during the time Madeleine was married to him. As far as we're concerned, we're following the evidence. We'll talk to him and see what he says. We could also ask him if he'd voluntarily allow us to examine his mobile phone. We can check for the app and for a photo of a male barely visible because of the sun breaking out behind him.' Dominic took another bite and listened as his stomach anticipated food again.

'Rhys, will you log all this on HOLMES, please, while I go and do the press conference with the boss?'

'You bet.'

'You said something about the app, what did she give you?' Hayley threw her empty paper bag into the bin under her desk.

'Surprisingly Gwen knew the app Madeleine was using to meet guys. She said it was a phone app called Close to Me. It's geared specifically for people over forty.' He rolled his eyes. 'Like you're supposed to be over the hill at that age and it's more difficult to meet someone.'

'Lucky you have the missus, eh, Dom?' Krish laughed.

'You mean she's lucky, don't you?' Dominic gave them a cheesy grin.

There was a collective groan and Dom shook his head and finished his sandwich.

Hayley spoke again. 'You want us to submit an information request to Close to Me and access Madeleine's account, see who this bloke is she was meeting? If it's the same photo — and we can check that with Helen Butler, once we have it — then it looks like we have our man and our MO.'

Dominic screwed up the paper bag his sandwich had been wrapped up in. It had filled a hole inside of him but for some reason he was still in need of something else. The problem with the job when they were this busy was it rarely gave you time to sit and eat anything properly. Your diet went out the window during an initial investigation. You ate nothing but easy, crap food. This left you feeling hollowed out and low and lacking in energy when you needed it the most. It was a time when you should be making the effort to take care of yourself better. The occasional cop packed themselves a salad the night before and tried to eat well but the behaviour soon stopped when the late nights tired you out so much you just wanted to slide into bed when you got home and not bother about your next day's meals.

The incident door opened and Kapoor stalked in. 'There you are, Dom. I wondered if you'd make it back in time. How did it go?' He paused, noted the tired faces. 'Never mind, catch me up later, we have to get this press conference done. Jonathan and Helen Butler are here, they're waiting for us in my office.'

He'd forgotten they'd be here for this. He was exhausted and drained just thinking about what was to come. Press conferences were not the most fun part of the job. Not that any of the job was fun, but some of it was interesting. He couldn't even put this in that category.

He stood, brushed away any crumbs that clung to him and stretched himself out, lifting his arms over his head and pulling them up, speaking to the team as he did. 'You know what you've got on. I'll leave you with it and if I don't see you after this I'll catch up with you bright and early in the morning.'

It had been a long day and unusually the press briefing had been put off to a late hour because of all the activity. The journalists and photographers were getting twitchy for their bite of news. They hated to be kept waiting and they had an idea that a family member might be up for grabs today. They loved the money shot of a loved one breaking down, no matter how sensitive they were at the time of recording, their viewership and readership went up and that's what they lived for. Everyone loved heartbreak. Mostly in their fiction, but if it was in the comfort of their own homes, while they were able to watch someone else's life collapse around them and they were able to stay safe but talk about it with their own loved ones or friends, then they lapped it up.

As they walked towards Kapoor's office, Dominic updated him on the name of the app that was being used by the women. 'I think we should consider mentioning it in the press conference.'

'Warn the women off?' Kapoor frowned.

Dominic understood why. Telling women what to do in their dating lives was not a good stance to take. Most women would tell you to get the men to control themselves. Keep their hands to themselves, their urges to themselves. Their nasty, violent thoughts to themselves. And they were right. 'Not exactly warning them off, no. But I do think we need to let them know what's been happening and let them make informed decisions when actively engaging in their love lives.'

'You're right.' Kapoor bit his lower lip, the tension of the day making itself seen. 'But we have to tread carefully.'

He would have to tread carefully. This was his press conference. Dominic was only here in a support capacity. This was all down to Kapoor.

They stepped into Kapoor's office and greeted the Butlers who had no idea what they were heading into. Running the gauntlet, sitting in front of steaming hot cameras and people crowding in at you, desperate for your pain. It was something indescribable. Intense. Intrusive. Inhuman.

'Do you have any news, DS Harrison?' Jonathan was eager to find out the latest the minute they clasped hands.

Dominic looked to Kapoor, unsure what had already been discussed, not wanting to go over old ground. Kapoor discreetly shook his head. The old goat had run shy of giving them this morning's information.

'I'm sorry, we're still working as hard as we can on the investigation. Nothing will slow us down. Unfortunately, I have to tell you that another woman has been killed. We're keeping an eye on the evidence to see if they're linked, but because of the timeframe, we're taking investigative control of that case as well.'

Helen paled and grabbed hold of Jonathan. 'Another one?'

'We're not sure yet,' he reiterated. He didn't want the press or the public to have this information. Not until they had ... what? They'd done the PM and the injuries were consistent. What were they waiting for exactly? Kapoor didn't

149

want to frighten anyone but there was a difference between frightening people and keeping them updated. He'd go with Kapoor. They could always update the hoards later. 'We still have some lines of enquiry. We'll let you know as soon as we're sure.' When would that be? 'In fact.' He looked to Helen. 'It may be that we have a photograph we want you to look at in the near future, if you'd be okay with that?'

'Anything I can do to help. Though I don't know what it is I can help with.' She paused. 'Oh, the dating app photograph. You do think it's the same person!'

Damn. 'We're not sure. If we get a photograph and we get you to confirm it then we can say positively.' Kapoor was scowling at him behind the Butlers. Dominic minutely shook his head that this was not his fault. This was Kapoor's own fault for not having a discussion with him before they got into his office. 'At this point we're not directing the press to any potential link between the cases because we don't want to jump to conclusions.' He had to warn them of this so they didn't blurt anything out during the press briefing.

'Okay.' Her voice was subdued.

Kapoor stepped forward. 'I'll talk first, providing a brief outline of the case so far and then I'll pass the baton to you at which point you can ask for witnesses or anyone with any knowledge to come forward. Then Dominic will close by taking a few questions.'

The couple looked at each other.

'Who's going to speak?' Kapoor asked.

'I will.' Jonathan took a physical step forward, straightened himself, brought his shoulders back, readying for the ordeal ahead of him.

'Okay. My advice is to keep calm. Don't speak until you're ready. Don't let them rush you. Take as many breaths as you need. There's no rush for this. You have the power in that room, not them. If you start to feel flustered, stop and breath and start again when you're ready. We're there to pick it up if you can't continue. Do the best you can.' This was Kapoor's forte. He was good under pressure. Always calm and composed and now Dominic understood how he managed that. It was in his breathing. He allowed himself to breathe before he made major decisions and when he was talking to people. Dominic liked it. He'd keep that nugget himself. He tended to lose his cool pretty easily. A trait he would like to change if he could.

'Are you ready to face them?' Kapoor asked, a hand on Helen's arm.

The couple nodded in unison.

They moved towards Kapoor's office door and towards the waiting media who were hungry for a story they could milk for as much emotion as they could manage.

Lights started to flash as soon as they stepped from behind the boards.

Bright and sharp. The constant whirr and click of the cameras was almost overwhelming, even to Dominic who had been here countless times before. He simply took in one deep breath and continued his walk to the chair he was allocated. In front of him Jonathan and Helen stalled. Helen nearly tripped over Jonathan as he stopped dead in his tracks.

Kapoor sensed what was happening behind him and turned and smiled at the couple, a reassuring, warm smile that said to them that they were okay, that they were not alone and that they were protected.

The line started to move again.

Chair legs screeched as they settled down behind the long row of tables that had been laid out, the sound exacerbated by the strangeness of the situation. A sea of faces stared expectantly at them. Hands clutching notepads, pens poised for the one remark they could cling to and analyse for the rest of the day. Behind this table everyone was on display. Every word was checked for meaning and secrets.

Jonathan and Helen were bolt upright, like they had broom handles up the back of their clothing keeping them in position. Their eyes were wide. Whatever they had been expecting, the reality had invaded and shocked more than they had prepared for. Dominic wondered how much

Kapoor's advice to breathe was going to help them. It was great advice but they needed to take it on board if they were to get through this.

Kapoor cleared his throat and the room which had been a hubbub of low chatter quietened.

'Thank you for waiting for this briefing today. We appreciate it's not the usual way of doing things, but it has been a long day here at Snig Hill Police Headquarters and as you can imagine with policing, we can't always run to a timetable. Sometimes things demand to be dealt with.'

Pens slid across notebooks. Cameras flashed. Jonathan and Helen stayed rigid, hands clasped under the table.

Kapoor continued, 'Today we want to appeal for witnesses to the murder of Julie Carver and to update the public on some new information that has come to light.

'We have become aware that a dating app has been used and that this is how the murderer identified Julie. Now while I'm loathe to name said dating app, I do think it is in the best interests of the women of Sheffield to be aware so they can make informed choices.'

Cameras clicked and pens scribbled their notes. He had everyone's attention. This was a scoop. Kapoor would get blowback from the app creator but putting the safety of the women of the city first was his priority. He could take whatever heat was coming his way. With quiet sincerity Kapoor named the app and asked the women using it to continue their lives but with a little added caution.

Dominic could see Kapoor let out a small sigh of relief but he knew the stress of this event was far from over. 'Now I will pass you to Julie's brother, Jonathan Butler—' he stared hard at the gathered press — 'who will *not* take any questions. Then you will be passed to DS Dominic Harrison, to my right, who *will* take some questions.'

He nodded to Jonathan, the hush over the room palpable. Jonathan took a huge gulp then picked up the glass of water that had been placed in front of his position — there was one in front of each of them — and swallowed the water like he'd been in the desert for a month. Gently he placed the glass back on the table and stared out in front of him, at the faces that stared back. Bright eyes in the darkened room.

'Thank you for letting me be here today,' he croaked and cleared his throat. He picked up his glass again, his hand shaking. He swallowed hard and then put the glass back on the table. Swallowed again, licked his lips, and was ready. 'As you know my sister was murdered three weeks ago.' His tongue came out to wet his lips again. 'It's a huge loss for my family. She was a special woman and I—' he looked to his wife — 'we, want to appeal to anyone who might have any information that can lead to the apprehension of her killer. He can't be allowed to be left to wander the streets. Not after what he's done. He will be your husband, your brother, your son, maybe even your father. You may have noticed him acting differently. He can't have done what he did to our darling Julie and not be a different person. Please, if you do suspect someone, or you think you saw something, let the police know.'

'Do you really want him to do it again?' blurted out Helen at the side of Jonathan.

It had been going so well until that point. Tears streamed down Helen's face and Jonathan was silenced. He was watching his wife intently.

Considering.

Dominic needed to stop him. 'I'll take some questions now.'

'He's already killed again. How many people does he have to kill for you to help us?' Jonathan asked quietly at the side of Kapoor. So quiet Dominic could barely hear him, but he had been heard. The room exploded.

Flashbulbs lit up the room. Voices began to shout out questions.

'Who has he killed?'

'How do you know it's the same person?'

'What are you doing about this, DI Kapoor?'

Dominic raised his voice and spoke out over the din. 'If you direct your questions this way, I'll try to answer what I can.' What the hell was he going to say? They hadn't agreed on a way forward for this scenario.

Every eye turned to Dominic.

The first question was shouted across to him. 'What's this about him killing again, DS Harrison?' Straight to the point.

Dominic cleared his throat. 'We attended a crime scene this morning. A woman in her forties. It hasn't yet been officially linked to Operation Halo,' he paused, made eye contact with the questioner, 'and we will inform you when it is linked. But there are some indicators to suggest that the team on Operation Halo should be the lead team on this murder as well.'

'What are these indicators?'

Dominic smiled. 'You know I'm not in a position to provide operational details. I'll give you as much information as I can, but we do need to keep some material close for investigative purposes.'

They walked out of the room in the line they had entered but backwards. Dominic leading the way out and Kapoor bringing up the rear. The back of Dominic's neck itched. Kapoor was going to blow a gasket as soon as he'd said his farewells to the Butlers and not a second before.

He was pleasant and kind to them. Shaking their hands. Reassuring them they could work with what had happened.

'The police are used to thinking on their toes, Helen. It's how we work. Please don't worry about it,' he soothed. His voice gentle and velvet-like.

The minute they were out the door he turned on Dominic. 'What the bloody hell?'

Dominic shoved his hands in his pockets. He may as well make himself comfortable for this one.

'I thought we said we weren't going to disclose the link between the two cases!'

'In case you missed it, boss, we didn't do any of the disclosing. The family did. There's little we can ever do to control the family. You did a brilliant job of trying to get them to slow down and think before they spoke before we went out but it was obviously preying on their minds.'

Kapoor was pacing back and forth in front of Dominic. They were in Kapoor's office, well away from the feeding press.

'How do you think they'll spin this?' Kapoor asked. 'We're going to get slaughtered, aren't we? We didn't catch the killer so he's able to have killed again, that kind of thing?' He scratched his head. 'Police incompetence leads to second murder.'

'Boss, I'd like to see them come in here and resolve this case any faster than any of us have done.'

'That's not the point though, is it? It's our job and their job is to comment on how we're doing ours. To hold us to account. You know Connelly is going to go ape shit when he reads the papers in the morning.'

'He might not need to wait until the morning. Some of those reporters will be able to load the reports online tonight.'

Kapoor spun on the spot. 'Shit, I'd forgotten about the bloody internet. I don't know how. It's the bane of my life. I'm going to have to update him straight away and he won't be happy because this one is going to be fed all the way up to the chief constable now it's a double murder case.'

'Look, we can't do anything about it. As you said to the Butlers, we have to work with it now. I'm just going to pop out to interview Madeleine's ex-husband, Alex Chapman. We couldn't get hold of him earlier and we're hoping we should be able to catch him now. But after that, we're all back in bright and early in the morning. It's a new day, we'll all be fresh and we'll go from there.'

Kapoor walked around his desk to his chair. 'Make sure you bring your A game, Dom, I want this case clearing up. Two murders is two too many. Tomorrow, you change the direction of this investigation and put us in the lead and him on the back foot.'

155

CHAPTER 28

Dominic

Alex Chapman was the picture of politeness. He moved around his large kitchen making drinks. There was a huge square island in the middle of the room with a line of white leather bar stools along one side. It was here Dominic and Hayley sat. The surface of the island polished to such an extent that it reflected their faces back to them. Dominic was perturbed by this and placed his hands on the granite.

'You say this is about my ex-wife, Maddy?' Alex placed cups and saucers in front of the officers. 'I'm not sure how I can help. I haven't seen her for a while. Our son is old enough that I contact him directly to sort our plans.' He paused as he collected his own drink and his eyebrows furrowed. 'What is this about exactly?' He stood opposite them.

'Shall we go and sit somewhere we can talk?' Dominic asked. He didn't like the dynamic of Chapman standing over them while they had this conversation.

Alex Chapman smiled. 'Of course.' He headed towards the door. 'This way.'

Dominic and Hayley climbed down from their stools and with some clinking, collected their drinks, and followed the ex-husband through to the equally large living room. He wasn't doing badly for himself. Divorce obviously hadn't hurt him.

'You haven't seen the news?' Dominic asked when they were all seated.

Chapman frowned. 'This doesn't sound good. Should I have? Again, I ask, what's this about?' The polite facade slipped as frustration niggled at the edges of the question.

Dominic was reminded of Gwen Grady's comments that Alex Chapman was not a good man and had made Maddy feel less than human. He was also suspicious the man wasn't already aware of why they were here. The press briefing had been done and had gone out on the local news channel. He'd expected to be walking into a torrent of abuse about not being informed. Not that he needed to be. He was the ex-husband now. But Alex was claiming to have no idea why they were there.

Dominic looked to Hayley who gave a barely perceptible shrug, then he turned back to Chapman. 'Madeleine Chapman was found dead yesterday.'

The cup in the saucer Chapman was holding quivered and the porcelain tinkled. His eyes shot down to look at his hands and he leant forward, placing the cup and saucer down on the low-slung oak coffee table in front of him. 'Maddy's dead?'

'I'm sorry to have to inform you, but she was murdered.' Dominic watched Chapman carefully.

His eyes misted up. 'Our boy . . .'

'Gwen is taking care of him.'

Chapman rose. 'He's my son. He belongs here.'

'He's sixteen, you'll need to speak with him and Gwen.'

Chapman's voice rose a level. 'No. He's mine. I want him here.'

Of course he would be concerned for his child, it was only natural, but he'd barely passed thought on his ex-wife. Dominic didn't like the way this felt. 'We're not going to get involved when the child in question is sixteen. Talk to your son and if you feel it's necessary then talk to a solicitor. Social Care will also be informed of Madelaine's murder and will be in contact.'

Chapman glared down at Dominic.

Dominic wasn't taking this aggression from anyone. 'Please have a seat, Mr Chapman. We need to ask you some questions in relation to your ex-wife.'

Chapman opened his mouth as though he was about to speak, but then closed it, paused, looked to consider his options, then retook his vacant seat.

Dominic inclined his head. 'Thank you.'

'I don't know what you want from me. Like I said, I don't have anything to do with Maddy.'

Hayley took out her notepad and pen.

'That's really necessary?' Chapman asked of her.

'It's so we remember the main points of the conversation and don't repeat the questions,' Hayley said.

Chapman lifted his head and looked down his nose at her.

Dominic bristled and quickly brought him back to the interview. 'When did you last see Maddy?'

The man didn't even try to hide his frustration. He let out a huge sigh.

Dominic waited him out. It didn't look like Chapman was going to respond, so Dominic prompted him. 'Mr Chapman?'

He sighed again. 'I don't even know. I've told you we don't engage with each other because I contact my son directly. Maybe at the beginning of the year when it was his birthday? I wanted to take him out but his mother had already made arrangements. We had words.'

'And that was the last time you saw her?'

'I didn't see her then. Yes, we had words, but it was by phone. I think the last time I saw her was at Christmas last year when I picked our son up from the house. She came out to wish me a happy Christmas. We're not on the best of terms and that was unusual for her. She's a flighty woman.' Another sigh.

'What do you mean by flighty?'

Hayley was taking notes as the two men spoke. Chapman glared at her as her pen moved across the page.

Then he waved his hands around in the air as though he was trying to grab the words he was searching for. 'You know, she was emotional. Irresponsible. She'd always give our boy his own way when he needed a firmer hand. Rules make the man. She wanted to mollycoddle him. Made the excuse he needed love.' He curled his lip. 'He had everything he could ever need. How was he supposed to grow into a decent man if he didn't know the rules of adulthood, I ask you? You would have less people to deal with in your job if more people taught their kids the rules of life and adulting.' He puffed out his chest.

Dominic had an unreasonable urge to cross the room and punch the guy. He'd just been told his ex-wife had been murdered and here he was slagging her off and telling them what a bad parent she was because she wanted to show her son what love was. 'Do you mind telling us where you were seven days ago?'

Chapman barked out a laugh. 'Do you want to be more specific than that?'

Dominic stared at him.

Chapman stared back.

Dominic really did not like this man. 'Seven days, Mr Chapman.'

'You're being serious?'

'I've never been more serious.'

Chapman looked at his watch.

'Are we holding you up from something?'

'I just want to contact my son.'

That was not unreasonable. He might not care that his ex-wife was dead, murdered in fact, but, Dominic realised, he probably did care how his son was dealing with it. 'Answer our questions and we'll be out of your hair.'

Chapman looked up at the ceiling and rubbed at the back of his neck, then straightened. 'I work and I come home. I haven't been anywhere unusual. I haven't seen my ex-wife.'

'And what is it you do for a living?' The house was beautiful. The man made a decent living whatever it was he did.

'I work in banking.'

It explained a lot.

'And your colleagues will be able to vouch for your movements on the day in question?'

'Of course. But do you really need to bother them with this?'

Dominic ignored the question. 'And what about the evening?'

Chapman sighed again. 'I work late but then I come home and as you can see, I live alone. Though sometimes I do have female company.' He smiled at them.

Dominic cringed. He could imagine how that comment made Hayley feel. It wasn't so much the comment but the way he'd said it. 'And what about that night?'

Chapman thought back then shook his head. 'No, not that night. I was alone.'

'Okay. Thank you.'

'I can call my son now?'

As much as Dominic wanted to make Chapman's life difficult, he didn't want to harm his son. He agreed they were leaving and contact could be made.

However, he was more than eager to inconvenience the man and follow up with his colleagues to see where Chapman had been when his wife had been murdered. He hadn't liked his manner at all when they'd informed him of her death. Dominic looked forward to turning Chapman's life upside down.

CHAPTER 29

Dominic

The first report to appear was, of course, online. Dominic slid into bed beside a sleeping Ruth and checked the news website before he went to sleep for what was left of the night. It was as bad as they had feared. The police were being trounced. Because of them another woman had lost her life. This wouldn't help Madeleine's mum. He would have to speak to the FLO in the morning and update him before he turned up for his shift at the house. He needed to be aware what he was walking into. Dominic hoped they had reassured Gwen enough when they visited her. But victim relatives could have erratic emotions and reading reports like this would do them no good whatsoever. It certainly didn't breed cooperation between families and police when it was needed the most.

He lay his head down and tried to switch off. There was a gentle snoring coming from beside him. Ruth was adamant she didn't snore, but she was asleep so how would she know. It wasn't loud and bullish, it was a mellow snuffle as she breathed in and only happened if she lay on her back. He stuck his elbow into her as the sound pierced his brain and irritated his tired head. She rolled onto her side and he closed his eyes. It had been a tough day and his mind was buzzing but he needed to switch off so he'd be prepared for the day ahead in the morning.

The alarm was going off before he'd even had the chance to realise he was asleep. He was dazed, his head fuzzy, cloudy and heavy, and he struggled to find his phone to switch it off. Eventually it was quiet.

Dominic lay back and relaxed. Ruth was still asleep. She had another hour before her alarm was due to ring. He was getting an early start. He stared at her sleeping form, irrationally annoyed she could still sleep on. He wanted to prod her, wake her, make it so that it wasn't just him who was awake and this tired.

He made a mug of tea and placed it with a clatter on her bedside table. She stirred, opened her eyes and looked at him.

'You're home,' she said sleepily.

Frustration fizzed through his body as she stretched lazily under the quilt. 'Yeah, I'm heading back into work now.'

'Have a good day.' She turned and saw the drink. Made just so he could wake her. She rubbed her eyes. 'Thanks for the tea.'

He gritted his teeth. He needed to get out of the house and get to work. It was no good taking his exhaustion out on Ruth. He walked to the door. 'I'll see you later.'

'Hey.'

He turned.

'No kiss?'

He ground his teeth, the tension running up to his tired head and building up behind his eyes, then strode down the stairs and out the door. The day was already bright and the sky clear.

In the station Dominic found he was one of the first in. He fired up his computer. He was relaxed once he was back in the station.

Staff trickled in and the noise level in the incident room increased. Hayley was the next person from their team to arrive.

'Sleep well, Dom?' she asked wrapping a cardigan around the back of her chair.

'Surprisingly, yes,' he lied. Could he call what had happened in his bed last night sleep? 'What about you? Getting enough rest?'

She smiled. 'I have no trouble sleeping. What mood do you think the boss is going to be in this morning?'

Dominic rubbed his chin. 'I have no idea. Depends on who he's spoken with this morning and how much grief he's been given about last night's press conference.'

Hayley pulled out her chair and sat behind her desk. 'It didn't go quite as planned, did it?'

'You could say that.'

'Were you in bother?' Paul had crept up behind them.

'Not really. Nothing anyone could have done about it. Though I'm not sure that's how the brass will see it.'

'Yeah, they like to have control and blame.' Paul had a mug in his hand and took a slurp.

'Hey, where's mine?' Hayley moaned pinning him to the spot with a look.

'I didn't know who was in yet, did I?'

'Well you do now, so get back and make more tea. I'm gasping.'

Paul saluted her, placed his mug on his desk and spun on the spot, heading out the incident room back to the kitchen.

'You've got him well trained.' Dom leaned back in his chair as Paul stalked out of the room.

Hayley laughed. 'You've got to be tough on this team if you want anything doing.'

'Is that right? Am I doing this leadership thing all wrong? Do I need to be tougher on all of you?'

She laughed some more. 'I think you're doing fine. But if I'm not tough with them they'll think they can walk all over me.'

Dominic was silent as he considered what she'd said. More people walked into the incident room. Krish came up

163

to his desk and greeted them with a good morning. They both responded with the same.

Dominic looked at Hayley. 'You think it's because you're female?'

'Oh, what've I walked into?' Krish was wide eyed.

Hayley laughed yet again, this time at Krish. 'You're fine. Nothing. I've sent Paul to make me a cuppa as he had one himself and not one for me.'

Understanding dawned on Krish's face. 'Nothing to do with being a woman, Dom. If you don't tell Paul what to do he'll forget or not have a clue.'

Dominic wasn't having any of it. 'You said you had to be tough, Hayley.'

She sighed. 'Yeah, we're in the police, you know, not some touchy-feely place, the stuff we have to deal with, we're automatically hardened. We can give and take some ribbing . . .'

'Or,' Krish pointed out, 'in Paul's case, direct orders. He needs them, Dom. I'm sure you know that. We don't see Hayley as any different to the rest of us. She makes the tea and she tells us to make the tea. It's swings and roundabouts.'

Before Dominic had time to mull Krish's point over, Kapoor entered the room closely followed by Rhys who had been out on enquiries. Kapoor brought the room to order.

'Okay gang, we all know what a disaster last night's press conference was. I've been summoned to see the chief this morning and I'm expecting to get my knuckles rapped for that. But as far as you're concerned, we're doing a great job and we have to continue. Connelly's already hauled me over the coals before I came in here. It's more about what was said rather than how they think we're handling it. When faced with the realities of the investigation they can't complain. But the press are not making it easy and more will be said today. So grit your teeth and get on with your jobs.'

Kapoor ran his hands through his hair. 'How's it going with the CCTV viewing?' he asked.

The officer at the back of the room responsible for viewing the hours and hours of CCTV spoke up. He was logging multiple vehicles that were in the area at and around the relevant time, but his job had just doubled with the case from yesterday. He asked if he could have another staff member to join him.

Kapoor shoved his hands in his pockets. 'I'm going to increase the size of the team by another fifteen officers. Expect them over the next week or so. I need to get them released from their commanding officers, but after seeing the chief later today I don't see it being a problem.'

The incident room team was growing. They were a huge enquiry team and if this case got any bigger, as Dominic worried it might, then they would probably expand to the biggest murder team the force had seen for a long time.

Kapoor turned to Dominic. 'How was your interview last night? With the ex-husband, wasn't it?'

Dominic thought back to the man they'd spoken with. 'I think we need to take a look at him. He's an arrogant prick, but if I take my personal dislike of him out of the equation he doesn't have an alibi for the time of death and he doesn't seem to speak very highly of Maddy.' He looked to Hayley. 'Or of any women, I imagine. He could very well be a suspect.'

Kapoor turned to Hayley. 'You agree with this?'

Hayley looked down at her notes from the meeting. 'Yes, boss. He's very unlikeable. But as the sarge said, he can't account for himself at the time Madeleine was killed.'

'What about the other murder, Julie Carver?' asked Rhys.

'Could be that he wanted to hide Maddy's murder and not have himself be the prime suspect,' said Dominic. 'It's not unheard of.'

'Anything solid on him other than your gut feeling?' asked Kapoor.

'Just the lack of anything that puts him in the clear. I definitely think he's worth a look,' said Dominic.

'Okay,' said Kapoor. 'We have our first real suspect, let's dig into him.'

CHAPTER 30

Dominic

By that afternoon they'd interrogated every police system at their disposal and nothing of concern had come up for Alex Chapman. He hadn't ever been arrested or committed a traffic violation as far as the team could see. There was no intelligence on the system relating to him or anyone connected to him. Even his car insurance was up to date.

Dominic scribbled a note into his pad. 'Okay, I'm going to his place of work. Check things out there.'

Hayley looked at him.

'Yes, it'll rattle him, but maybe that's what we want? If he does have something to do with this we need him to make a mistake. Whoever is behind this hasn't put a foot wrong so far. A rattled killer is a sloppy killer.' Dominic grabbed his jacket. 'Are you coming with me?'

Hayley rose. 'Me?'

'Yeah. You were with me yesterday. You may as well follow through, hadn't you?'

She shoved her notebook into her bag. 'Okay, let's go do this.'

* * *

Dominic knew when Alex Chapman had stated he was in banking he didn't mean he was a teller handing out ten-pound notes over the counter to the men and women of Sheffield.

The building they entered was a huge glass-fronted affair. In the centre was a beautiful atrium with a water fountain surrounded by plush sofas facing outwards. A couple of people were sitting there having conversations, disposable coffee cups in hand, expensive looking briefcases on the floor at their feet. The women in heels so high Dominic wondered how they could stand in them never mind walk in them. All the women he worked with wore sensible shoes they could stand in all day or chase an offender if needed.

To the side was a glossy, white, long desk with a smartly turned out male sitting behind. Dominic and Hayley approached. The young man looked them up and down barely disguising the comment that he thought they were in the wrong place.

This, thought Dominic, is where Alex Chapman's whole demeanour came from.

Eventually, after warrant cards were shown and a strong refusal by Dominic to return later, they were hand-delivered to the floor where Chapman's boss resided. Chapman, it turned out, worked in the financial crime threat mitigation department.

'You protect individuals from fraud?' Dominic asked as they settled around a table.

The woman smiled. 'That's a simplistic way of putting it. The FCTM department is responsible for all financial crime, individual and big business, in every country the bank operates in. It's a challenging, global role.'

Dominic inclined his head, little understanding the scale of banking across the world. It wasn't important though, having no bearing on why they were there. 'You supervise Alex Chapman?'

'He's part of the team, yes.' The tip of her tongue ran along her lower lip which was glossy red.

'Was he at work eight days ago?'

'Yes,' she said.

'How can you be so sure, without checking?' asked Dominic.

She crossed one leg over the other. 'I don't need to check. Alex is dedicated, like everyone here, and I can't remember the last time he took a day off.'

Hayley scribbled in her notebook.

'What's he like?' asked Dominic.

She let out a sigh, which reminded Dominic of Alex. Was everyone here impatient with the world around them?

'Like I said, he's dedicated.'

'As a person,' Dominic clarified.

The woman leaned back in her chair. The chair relaxed with her, then bounced back to its original position. Behind her, through the huge window that framed her desk, the sky was grey and heavy. 'I'm not quite sure what you mean.'

Dominic tried to keep his own patience. 'Is he a calm man? It must be a very stressful job.'

'Alex is excellent at his job. The team couldn't run without him. He gels very well with his colleagues and we've had no complaints about him.'

It wasn't much. 'Has he said much about his divorce, his ex-wife?'

'Not to me. He tends to keep his personal life personal. This is a busy office, we don't have time for heart-to-hearts.'

It sounded like a pretty cold place to work if you asked him. He thanked her for her time and they were, again, hand-delivered back downstairs to the atrium.

'We didn't get much from this visit.' Hayley tucked a strand of hair behind her ear.

'No, but we did get a bigger picture of a cold-fish of a man. One who isn't really connected to people. Who works with numbers all day and goes home to an empty house. Who will view the fact that Maddy had custody of their son as a loss in his eyes. He won't have liked that.'

They handed their lanyards in to the man behind the glossy white desk and walked towards the huge glass entrance doors.

'You really do fancy him for this, don't you?' Hayley was mesmerised by the silent hush as the doors slid open in front of them. There was real money here.

'I'm not making the narrative fit the man. I'll wait him out until we have real evidence. But, yeah, I get a real uneasy feeling from him.'

* * *

Back in the incident room Dominic updated the team and HOLMES. Hayley sent Rhys into the kitchen to make a brew. He grumbled as he stalked out of the room, a tray of empty mugs clattering in his hands.

Dominic was engrossed in HOLMES when the door to the incident room was quietly opened and one of the front counter staff crept in and handed the day's post out onto the relevant desks. There were two items for Dominic which she placed beside him. He ignored them and continued tapping away at his keyboard, writing in reasons Alex Chapman should remain a person of interest. One whom they should refer to when any evidence came to light or God forbid, any further murders occurred. Dominic was aware there was an underlying personal dislike on his part, but there was also sound logic dictating Chapman be kept in mind.

He finished typing as Rhys walked back in with a tray filled with fresh drinks, followed by Kapoor. He was looking for an update.

'Just what I need.' Dominic grinned at his DC. 'Thanks, mate.' He lifted a mug from the tray that was presented to him and placed it on his desk. 'We haven't got much to tell,' he said to Kapoor. 'I've just typed it all up on HOLMES.'

'You think he's good for it?' asked Kapoor.

'Thinking he's good for it and being able to prove anything are two different things entirely.' He looked down at the two envelopes that had been left on his desk. One in a brown, official looking envelope. It was a report from Social Care on a couple of children that were involved in a case they had picked up six months ago.

'Did you even boil the kettle?' asked Paul, scowling at his coffee.

'Make it yourself next time.' Rhys wasn't impressed.

Dominic picked up the second envelope. This one was white and slim.

'Any further work to do on Chapman?' Kapoor asked.

Dominic shook his head as he ran his finger along the edge of the envelope to tear it open. 'I think it's just a matter of waiting to see what evidence we get and bearing Chapman in mind.' He pulled out the single sheet of paper that was contained within. He read it, his brain not quite connecting with what his eyes were seeing. He raised his arm as though in school. 'Erm, sir.'

Kapoor looked at him. 'What is it, Dom?'

'I think we might have a problem.'

'More of a problem than the one we're discussing?'

Dom looked down at the paper again. 'Well it's related.' He waved the sheet in the air. 'We've had contact, boss.'

Kapoor's eyebrows shot up to his hairline. 'What?'

'I've received a letter that appears to be from the killer. Sent directly to me.'

'Drop the letter onto your desk,' demanded Kapoor. 'We need to get a CSI up here to retrieve it and get it fingerprinted, and tested for DNA if he's licked the envelope.'

As Dominic let go of the sheet of paper it fluttered down to his desk. A desk he was now unable to work from.

'Can you still see what it says?' Kapoor asked.

Dominic peered at the sheet. It had been folded into the envelope so had rigid fold marks, but if he bent his head at an angle he could still read it. 'Yes, boss.'

'I have so many questions,' Kapoor started, 'but the first one has to be, what does it say?'

Dominic checked the sheet he'd dropped on the desk and read from the page:

'*DS Harrison, please don't worry that you are failing the families as the press are making out. You are not. It's just that I'm too good for you. And if you fear this is a hoax, I left the women with a little red kiss.*'

CHAPTER 31

Claudia

Twenty hours since Ruth's attack

'I heard that the killer was in contact with someone on the investigation team, I just never realised it was you. Why did you keep it a secret from Ruth and me?' They were back in an interview room in the custody suite. Claudia's surprise and horror at this disclosure was plain to see.

Dominic sighed. 'How do you think you both would have reacted if you'd known it was me he was talking to?'

'We're cops, you know?' Claudia spat back at him. Now they were talking about their personal life the frustration she felt spilled over.

He laughed. 'You sound so much like Ruth.'

'I'm glad we're not pretending that you're not my dad anymore.' She waved an arm between them. 'It was a damn strain trying to run this like any other case.' Her head was tight and throbbing at the same time, like it was going to explode. First there was the excruciating concern for Ruth — she was family. Not only family by marriage, but they were close, they were friends, and good friends at that. They spent time together, away from her dad, shopping, tea and coffees, wine, chatting, putting the world to rights. Her heart was breaking. Then she'd been placed in this ridiculous position of interviewing her own father about the situation. A father where tension easily flared up at the best of times. They both had issues. Silent fears that mostly left unsaid managed to leave a rumble of disquiet. Ruth had always been great at smoothing things out between them. But now she wasn't here and it was like the world was splitting apart.

Dominic put his head in his hands. 'They knew what they were doing putting you in here to interview me.'

'Why do you say that?' Claudia looked to Kane who shrugged his shoulders. She didn't believe anything between them was obvious at work. After all, they'd never actually worked together on any jobs in the past.

'Just look how emotional we're getting. If I had anything to let slip, we're heading into the time when it's going to happen, don't you think?'

Claudia dropped her voice, fear curdling in her stomach. 'Do you have anything to let slip? Do you know what happened to Ruth?' Sharpe had played her cards well asking Claudia to run this investigation, but it was harder than she could ever have imagined. No one could have considered that it would get this dark.

He lifted his head. 'I'm not a killer, Claudia. How can you ask these questions?'

'Because that's what I've been sent in here to do, you've acknowledged that.'

Dominic nodded.

'You know the rules, Dad. For the recording.'

He sighed. 'Yes. I know that's why you're in here.'

'So why all the secrecy around the contact?'

Dominic leaned back and crossed his arms. 'It wasn't just to protect myself from getting grief from you and Ruth about the danger I could be in. It was to protect the pair of you.'

'You were protecting us? How?'

'If I kept my two lives apart, my home life and my work life, then I hoped the Sheffield Strangler wouldn't realise you were both important to me. And hopefully you wouldn't be targeted if he ever became angry with me. Which he did at times. It's not easy liaising with a killer through the press. And this was why I was so up in arms when Ruth was given the task of going undercover to try to trap him.'

'You really thought he'd risk himself by coming after us?'

Dominic rolled his eyes. 'He's a dangerous man, Claudia, you must know that? You haven't worked the case but you know enough from the chatter within the force and from the press. Plus the little I've told you myself.' He let out a sigh. 'What happened if he wanted to send me a more personal message? Not one printed on paper? One to get under my skin? How do you think he would do that?'

Claudia rose from her chair and paced around the room. 'You think he would hurt someone you love to send you a message?'

Dominic nodded.

'Dad . . .'

'Sorry. Yes. Yes, I do think he'd hurt someone I love to send me a message. He liked to have the upper hand. He gloated and he taunted and he hated it if we made any steps forward. He wanted to put me back in my place.'

Claudia paced around the room some more. Kane sat silently. He was here for support. This was her interview. Her investigation. He would do as she wanted and he'd keep quiet until she needed him.

Dominic kept his head down.

'So,' she said, 'You think he's found out Ruth is your wife rather than her going missing as part of the operation?'

'Have you spoken to her team? Was she going on a date? If it was part of the operation they'd know about it and she wouldn't be missing because they'd have been there to back her up and support her. No matter how pear-shaped it went, she'd have come home at the end of the day. No, this is her going missing because he found out somehow that she's my wife and he's playing a game with me for some sick reason. Maybe I was getting too close. Think back to the witness we're talking to who saw the man lurking near the scene. If we ID that guy we might have him.'

Claudia stared down at him.

'If he wants to send a message, she might still be alive. He might want to talk. We have to do something, Claudia. Being locked inside this tiny room is doing no good. It's not doing Ruth any favours. I need to be where he can contact me. It's me he's playing a game with.'

CHAPTER 32

Dominic

Five months ago

Kapoor was focused. 'Tell me what it said again. I want to make sure I have it straight in my head.'

With his head bent Dominic read it for the office again. '*DS Harrison, please don't worry that you are failing the families as the press are making out. You are not. It's just that I'm too good for you. And if you fear this is a hoax, I left the women with a little red kiss.*'

'He's directed it to you personally,' Kapoor noted.

'Why would he do that?' Dominic straightened up in his chair. 'What did I do to draw his attention?'

'Maybe it was because you took the questions after the Butlers gave the press the link between the murders. It was either going to be me or you as we were the ones out there with the media. Is it hand-delivered or has it gone through the postal system?'

The envelope was face down so he couldn't tell. Dominic shrugged. 'I can't see, boss.' He picked up a pen and flicked the envelope over.

Kapoor tutted.

'It was posted. Postmark is Sheffield so I'm not sure if it's going to help us any.'

'We're not going to get DNA from the stamp, but we may well get some from the envelope. Stamps are self-adhesive, but not all envelopes are.' Kapoor rubbed his chin. 'He's gloating. He thinks he's well ahead of us and he wants us to know he's out there.'

'Not that we could forget that.' Rhys shook his head.

'Quite.'

The door to the incident room opened and Catherine, a CSI, walked in with a black bag in her hand. 'I heard you have something for me?'

'Hi Catherine.' Dominic waved her over to his desk. 'It's over here. A letter from the killer.'

'It's real?' she asked.

'Seems to be. He knows details we haven't released.'

'Ooh, he's brazen.' She snapped on her blue gloves and opened up her bag. 'Who's touched the paper? Including the envelope.'

'I'm the only one who's touched the inside letter, but the envelope, I can't say for sure. Me, and Dawn from the front counter brought it in. You'll have to check with her if anyone else had contact with it out there. Then you've got a whole host of people on its journey through the postal system.'

Catherine snorted through her nose. 'That's not very helpful, but hopefully we'll get a print off the contents inside. Can you wheel yourself away from the desk very slowly so I can get in and work, please?'

Dominic placed his feet against the floor and pushed away from his desk, one of the wheels on his chair squeaking as he wheeled away. Catherine moved in closer and started to work.

She took a camera from her bag and began by taking photographs of the paper and the desk it was sitting on. Once she was sure she had an image from every angle she grabbed some tweezers from her bag and selected a couple of paper bags to store the items in. This was to prevent the paper from sweating in a plastic bag which would degrade potential fingerprints. Then she gently picked up the letter and the envelope and placed them in their own evidence bags.

'I'm going to check your desk for trace particles that may have dropped out of the envelope when you opened it.' She let them know what she was doing as she worked.

'What do we think he wants from this letter?' Kapoor asked of the room.

'A response,' said Paul.

'And how are we going to respond?' asked Dominic.

Hayley pursed her lips. 'Through the press is the only way I can think of.'

Kapoor considered this. 'What do you suggest we respond with?'

'Do we respond at all?' Dominic asked, countering his initial query.

'That's a valid question.' Kapoor was concerned. 'What's his end game? What's he want from this dialogue? Why does he think he's going to get it from Dom? All questions we need to consider before we even contemplate engaging in any kind of interaction with him.' He checked with his team. 'And do we believe it's him?'

'I'd suggest it is, with the mention of the lipstick,' said Dominic. 'It's a detail we haven't released to the press and yet he knows about it.'

Kapoor blew a breath out. 'The only way we can talk to him is through press releases. Anything we say, now we know he's watching and listening, has to be agreed at a higher level. I'm running this up the flagpole to Connelly. He has to sign-off on any release we put out.'

'Do we think Dom is safe?' asked Hayley.

Kapoor furrowed his brow. 'What do you think, Dom? Do you sense any threat? I don't pick up any aggression, it feels more like a gloat to me. But if you see it differently then speak up.'

Dominic shook his head. 'No. No, it's fine. I don't feel threatened at all. I think he wanted to let us know he's watching us and couldn't help but tell us he was there.'

Catherine stood up and backed away from Dominic's desk. 'All done. I'll let you have the results as soon as I've processed these. With any luck we might get a fingerprint on the paper.' She looked at Kapoor. 'I'm presuming this is also urgent.'

'You presume correct.' He smiled.

She clipped her bag shut and walked towards the door. 'This is the first time I've seen anything like this. Keep yourselves safe, guys.' And with that she was gone.

'She's right,' Kapoor said. 'I want you all to make sure you take extra precautions. He's obviously paying attention to the investigation team. So pay attention to yourselves and your surroundings. Do not let yourselves get caught in any dangerous situations. I don't want to have to visit a crime scene with one of you as the victim.'

The words cut through the room like a blade. Everyone looked at him. The words sinking in. The implications of what he was saying imprinting on brains. This guy knew who they were and he wanted their attention. They would be foolish to think he wouldn't go after a cop. They'd have to keep their guard up.

CHAPTER 33

Claudia

Twenty-one hours since Ruth's attack

They'd been at it for hours now. Claudia was exhausted. Dominic surely must be. Not that he'd admit it or agree to a break, but a break was what he would get. She needed to follow up with her team. See where they were in the investigation. If they had any leads or information she needed to be aware of.

She looked at her dad, sent a silent prayer up — though she wasn't one to pray — that Ruth would be found and that the man in front of her had nothing to do with this.

'Interview ended at—'

Dominic exploded. 'What?! What do you mean interview ended? Why? What are you doing? We haven't finished.'

Claudia kept her calm. She'd expected this. When she was a child he'd worked all the hours the job had dictated, regardless of what effect it had on his family. She'd felt his absence keenly and it wasn't until she became a detective herself that she understood the drive her father might have felt. But she also recognised that he could have walked away some of the time and left it to someone else. He'd chosen the job over his family. And that loss of time had driven a wedge so deep she didn't know if she could ever drag it out. She felt Kane shift in his chair and continued her closure for the recording. 'Eighteen oh-two hours.'

Kane pressed the stop button and started the procedure of wrapping the discs up and labelling and signing the seals.

Dominic glared at Claudia, waiting for a response.

'You need a break. I'm going to ask the custody staff to feed you. We should have done this sooner but it's been too important to stop.'

'It still is,' he barked. 'I don't need to eat.'

'Maybe not, but you're having a break and I'm going to check in with my team and see what's been happening in my absence.'

With that he settled a little, his shoulders relaxed, rounding off again.

'Don't worry—' she tapped at the table with a finger — 'I'm not going to sit and relax while you have a break. I'm still working. I'll come back and we'll pick up where we left off as soon as I know what's been going on.'

'Check in with my team, see if they've made in-roads with identifying the witness.'

Claudia stayed silent. She didn't want to antagonise him any further by informing him that her team was also working the Sheffield Strangler angle as he'd made it such a prominent part of Ruth's case. She rose from her chair. 'I'll be with you as soon as I can.'

Kane would return Dominic to his cell while she made a call back to the incident room.

Exiting the interview room and heading into the bowels of the custody suite, Claudia could hear detained people locked in cells, banging on doors and shouting for attention. The clatter and shrieking was a regular soundtrack of the suite. People were very often angry, frustrated. It was a space of helplessness. And that's how she felt. It covered her like a heavyweight blanket. Bearing down and smothering her.

Running a hand through her hair, Claudia turned right and into the report-writing room where the computer terminals and phones were housed for attending officers to use. She picked up a phone and dialled in to her incident room.

Graham answered. He sounded hassled. Stressed.

'What do we have?' she asked him after checking he was okay. She was eager for news and Graham didn't bore her with details of his welfare. He was fine, just busy.

'About half an hour ago we identified the second witness at the abduction site of the Sheffield Strangler's latest victim — the one eating from a bag of chips.'

A full working day had passed but she hadn't expected this progress. 'How did you manage that?'

'We narrowed down the time, went to the closest two chip shops and asked about customers. A couple of them had paid by card. We identified them, made contact, and we have a winner.'

Claudia couldn't believe it. If she was with him she could have kissed him. She realised her emotions really were running around unchecked with this case and reigned herself in. 'You've spoken with him?'

Graham made a grunting sound. 'Not as such. We had a landline number. It was his wife we spoke to. She confirmed he was out the evening in question and provided his mobile number so we could contact him. He's at work at the minute. We were just about to call him before you rang in.'

Her skin itched. She was desperate to speak to this witness herself. So much of her life was invested in this case. It was fine to keep detainees in their cells while lines of enquiry were followed up and she had the time. He'd be frustrated, but if the end result cleared him and found Ruth then he'd soon get over it. 'Text me his work address, don't bother calling him, I'll go and see him.' Hers was a work mobile so it was fine to transfer personal information like this.

'You're sure? We can deal with it while you're there.' He wanted to be helpful but Claudia was twitchy. It was like her skin was going to crawl from her bones of its own accord.

'It's fine. I can fit it in.'

* * *

Mike Bell was a butcher. It was late in the day for a shop and the premises were quiet. Claudia and Kane entered, a small chime tinkling above their heads as they walked through the door. The smell of cold dead meat assaulted her nostrils. Metallic and raw. The temperature chilling her skin. Pimples rising on her arms.

A large man, round with red cheeks, greeted them from behind the counter. The kind of man you'd imagine on the signage of a butcher's shop. You'd describe him as jolly. Was this their guy?

'Mr Bell?' Claudia asked.

'Ooh, no,' the man laughed. 'He's out back. Anything I can do for you?' He rubbed his hands together. To stave off the chill or with eagerness for the task in front of him?

'We need to speak to Mr Michael Bell, please.' Claudia showed her identification. The jolly man's mouth clamped shut into a tight line and he glanced to the doorway that led to the rear.

Claudia's hackles rose. She parted her feet ready to run if necessary.

Then the man spoke again. 'He's not in any trouble, is he?'

Claudia shook her head. 'We just need a word with him.' Her patience was wearing thin. She wanted to get on with this. Find out what Bell knew. What information he was holding. She needed to know if they were on a wild goose chase.

'Mike,' the man shouted through the space between the store and the back. 'You'd better come out front, mate.'

Claudia heard him first. His footsteps on the hard floor echoing in front of him as he moved towards them. He walked into the shop, rubbing his hands down the front of his apron. He was small. Slim build with a head of red hair.

'What is it, Tim?'

'Police, mate.' Tim stood stock still.

Mike Bell looked at Claudia and Kane. 'You're after me?'

'Is there somewhere we can talk?' Claudia asked.

'I'm supposed to be working.' He turned to Tim.

Tim shrugged.

'We need to talk to you, Mr Bell.'

Bell pursed his lips. There was a second door at the side of the opening he'd walked through. He indicated they should go through there. Claudia and Kane followed him in. It led down a narrow corridor the length of the building and out the back where large industrial bins stood. It was shaded from the sun here and cool. Claudia shivered.

'What is it?' Bell asked.

'You were recently seen eating a bag of chips on the corner of Well Road and Gleadless Road, can you first confirm that was you?'

Bell cradled his chin as he thought about it. 'I don't understand?'

'A woman, who would later become a murder victim, was abducted from there around the time you were seen.'

His lips parted in an 'Oh'.

'We need to know what you saw.'

Bell swallowed. 'Yeah, there was a woman with a man. He had his arm around her. She was unsteady on her feet. I thought she'd maybe had too much to drink. He was keeping her upright.'

Claudia's adrenalin burst through her veins and she shared a look with Kane. She could see he was as excited by this as she was. 'Did you get a good look at the man?'

'Oh yeah, they walked right under the streetlight in front of me. I was messing about with my phone and nearly walked into them. The guy apologised and carried on walking, controlling the woman.'

They finally had a real witness. One who had come face to face with the Sheffield Strangler.

CHAPTER 34

Claudia

Claudia and Kane drove Michael Bell back to their home-base police station, Snig Hill, and to the incident room where the team could follow up with him.

For his part, Bell wasn't happy. He'd stripped out of his whites complaining about the fact that he was supposed to be at work. Tim had tried to reassure him that he could hold the fort down until they closed, which Claudia realised wasn't going to be long. Tim would hardly be standing alone for hours. It was getting close to seven p.m. They were probably going to close soon anyway. She wanted to remind Bell of this but kept her mouth closed. The guy was doing them a favour, best not to antagonise him.

'We're grateful for your help,' she said as Kane manoeuvred the car into its parking space.

'What is it you want me to do?' He looked down at the phone in his hands.

Claudia rolled her eyes. She'd been through this with him already. 'We're going to get you to work with someone to create a photofit for us. Of the guy you saw that night.'

Bell opened his phone. Claudia raised an eyebrow.

'I'm letting my wife know I'll be late home.'

Claudia thought of her empty house. She had no one to keep up to date with her movements. Not even a pet she could talk to. Ruth was the person she turned to when she needed someone. Ruth was there regardless of what was happening in her own life and Claudia loved her for it. She was aware she had given too much time to the job. That her body clock was ticking by. She'd had that very conversation with Ruth who had told her she didn't need a man. She was an independent woman and could raise a child on her own. But Claudia didn't know if that was what she wanted. She looked at other couples and liked what she saw. She wanted some of that for herself.

She shook herself free of her melancholy and climbed out of the car. She had a job to do. If she were to have such intimate conversations with Ruth again she needed to focus, not drift off in a world of her own.

In the incident room Claudia introduced Bell to Harry and asked him to take care of the photofit. Harry's face lit up.

'You mean we have a real lead on the Sheffield Strangler?'

Bell stood mute. Hands by his sides.

'It certainly looks like it, if Mr Bell here can create us an image of him.' She smiled at Bell who decided the floor was a more interesting proposition. She'd have thought he'd be more excited to be involved in the investigation, especially in such a pivotal way. But some people were worried about repercussions, blowback. She'd have a quiet word with Harry and ask him to reassure Bell that this was not likely to happen. His details would not be made public.

With Bell ushered out of the room, Claudia turned to Kane. 'I suppose we'd better head back to the custody suite to interview Dominic.'

'You going to tell him about Bell?'

Claudia thought about this. What were the pros and cons of telling her father they had a lead on the Sheffield Strangler case? Would it distract him from recounting his knowledge of the Strangler or focus him more? 'I'm not sure.'

Kane read her mind. 'You're worried he'll lose concentration?'

They headed back to the car. 'Yeah. You never know what might be valuable in the telling. So much has happened over the last six months. Our fresh eyes over events might be what's needed. But if he clams up . . .'

'It's a risk but he's going to want to know what we've been doing all this time.'

Kane was right. Dominic wouldn't let it go until he knew what they'd been doing.

At the custody suite Kane went to bring Dominic out of his cell while in the interview room Claudia considered the impending conversation.

'Where've you been?' Dominic was speaking before he was fully through the door.

'I told you I was giving you a break.' She kept her voice calm. There was no point in getting into it with him.

'I've been locked in that cell for what feels like well over an hour.'

It was a good guess. And that was all it was because he'd had his watch removed when he was booked into custody.

'Tell me, Claudia.' He was using his parenting voice again.

She glared at him as Kane unwrapped the discs to start the interview.

'Let's get the interview started first, shall we?'

Dominic folded his arms. 'So it's relevant to the investigation?'

'You think we've just been sitting having some tea?' she snapped at him, losing her temper. She didn't want to but sometimes he was just too ridiculous.

The room fell quiet as each of them contemplated the situation. A buzz filled the space as Kane pressed record on the machine and the interview was commenced again.

Once they had run through the preliminaries, Dominic tried again. 'So, are you going to tell me where you've been?'

Claudia looked to Kane.

'Stop looking to him for answers. Just tell me.'

She balled up her fists in her lap. Yes, he was in a difficult position, but did he think she wasn't? How did he think she was feeling having to interview him, considering him a potential suspect for this? She ground her teeth before answering him.

'The witness you were looking for . . . the one eating chips . . .'

'Yes?'

'We've identified him and been out to speak to him. He saw a man holding a woman up and helping her along. He's doing a photofit as we speak.'

Dominic opened his mouth but nothing came out. For a change, figured Claudia, relishing the peace.

Eventually Dominic let a breath go and spoke. 'You've managed to find a real witness? After we've been at it all this time . . .' His voice was barely a whisper. There were tears in his eyes.

'Hey,' Claudia said. 'You put in all the hard work. We were simply working from where you'd got to.'

'But still.' He scrubbed the back of a hand over his eyes. 'If you locate him you can find Ruth.'

Claudia's breath caught in her throat. She struggled to compose herself.

Kane leapt in for her. 'Shall we go back to the letter you received?'

CHAPTER 35

Dominic

Five months ago

The rest of the press releases that morning were pretty scathing of the police. Dominic read them with a sinking heart. He hated when the police were under such negative scrutiny and this time it was one of his cases. It felt personal.

They were doing everything they could but murder cases were complex investigations. You couldn't just run a set of prints from the body and then identify the killer. It was never that simple. He wished it were. For the sake of the family and for the clear-up rate of the investigation teams.

Linking the two murders like this was going to make people anxious. It was going to make the women of the city anxious. Did they have cause, he wondered? The fact that they had been contacted by the killer pretty much guaranteed they now had a single murderer for both victims. Kapoor had informed the team they were officially working both cases and he was linking them. Much as he hated to. There was no way out of it now they had the letter.

The day dragged on in a blur of work. Dominic had managed to stuff a sandwich down his throat at his desk when his phone rang. It was Catherine.

'What do you have for me? Please tell me it's good news.' He tapped his fingers on his desk.

'I'm sorry, Dom. There's nothing on the letter or the envelope. He knows how to avoid forensic detection. I imagine he used gloves and he bought a self-sealing envelope. He didn't need to lick it. Both the paper and the envelope are commonplace items. I can't give you anything to chase up. I've photocopied the letter and sent it back down to you so you have it for your records.'

Dominic let out a deep sigh. 'Thanks, Catherine.'

'I'm sorry it's not better news.'

'Don't worry about it, it's not your fault.' He'd been hoping there had been a print, one they could compare against Alex Chapman. Not that they had his fingerprints, but it would come with time as the evidence gathered.

'Sarge . . .' Hayley broke through his thoughts. He turned and looked at her.

'The DI wants you. He tried your phone but it was engaged. He said can you go to his office.' She looked worried.

'Did he say why?'

'No, but he didn't sound happy.'

Dominic knocked on Kapoor's door and walked in. 'You wanted me, sir?'

Kapoor stopped typing. 'Come in and close the door, Dom.'

Dominic did as he was asked and took the seat in front of Kapoor's desk.

'Don't get comfortable, another body has been found.'

Dominic couldn't believe it. They'd only just dealt with the one from yesterday. 'What?'

'The cops on the scene are saying it looks to have been in the ground longer than the last two. It seems he's been more active than we've given him credit for. I need you to go out there and supervise. We need to get something on him. We can't allow this to continue.'

Dominic stood. 'The press are going to have a field day.'

Kapoor rose from behind his desk. 'Yeah, and what's the killer's reaction going to be? Be careful, Dom.'

'I will. But I don't think there was any threat in the letter. It was more gloating than anything.'

'Well, I can do without the bastard gloating. Panic will be growing. I have no idea how we'll contain this.'

Dom walked to the door. 'We work it as we work any case. We'll get him.'

Kapoor stroked his chin. 'I'll get the extra staff in. We're going to need it. I'm sorry to dump the body on you again, but as you attended the first two, you know what his MO is. You're best placed to attend.'

'It's fine. I'm happy to do this for the victims.' And he was. It was a grim job but he felt that once officials were at the scene the victims were finally at peace. Justice was being worked on.

She had been left in Grenoside Woods. She had definitely been in the ground a lot longer than the first two women he had seen. She was decomposed. Fluids were being released and she was a squirming mass of maggots and flies, eyeballs and finger ends eaten away. He couldn't even guess how old she was.

The process to examine her and remove her from the ground was slower than the other two women, but Dominic stayed by her side for the entire time.

He returned to the station an exhausted mess. No one had identified a possible missing person who would match the murdered woman. At this point she truly was a Jane Doe. An unidentified, unclaimed woman. This made their task all the more difficult because they couldn't track her last movements or the last people to see her alive. They knew nothing about her life or her activities. Dominic was frustrated. He hoped she'd be identified within the next day or two.

The post-mortem was grim. There were no fingerprints to help with identification because of the start of decomposition and animal activity. But the signs were there that she was again a victim of the now named Sheffield Strangler. She had bruising around her throat as well as a knife wound, and lipstick — barely visible but there — was found in the creases of her mouth.

They had to create a press release that informed and at the same time asked for the public's help in identifying the unnamed woman. Items of clothing were listed, a blue floral blouse. It was in a pretty tatty state but they'd laid it out and photographed it in case anyone recognised it. The days were hectic, busy and yet sluggish. Dominic was frustrated with the lack of progress being made on the case.

By Wednesday morning Dominic had started to flag. The fatigue starting to settle into his bones. But he wasn't going to let it slow him down. The victims deserved more from him, from them.

Kapoor walked in for the morning briefing. 'Okay gang, where are we on identifying the third, or is she potentially the first victim?' He was straight into it this morning. There was no welcoming small talk. He was obviously getting pressure from the top.

'Several calls came in late yesterday from people who think they recognised the photograph of the blouse we put out. We're following those up and we're hopeful we'll be able to identify her, maybe today,' said Rhys.

Kapoor looked tired. 'Good. We need to progress this. She has family out there who want to know what happened to her. People who are scared she's theirs and they don't know. People are scared anyway. Three dead women, all of a similar age, over forty, he has a type. We have the linked dating app between the first two, once we identify the third woman we need to see if there is any overlap between the three of them. Have we got anywhere with Julie Carver and knowing what app she was using?'

'We've contacted her service provider and have a list of the apps she was using. It's the same dating app as Madeleine Chapman. We're waiting on the app company to get back to us with the profile information for both women. The problem is, it's a US company and as you know they're not obliged to comply with our laws, but most do to keep on side. If the app was created by a UK company we'd have the information by now. Our country, our laws. Going by the communication we've had with this company, I think they're getting the information together, but they're not particularly pulling their finger out.' Krish let out a sigh in irritation at the foreign app designer company.

'Keep on at them. Chase them up today.'

Krish made a note in his pad.

'You've all got work to be getting on with. Let's move this investigation forward please. The city is scared. You know they're saying we have a serial killer in the city. I don't want this to be the case for long. I want him found and I want him in our cells. Have I made myself clear?'

There were murmurings of 'yes, boss' around the room.

'We will not have a serial killer and all the press trappings and fear that brings with it,' he said. 'This is Sheffield not New York.' And with that he stalked out of the room.

'What's with the boss?' Paul asked.

'I presume he's getting a lot of pressure from Connelly,' Dominic answered. 'It's a high-profile case. Even Connelly will be getting pressure from higher up. The chief is watching this one. And it doesn't stop with him. He'll be getting grief from the Police and Crime Commissioner. It won't be good for his figures and he's voted into office. Policing is a political game nowadays.'

Krish shrugged. 'I don't know about that. I come in and do my job and leave again. I'm only interested in catching the bad guys. I'll leave all that to those who get paid a hell of a lot more than me.'

'Best way to be,' said Paul.

Hayley stood. 'I'll go talk to the intel unit. Let them know we need the pressure putting on for the US app developer.' She pushed her way out of the incident-room doors and Dawn from the front counter nearly walked into her. They exchanged apologies and Hayley let her through and then walked to the kitchen.

Dawn handed out the mail and escaped back to the front counter as fast as she could. As far as Dominic was aware, she'd left George alone, manning the front counter, and he wasn't always the most amenable person. He'd heard that George had problems at home these days and his mood seemed to be worse than usual for it.

Dominic picked up the four pieces of mail and opened the first one. Distracted, half-listening to a conversation between Rhys and Paul about the footie on the TV the night before. He hadn't managed to see it himself. Ruth had wanted to sit and talk. She'd told him he was too tightly wound lately and needed to relax. This had only served to wind him up and resulted in them screaming at each other. Or rather he'd yelled at her in utter frustration and then stormed off into the garage to fiddle, in the pretext he was tidying up. He didn't need telling how to behave, he was a grown man, leading a small team in a vital part of a serious investigation. Of course he was going to be wound a little tightly. But trying to control him wasn't going to work. He'd left home this morning without saying a word to her and now he was getting a running commentary from the lads on how the game had played out.

His attention was soon drawn back to work when he saw the familiar start to the typed letter in his hand.

DS Harrison,

How does it feel to be lagging so far behind at this stage in an investigation? I'm not usually one to gloat but you make it far too easy. I can't say I'm always happy with the words you use about me in the press. Please remember who you're talking about. Words have meaning and I'd hate if your words did more harm than good.

I trust that we all believe in who is talking in this conversation and I no longer have to prove myself.

Tread carefully please.

Again he dropped the letter onto his desk and picked up his phone and called the CSU. He had presumed the first communication was a one off. To say hello, hi, I've done this.

'What is it, Dom?' Paul had spotted him.

'Another letter,' he admitted.

'From the killer?'

'Yeah.'

Paul, Rhys and Krish walked over to his desk and peered over at the single white sheet of paper. Hayley walked over from the printer in the corner of the room.

'What've I missed?'

'Dom received another letter,' said Krish.

Hayley put down the pile of hot paper. 'Another one?'

They all stared at it and read the contents. 'Is he threatening you?' she asked, eyes wide.

'I'm not sure,' Dominic answered. 'I think he's gloating but it's turned into a bit of a warning. Seems he doesn't approve of his press.'

'Shouldn't be a crazed wacko killer then, should he?' said Rhys.

Paul snorted.

'You're not supposed to use words like wacko,' said Hayley.

'What word would you use for him?' Rhys asked.

Hayley shrugged. 'Just don't let the boss hear you.'

'Talking of the boss, I'm going to have to let him know.' Dominic pulled his mobile phone out of his pocket and took a photograph of the letter, then rose from his chair.

'Anything you want us to do?' asked Hayley.

'Keep an eye on that.' He pointed to the sheet. 'And direct the CSI to it when they arrive.' He strode out of the room and headed for Kapoor's office.

The door was closed. Dominic knocked and waited to hear Kapoor's voice so he could enter. Once inside he sat himself in the visitor's chair.

'What is it?' Kapoor asked. 'I've just seen you.'

'Yeah. We had another letter.'

Kapoor lifted an eyebrow. 'From the killer?'

'That's the one.'

Kapoor leaned forward. 'What did he say this time?'

Dominic pulled his phone out of his pocket, scrolled through to the photograph he'd taken and handed it to his boss who took the phone and read through the letter.

Kapoor was silent as he read, then he looked up at Dominic. 'What do you want to do?'

'About what?' asked Dominic.

'The threats in the letter.'

'I don't feel threatened. He hasn't said he's going to do something to me if things don't go his way. He hasn't been explicit.'

Kapoor let out a long sigh. 'We don't always need things to be explicit to understand them, Dom. It's quite clear that he's not happy with some of the press releases and he takes it that you're behind it all.'

Dominic ran a hand through his hair. 'Look, I'm fine. I'd rather Ruth didn't know about this though, so if we can keep it quiet as to who's receiving these letters I'd appreciate that. I don't want to worry her. She knows too much about the job as it is without thinking the psycho behind it all has a crush on me.' He laughed.

'Is this your way of brushing it all off?' Kapoor asked.

'Is it working?'

'I can give you some leeway, but if he becomes any clearer in his messages then you're going to have action taken. A guard in the evenings while you're at home, at the very least.'

It was Dominic's turn to let out a sigh. 'This job is hard work.'

'Tell me about it.'

'You're getting grief from Connelly, I take it.'

'He's getting it from the chief who doesn't like that his county is scared witless and we're getting slaughtered in the press for not having caught him. Shit rolls downhill.'

This was why the briefing had been short and not so sweet this morning. Kapoor was trying not to pass it down, but it was hard. 'Anything I can do?'

Kapoor laughed. 'Yes, you can catch this bastard.'

'He's forensically aware and we're at the mercy of a US app developer.'

Kapoor stood, his face like stone. 'I want you to chase that today. I want you to push them. I don't care what it takes. Let them know this is a multiple murder enquiry and we want the information we've requested and we want it today.'

Dominic rose from his chair. 'I'll get right on it. We've plenty to be getting on with. There has to be a positive lead come out of it all at some point.'

'I hope you're right, Dom. With three women dead we can't carry on this way. We need to make progress, not look like we're running around like a bunch of headless chickens.'

CHAPTER 36

Dominic

The results came back from the lipstick tube found near the third woman's body. As with the previous two, there was nothing of substance they could use. No fingerprints and no material they could test. If there was any DNA on the lipstick, if it was the actual tube he had used on the woman, it had broken down in the time she had been buried with it.

She was still a Jane Doe. A drawing was mocked up of what she probably looked like before the ravages of death, decomposition and animal feasting took her. Dominic had contacted the press office and requested a briefing so he could share the image they'd created. He hoped it would lead to an identification. Maybe she had been reported missing out of the county. Maybe the killer was crossing county borders. Or maybe the poor woman had no one in her life to miss her. He hoped it wasn't the latter. Everyone deserved someone.

The media briefing room was even more rammed this time than the first briefing they'd conducted. With three murders, there was national attention as well as local press interested in what was happening. Everyone pricked up their ears when the phrase serial killer was used and they were throwing the words around like sweets at a children's party. They were giddy and excited. To them this was news. To Dominic and his team it was hurt and pain as they dealt with the families left behind. As they dealt with the women he had murdered. None of this was exciting or fun.

He took his seat in front of the boards with the force's logo printed on them. The table held glasses and jugs of water. Dominic poured himself a drink and took a sip. His mouth was dry. His tongue like a piece of felt, sticking to the roof of his mouth. Kapoor sat rigidly beside him.

They had information to impart. They needed the people in front of them. But in needing them they were opening themselves up to even more pressure and needling about their performance on the Sheffield Strangler case. It was a difficult relationship but one they couldn't do without.

Kapoor coughed into his hand bringing the room into an unsettled quiet. Reporters were shifting in their seats, eager for news and ready to send it to print or online before any of their colleagues. They had to let the police speak first. Nothing could happen before they had said their piece.

'You will see on your left DC Rhys Evans moving down the room. He has a stack of paper in his hands. This is the image of the most recent woman found. We would like your help in identifying her.'

Rhys moved along the rows of seats, handing out small piles of paper for the reporters to hand on to their colleagues.

Kapoor continued. 'The helpline number is still the same and is listed on the bottom of the image. If anyone thinks they recognise the woman can they please contact us so we can follow it up and identify her as soon as possible.'

The sound of paper crinkling as reporters reviewed the image in their hands and photographed it filled the room.

'This woman deserves the decency of being known. And to thank you for your help, we will answer a couple of questions. Though obviously if it falls within investigative parameters we'll not be able to respond. We don't want to give any information away that will hamper our investigation.'

A hand went up at the front. Kapoor pointed to the man it belonged to.

'Nick Holmes, BBC. Do you think you could have done anything differently and prevented any of the deaths that have occurred at the hands of this killer?'

Kapoor stiffened. 'The team working on this are excellent. I have complete faith in them and no, I don't think any action we could have taken would have prevented events so far. But what we need to do is make sure we're progressing the investigation and that means we need help from the public. If we identify this woman then we can see how he got to her and work the case from there.'

He was keeping the focus on the Jane Doe and on moving the investigation forward. This was why Kapoor had the managerial role and not Dominic.

Another hand went up, further back this time. 'Danielle Spicer, Sheffield crime beat.'

'Go ahead.'

'Have you had any contact from the killer?'

CHAPTER 37

Dominic

How the fuck did she know that?

Kapoor looked thrown off guard. 'Can you repeat the question please, Danielle?'

Dominic thought he was stalling for time. Probably trying to get his head around the question. They hadn't disclosed this to the press. Not officially anyway. Kapoor had no response ready.

'Yes.' she smiled. It was kind enough. 'Have you had any contact from the killer?'

'Why would you think that?' Kapoor asked.

'That doesn't answer the question, DI Kapoor. Does that mean you've had contact with the killer known as the Sheffield Strangler?'

Kapoor's cheeks darkened and his jaw clenched. He was definitely not happy. Dominic could understand why. This was disastrous, that something so personal to the investigation had been leaked this way and was out in the public domain. It was not how investigations were supposed to be run.

'DI Kapoor?' she prompted again.

'We have had a letter from the killer,' Kapoor admitted. It was never good to outright lie to the press. Now they had to try to manage this.

'What did he say?' She was eager, sitting forward in her chair. Pen poised over her notebook. Cameras were flashing and there was a rumble of voices as reporters took in what Danielle had shared.

'He said we were not failing the families.'

'He did?' She lifted her eyebrows.

'That surprises you?'

'It does a little. How would he come to that opinion if you haven't caught him?'

'He seems to think he's too clever to be caught and this means we're not failing the families.' He closed his mouth and stood. 'That'll be all for today. Thank you for your time and for sharing the image of the woman we need to identify. We appreciate your help with this matter.'

Dominic rose.

'DI Kapoor!' Several voices spoke at once. Hands went up in the air in an attempt to gain his attention. He turned on his heel and headed towards the door keeping his eyes forward. Once they were both out of the door and away from the press he exploded at Dominic.

'What the bloody hell happened in there?'

Dominic shook his head. He was in shock as much as Kapoor was. 'I don't know, boss. I have no idea where that came from.'

'We have a leak, Dom, and I want to know who is giving this to the press. This is inexcusable. We can't have sensitive details like this shared in that way. Not only could it hurt the investigation, but if the wrong thing gets leaked it could potentially create mass panic. This case is delicate. We need to be careful.' He paced up and down the corridor. 'Who knew about the letters?'

Dominic thought it through. 'It's quite a wide net. There's everyone in the incident room, then you have every-one in the CSU, the front counter staff as we had to take statements, and the killer himself.' He concluded. 'Maybe it didn't come from us. Maybe, if he's contacting us, he's also contacting the media. I haven't seen anything like that in the press, but we should keep an eye on Danielle Spicer's column over the next day or so.' His hopes were up that this wasn't one of his team. He would hate to think one of them had done something so unprofessional.

'If he contacted her then she should be telling us not blindsiding us with such a question,' Kapoor shouted. 'She has a duty to tell us if she's heard from him and if she hasn't then there's a mole in the organisation and I won't tolerate that, Dom.' He stared hard at him. His dark eyes boring a hole into Dominic.

'I don't know how we're going to narrow it down.'

Kapoor sighed and ran a hand through his hair. 'We first talk to Danielle. Not that she's likely to tell us her source if it is one of ours. Then we ask everyone who knows, if they've leaked the information. Ask them to do the right thing and come forward.'

'They'll never do that. Not knowing they'll lose their jobs because of what they've done.'

'I don't know how else to get to the bottom of this, Dom. If you have any bright ideas please do let me know.' He was frustrated and Dominic didn't have any of the answers he needed. Dominic was pretty furious himself. How dare someone they trusted do this to them. He would give them what for if he found out who it was.

'It'll have to be referred to Professional Standards,' Kapoor said walking towards the stairs that took them back up to the incident room.

'You never know,' said Dominic, 'They may have sent Danielle an email and it could be traced. It might be as simple as that.'

Kapoor laughed. 'We're talking about cops, Dom. I'd hope if they were going to do something where they didn't want to get caught that they'd have a bit more sense than that. But we can but hope.'

'It might not be a cop, it could be civilian staff.'

'Yeah, forensic civilian staff. The people who think about getting caught all day long. I don't hold out much hope but I'll put the referral in to PSD when I get into my office. We'll leave this messy investigation in their capable hands, we have enough to be getting on with without twisting ourselves inside out with this.'

Dominic couldn't believe it. Not only were they dealing with a serial killer, they were also facing a professional standards investigation because they had a snitch on the team somewhere. This was dangerous because if the killer got too much information it could help him stay one step ahead. It was also not good for the morale of the city where people were already frightened and twitchy.

He said goodnight to Kapoor and headed towards the incident room. It was time to brief his team before heading home for the day.

'DS Harrison?' A voice called out behind him.

Dominic turned. The man standing behind him was familiar but he couldn't quite place him. He was in his thirties, medium build with a full beard.

The man could obviously sense Dominic's misremembering as he strode forward, holding out his right hand. 'Samuel Tyler, Victim Support, we met about four weeks ago when I spoke with you about Julie Carver and seeing her family?' It was phrased as a question. A question about Dominic's memory.

The conversation returned to Dominic. He kept his eyes up, looking at Samuel's face, but remembered the burnt hand and his faux pas in staring at it when they'd met. 'Oh yes. Sorry about that. Busy day.' He was embarrassed. He was usually pretty good with people.

Samuel smiled. 'Don't worry about it. I imagine you're struggling to recognise yourself in the mirror in the morning, the pace this job is going, never mind remembering a stranger from a month ago.'

Yes, Samuel would know all about the pace of the job working in Victim Support. 'You're not far wrong there.'

Dominic laughed at how well Samuel had zoned in on the fatigue the job was creating. 'You're assigned to the family of the second victim?'

Samuel's smile slid away. 'Afraid so. They seem to think it's best that one person deals with the families so it keeps the information contained.'

Dominic could understand that. 'It has to be tough on you though. Picking up every job that comes in. I'm sure we'll ID the third victim any day now.'

'No tougher than you're finding it, DS Harrison.'

'Call me Dominic.'

Samuel inclined his head. 'Dominic. I make sure I find ways to relax when I'm not working.'

Dominic rubbed his head. He wasn't sure he was as well balanced as Samuel. He was pretty caught up in the case and barely had any free time to relax outside of it. 'How are the families bearing up?' He was kept up to date through the daily briefings of any case-relevant information the FLOs were feeding back to the team, but he wasn't aware of the families' emotional stability.

Samuel rubbed his left hand. Dominic couldn't help but look down as the action caught his eye. He dragged his gaze away quickly.

'As you'd expect really. They swing between disbelief, anger and denial. Every hour is a new hour, never mind every day. In fact it's a minute-by-minute process. Grief is difficult at the best of times, but when a loved one has been snatched from you in such violent circumstances it becomes pretty hard to accept and process.'

'And that's where you come in.' Dominic didn't envy the man. He'd rather be following the leads on the investigation than be mired in the turmoil of the relatives' emotions. Not that he was heartless, but because he didn't think his heart could take it. It would break him.

'I try.' Samuel shrugged.

'Don't undersell yourself.' Dominic liked the man. It was a tough job and he was grateful to him. 'What you're doing is invaluable. To us as well as the families. If I can ever do anything for you then you only have to ask.' He fished in his pocket and pulled out a contact card handing it over to Samuel.

A small flush crept up the top of Samuel's cheeks, the part that wasn't covered by his beard, as the man took Dominic's card. 'I don't know what to say, thank you.'

Dominic clapped him on the shoulder. 'We're going to get this bastard.'

CHAPTER 38

Dominic

The incident room was half empty. People had started to taper off and head home. His team was still here, waiting for him to finish his briefing.

'How'd it go?' asked Hayley.

'Not good.'

'What happened after I left?' Rhys closed down his computer and stood from his chair.

'Someone leaked to Danielle Spicer that we'd had contact from the killer.'

'Jesus.' Hayley's face dropped. 'Who the hell would do that?'

'That's a serious question, Hayley, and one the boss is taking up with PSD as we speak.'

'I'm not surprised.'

Paul pulled on his coat. 'How about we go for a drink? We know it's not one of us. It's been a long day, I think we all deserve it.'

Dominic was tired. Paul was right, it had been a long day and he could do with a stiff drink right about now. But what about Ruth? She'd be at home expecting him. He could text her, let her know it had been a tough day and he was taking the team out to boost morale. She'd accept that. He liked to keep his team ticking over and not let them be pulled too far down in difficult investigations.

'Come on, Dom.' Hayley pushed her chair under her desk. 'We're all going, it won't be the same without you.'

He pulled his phone out of his pocket. 'Yeah, okay. The first round is on me.'

There was a small cheer as they jostled past him towards the door.

'It's the only reason you ask me to come with you,' he moaned.

'We like you really,' Hayley laughed.

Rhys nudged her. 'We have to tell him that to keep him onside, obviously.'

'I can hear you, you know.'

'Oh, really? Did I say that out loud?' Rhys feigned shock.

Dominic moved with the group to the incident room doors. Waved to the rest of the homicide team who were at their desks. They wouldn't stay long. A couple of hands went up in response. He tapped out a message to Ruth letting her know where he was going. He got a response straight away letting him know there was some food in the oven should he want it when he got home. She didn't have anything too serious on at work at the moment so was getting home at a reasonable hour and that meant they were getting proper food inside them instead of the crap they tended to eat when they were both working long shifts. Right now though he would rather be with his team than at home. Ruth couldn't understand this case and he was tired of trying to pretend everything was okay when it was far from okay. All he wanted to do was work the case and be with the people who understood that feeling. Anything else was irrelevant.

Home was simply a place to sleep. To put his head down. Right now Ruth was irritating him. He couldn't cope with the constant bickering. The barrage of inane questions. How had they got to this place when they'd started with such passion and love? Now the love seemed like a distant star. Unimaginable and so very far away. Dominic couldn't see a way back. But it wasn't something he was willing to share with his team or with anyone. It was private, between him and Ruth.

This case was consuming his team and it was crucial they have this release together. It was also essential he went with them. His reputation within the team was important to him. What others thought of him and the work he was doing meant so much. It didn't really matter if Ruth was upset that he was late from work. He pushed his phone into his pocket.

The Church House was a Grade II listed building that once used to be — as the name suggested — a church, but which had been converted into a pub about thirty years previously. Dominic liked the vibe in the bar. The dark blue of the ceiling and some of the walls, along with exposed brickwork, gave him a comfort he could settle in.

Dominic bought a round of drinks, buying a whiskey for himself. He needed it. It was mid-week so they managed to find a table fairly easily and gathered around it. Once settled Dominic took a slug of his drink, the familiar warmth of it spreading through him. He tipped his head back, resting it lightly against the wall and savoured the feeling.

'That good, eh?' Hayley leaned in close to his ear.

Dominic smiled. He didn't think anyone would be paying him any attention. He thought he could have a minute alone with his drink and his thoughts before he had to engage with the rabble of the team. Obviously he was wrong. 'It's been a long day. I needed this.'

Hayley raised her glass to him. The clear gin swirling round the ice piled up high inside leaving a transparent slick against the edge of the glass in its wake. 'A lot of grief from Kapoor?'

Dominic shook his head. 'Not really. He vented a little, but that's only to be expected. He has a lot on his plate.'

'Don't we all.' She brought the drink up to her nose.

'Yeah, but the higher up the food chain you go, the worse the pressure you're under, from those above you and from the general public.'

'Ah, our beautiful public.' Rhys leaned in. 'Our job would be great if it wasn't for people.'

Paul laughed. 'They do rather have quite a lot to do with how our day goes.'

'Do you think we'll get anything from tonight's press release?' Hayley asked.

Dominic pursed his lips. 'I don't know. I hope so. I hate to think the poor woman is laying in Nadira's fridge unclaimed, especially after such a brutal death. Everyone should be claimed by someone.'

Hayley took a sip of her drink. 'That's very sentimental, Dom. I didn't know you had a deep and meaningful side.'

He swirled the amber liquid in his own glass. 'I think this case is getting to me if I'm honest.'

Krish leaned forward. 'It is pretty dark. A bit different to the domestic assault murders that usually come through the door.'

Dominic looked around him, he didn't want any of the pubs clientele to overhear their conversation. Krish took note, lowered his voice. 'I usually talk about work when I go home but with this one, I can't tell her anything. There's nothing I feel is suitable or safe.'

'What do you mean by safe?' asked Rhys.

'Well, I don't want to give her nightmares, do I? She gets enough information from the press and when she asks me about the job I tell her it's as bad as she's reading about and she doesn't need to know anything else. Surely none of you are going home and telling all?'

Hayley shook her head. 'Not that I have anyone to tell all to. But when I visit my mum she asks me what's happening and I tell her it's lots of paperwork. It's not a lie.'

'Same here,' said Paul. 'I tell the missus that the investigation team is huge and I'm a minnow in a large pond. There's not much for me to tell her. She leaves me be. I think she's proud that I'm on this case though.'

Dom was puzzled. 'Proud, how?'

'Well, it's high profile, isn't it? She thinks we'll be getting the glory when we catch him because she has all the faith that we will. It doesn't even cross her mind that we couldn't catch him.'

'It crosses yours?' Hayley slugged back the last of her gin.

'Of course. We're three bodies down. He's way in front of us. He's forensically aware. He's also taunting us by being in contact, he has to be pretty confident in his own ability to do that. Of course it's crossed my mind that we might not catch him. We don't solve every case we land.'

'I know, but . . .'

'But, what?'

'It's the Sheffield Strangler.'

'And that makes it different how?'

'Because we have to catch him. We can't leave him out there for members of the public to keep getting murdered.'

Paul slammed his empty glass down on the table. 'You think we'd be leaving him out there? Like, out of choice? That's so not what I'm saying and you know it. I'm saying we might not be able to solve his crimes. He might be too advanced for us, that's all.'

Dominic rose from his seat. 'I think I get it. But let's hope you're wrong, eh? Who wants another drink? I think we deserve it this evening.' He wanted to diffuse the situation.

'You're buying again?' asked Hayley.

'Anything to stop you two bickering.'

Paul laughed. 'We should fight more often if Dom puts his hand in his pocket.'

Hayley looked at him, all serious. 'I wasn't fighting with you.'

'I know that.' Paul put an arm around her. 'Come on, this is a shit case and it's getting to all of us. Let's drink up while Dom is paying and make the most of it.'

Hayley smiled. 'Well, there are obvious benefits.'

Dominic came back from the bar with a tray loaded with another round of drinks and slotted back in the other side of Hayley.

'What about you, Dom?' asked Rhys.

'What's that?'

'Well, you're married to a woman in the force. Can you go home and talk about the job? It must be so much easier for you. You don't have to worry about scaring her—' he winked at Krish who threw a beer mat at him — 'because she's a toughened old cop anyway.'

'Less of the old,' said Dominic. 'But no, I don't go home and talk to Ruth about it. Much the same as you guys. I think this job deserves to be left at the office. Yes she's interested in it and asks for details because she's only getting the same information the public are. I give her a little more to keep the peace, but I don't unload on her. I don't think it's fair.' The reality was he didn't want to talk about it with her. His skin crawled when she asked him about the case. He wanted to climb into bed at home and get some rest. These were the only people he wanted to talk to about the Strangler. 'She has her own workload to worry about. She's in a tough area of work being undercover and she needs to focus when she's doing that and I have no intention of distracting her by telling her what my day involved.'

There were nods all around. They all knew and liked Ruth and could understand Dominic's argument for keeping her in the dark.

The conversation continued between them. Rhys, Paul and Krish got into a deep and meaningful about the football.

Hayley turned to Dominic. 'I couldn't think of anything more boring. How come you're not getting all wet about this?'

'I'm not much of a fan to be honest. I hate to admit it in front of the lads, but for some reason it never appealed to me.'

'How did I not know this about you after working with you all these years?'

Dominic smiled as he sipped at his drink.

'How long has it been anyway?' she asked.

'What's that?'

'How long have we worked together?'

'You know you're asking a bloke, don't you? We're not known for remembering dates and suchlike.'

Hayley knocked back her drink.

'You thirsty tonight?'

'Like you I'm feeling the strain of the job, I think.'

Dominic went quiet at the mention of the case again.

'So, how long?' Hayley asked again.

'What?'

'Us?' She slapped his arm.

'Oh.' He tried to think back. 'Five years? Yes, it will be. You were already on the unit when I joined as a DS and that was a little over five years ago.' He grinned. 'See, I can remember stuff.'

'I'm impressed.' She returned his smile. 'I'm going to get another round.' She lifted her glass to show him it was empty. 'Are you staying for another?'

'I should get off. We have another early start tomorrow.' He tipped the remains of his drink down his throat.

Hayley looked at him and waited.

'But as you're buying I suppose I could have one more.'

CHAPTER 39

Claudia

Twenty-three hours since Ruth's attack

There was a knock on the interview-room door. Claudia, Dominic and Kane all looked at one another then at the door as though they'd get the answer to their unspoken question without getting up to answer it.

Eventually Claudia spoke and suspended the interview for the recording, then stood and opened the door. Sharpe was standing in front of her. Face pale and drawn, her lips pinched.

'What is it?' Claudia asked.

'With me.' Sharpe clacked down the bare corridor not waiting to see if Claudia was following her.

Claudia didn't like this, she didn't like it at all. Sharpe knew better than to interrupt an interview. Especially this interview. It had been at her behest that Claudia was in this one in the first place and now Sharpe was here knocking on the door and pulling her out of it. It could only mean one thing.

Bad news.

She turned back to Kane. 'Can I ask you to put Dominic back in a cell temporarily as I don't know how long this is going to take and we can resume as soon as I know more. Come and find us when you've done that.'

'Sure.' Kane stood. The strip light above shining on his head.

'Claudia?' Dominic rose, anxiety oozing from him.

'I don't know,' she said, closed the door on them and followed the direction Sharpe had walked off in. Sharpe was nowhere in sight and she had to find her. An emptiness gnawed at the pit of Claudia's stomach and nausea rose in her throat. Claudia walked into the open custody area and couldn't see Sharpe so doubled back and reviewed the closed doors she had passed. There was a consultation room. She placed her hand on the door handle. A prickle of sweat slicked over the metal shaft as nerves made her palms damp. Then she pushed down and entered the room.

Sharpe was standing with her back to the door. She didn't flinch as Claudia entered the room and quietly closed the door behind her. Her arms were crossed in front of her, her face still rigid and stern.

'What is it?' asked Claudia, wanting to get straight to the matter at hand.

'Have a seat.' Sharpe waved to the table and chairs in the middle of the room but made no move herself to sit.

Claudia stayed where she was in front of the door. 'Tell me why you've dragged me out of the interview you pushed me into.'

Sharpe turned her back to Claudia for a moment, paused, then turned back to her. 'I'd rather you had a seat, Claudia,' she said. 'Stop being so stubborn.' This last was pushed out emotionally. Claudia was not used to seeing this side of Sharpe and she took an involuntary step back.

'Sit,' said Sharpe again. This time she pulled out a chair herself and looked Claudia in the eye, daring her to go against her.

Claudia stepped forward, her stomach swirling, and pulled out her own chair. They both sat, each mirroring the other. Sharpe let out a small breath as though the hardest part of the job had been done.

It was far from done. This was just the beginning. She was tense. Her muscles clenched in fear of what was headed her way. She bent her head from one side to the other in an attempt to relax herself, but it was no good. The one thing she needed right now was to hear why Sharpe had interrupted the interview. Whatever the reason, it wasn't good.

'What is it?' Claudia asked again.

Sharpe placed her hands on the table and clasped them tightly together. 'We've had the results back on the blood recovered from the Harrisons' garage this morning.'

The swirling in Claudia's stomach flipped over and she had to grit her teeth to stop herself from vomiting up her breakfast. She had expected this and yet hearing the news as a definite with no hope left scooped out her insides.

'Did you hear me?' Sharpe was peering at her over the table. Her lips pursed in concern.

Claudia shook herself free from the darkness that was circling her. 'Yes. Yes, I heard you. I take it . . .'

'I'm afraid so. It was a match for the DNA of Ruth Harrison. I'm so sorry, Claudia.' Sharpe did something Claudia had never seen her do in her career, she reached out a hand and placed in on Claudia's. It was warm and soft. All unexpected. Claudia looked up at her in shock.

'Even though we suspected as much, it's not easy to hear, is it?' Sharpe added. Tears pricked at Claudia's eyes but she refused to let them fall. She was working, she was responsible for trying to identify what had happened to Ruth. Breaking now was not an option. She blinked hard.

'Is there anything I can do for you?' Sharpe asked.

Claudia shook her head, unsure of what she was supposed to be thinking. Everything had been twisted inside out. She'd been interviewing her father all morning and now this — it had been confirmed that it was Ruth's blood in the garage. How could this be? If it was her father, it would be stupid to have left it there . . . She mentally shook herself. She needed to focus.

Sharpe withdrew her hand as quickly as she'd placed it there. 'This doesn't mean she's dead, Claudia. Ruth is a strong woman. Yes, there's massive blood loss, but she could survive it. We need to get to her quickly. How's the interview going?'

'He's saying he didn't do it, of course. That he's being set up. He believes it's something to do with the case he's been investigating for the last six months.'

Sharpe was all business again. She straightened in her chair. 'And what do you think?'

Claudia shook her head. 'You do know that's my father in there, don't you?'

Sharpe tutted. 'I'm well aware of who he is, Claudia. We had this conversation this morning. If he's had something to do with it you're the best person to rattle and unnerve him and get relevant information out of him. Yes, of course we know your relationship, that's why you were chosen. We're as invested in finding Ruth as you are. She's one of us.'

Conflicting emotions raged inside her. She had mostly managed to box them off so far today, but now the blood type had been confirmed everything had come crashing in.

'Do you think this is the Sheffield Strangler?' Sharpe asked. 'And if so, for what reason?'

Claudia tucked a piece of hair behind her ear. 'I don't know yet. I don't know if it is the Sheffield Strangler or what the reason would be, we're still talking about it and getting to the point of all this.'

'Well you need to get to the point a whole lot quicker. Ruth doesn't have time for you to be messing about in there because he's your father.'

Claudia jerked to her feet, pushing the chair backwards with her calves, the feet of the chair grating on the floor and squealing loudly in the small box room. 'I'm not slowing this down because he's my father! I want to find Ruth and if he did this I want him to pay for it. But I want the truth. I don't want a witch hunt. We need to find Ruth, not target someone because of where the blood was found. Interviews take time.' She paused for breath, lowered her voice. 'And we don't have time.' She ran a hand through her hair, exasperated. 'I don't know what you expect me to do.' The nausea of earlier circled her stomach.

'Calm down, Claudia.' Sharpe's voice was cool. 'You're doing a good job so far. I just wanted to make you aware of the time issue for Ruth of which you're obviously mindful and I'm sorry for bringing it up. I'll leave you to continue your investigation.'

Claudia lowered her voice, 'Talking of the investigation, how is the rest of it going? I haven't had a chance to catch up with my team because you've forced me into the interview room.'

'House-to-house enquiries have been conducted but nothing has come of it. No one has seen anything out of the ordinary. No strange vehicles, no sounds of screaming, not even from the neighbour who heard the argument before. CCTV is being seized and trawled through to check Ruth's movements from leaving the station last night. Though with her blood being at home we fully expect to find her heading there. We need to make sure she didn't pick anyone up on her way home or divert somewhere that could give us a lead. A separate life somewhere else that is impacting on her now, that kind of thing.'

Claudia understood the process. Investigate the victim as much as any potential offender. 'You've seized Dominic's car?'

'We have. It's being examined as we speak. If there's a drop of blood that belongs to Ruth in there, we'll find it.'

Claudia was nauseated.

'Are you okay to continue with this, Claudia? We want you to do it, we think you're the best person for the job in such dire circumstances, no matter how unusual it is, but we're aware of the effect it must be having on you. Don't

218

misjudge us. We're desperate and that's why we've taken such unconventional action, but . . .' Sharpe rose from her own chair. 'I'm not prepared to recover one officer at the expense of another.'

Claudia smiled. It was weak, a half-attempt, but a smile nonetheless. 'I think Ruth's life is more important than my currently fragile mental health, don't you?' And with that she turned and walked back out of the room.

CHAPTER 40

Claudia

Claudia found Kane and updated him. His shoulders drooped at the confirmation they'd been dreading. He had previously worked with Ruth on a job and, as with everyone, had got on well with her. She was kind and generous with her time and energy.

'Back into interview with your dad then?' he asked.

'Yeah, we have to update him on the blood as well as progress the interview.'

'How are you bearing up?' They were in the custody block kitchen which was a small affair. It wasn't meant for gathering in, it was meant for making a drink for detainees and microwaving their meals and nothing else. They were both leaning on cupboards and the kitchen felt busy and overwhelmed with people even though there were only two of them.

Claudia's stomach gurgled. 'I could do with some chocolate, I can't remember the last time I ate.'

Kane fished in his pocket and pulled out a couple of coins. 'I have some cash for the machine.'

Claudia held out her hand and he dropped the coins into her palm.

'Other than chocolate?' Kane pushed.

'This is my dad we're talking about. We might have a strained relationship because I outrank him but he's still my dad and I can't believe he would kill someone. Never mind Ruth.'

'And Ruth? I know you two were . . .' Kane paused. 'I'm so sorry, Claudia, I didn't mean to talk about her in the past tense. Of course I mean I know you two *are* close. This must be incredibly difficult for you.'

Claudia fiddled with the coins in her hand. 'It's okay, Russ, I know what you meant. We are close. Today is hard in multiple senses of the word. I keep expecting my phone to buzz in my pocket and Ruth to send me a text with laughing emojis telling me this has all been one big joke and she'll see me for a glass of wine later and catch me up on what's been happening. My phone doesn't buzz and the text doesn't come. Interviewing Dad for killing her . . .' She stumbled over the words and Kane looked at his feet. Claudia was aware he'd never seen his boss so fragile. It was so damn hard to keep herself together.

'Interviewing Dad for killing her is like some sick joke and there's no amount of emojis that can make that right.'

'How do you think he's going to take the news about the blood?'

'If he's innocent, then he's going to be more driven to find her. Knowing for definite how hurt she is. He's going to want to be out there helping to look for her. Hell, it's where I want to be, not stuck inside like this.'

'Yeah. And if he's . . .' Kane let the rest of the sentence trail off.

Claudia finished it for him. 'If he's guilty—' she gave Kane a rueful smile — 'then he'll pretend those things. I would. So who knows what it's going to look like in there when we get him back in.'

'You go and grab some chocolate and I'll get him from his cell and we'll wait for you in an interview room.'

'Thanks, Russ.' She bounced the coins from her palm into the air and walked out of the kitchen.

With her fill of chocolate Claudia waited a beat outside the interview room and listened. She could hear murmurings but not what they were saying. Russ couldn't talk about the case with her dad while the recording equipment was off so any conversation had to be small talk. Difficult in the current circumstances. But both Russ and her dad would make sure they stuck to the rules so as to not jeopardise any potential trial. What would Ruth think of them all now if she could see them? It was the six million pound question that her best friend was at the centre of today and she held all the answers. Answers Claudia was desperate to know.

Claudia walked into the room and the minute she had she wished she had waited a little longer. Her dad was sitting facing her and he looked up at her expectantly, waiting for information on what Sharpe had wanted. Like her, Dominic knew Sharpe had only stepped into an interview midway through because there was news of some description. He was desperate to know what that news was. He cut Russ off immediately, his focus targeted in on Claudia.

She closed the door behind her and started the recording again, repeating the introductions and interview procedure. Dominic waited but it was far from patiently. He was twitching in his seat. A knee was bouncing up and down and fingers were drumming hard on his crossed arms.

As soon as she had finished the necessary verbals she spoke. 'So?'

Claudia didn't want to tell him yet. She needed to get on with the rest of the interview. She needed to get his account from him before she gave him information. 'Can we continue from where we were before we get side-tracked?'

'It's a bit late for that, don't you think? We were side-tracked the minute Sharpe barged her way into the interview.' He leaned forward on his chair, hands on the table. She could see he wasn't going to let this go.

Claudia closed her eyes and thought through the consequences of telling him at this juncture. As already discussed, he would flare up. Whether it was real or he was putting it on, they would have to deal with it and that would delay the rest of the interview and delay the gathering of information from him which could ultimately help in recovering Ruth, whatever state she was in.

'Claudia.' His voice was firm.

She opened her eyes. He was her dad. Telling her off. She looked to Russ for a reminder of where she was and who she was. A DI of higher rank than the man in front of her. She had the upper hand and she had the right to make the decision she was currently contemplating. She would not be bullied into making the one which was best for him.

Russ looked hard at her and nodded. He was trying to convey that she had this. That she was in control. She inhaled.

'If the news was something to do with Ruth then I have every right to know.' Dominic was still pushing her to talk.

'To find Ruth we need to progress this interview,' she said.

'I won't talk any further until you tell me what you know.' He folded his arms across his chest.

She narrowed her eyes at him. Furious at his stubborn streak and at how he was derailing the investigation. 'You know you're putting Ruth more at risk by doing this?'

'You're the one doing it by refusing to share what you know. As her husband I have every right to be updated.'

'As the arrested suspect you lost that right.' Her jaw was set like stone. Her anger at him was building.

'It seems like we're at an impasse then, aren't we?' He leaned back, arms still crossed.

Claudia glanced at Russ and then back to Dominic. She was cornered. She had to go through this if she was to move forward, much as she hated it, especially as she was being forced into the decision when she had wanted to wait until the interview was over to inform him. 'We've had the results back from the blood in the garage,' she said at last.

Dominic's arms dropped to his lap, his jaw gaped slightly. As Claudia had when Sharpe had said the same to her, it was obvious he had come to the same conclusion. 'No.'

'I'm sorry,' she said. 'It's a match for Ruth.'

'No,' he said again, his eyes like saucers.

'I'm sorry, Dad.'

He stared at her. Claudia couldn't tell if he was looking at her or if he was looking through her or was somewhere else altogether.

'Are you okay?' she asked.

'Is she still alive?'

'I don't know. There was a lot of blood but I've been told it's borderline if a person can survive with the amount lost. She desperately needs to be found which is why I want to get on with the interview. I know it's hard, but it's in her best interests that we carry on.'

'I want to get out of here. I need to be involved in the search for Ruth. I can't be caged up like this while she's out there hurt and bleeding and needing me.'

Claudia choked on the lump in her throat. 'I'm sorry, Dad. You're most helpful in here. If you truly believe it has something to do with your current case then we need to look at it and we need you to run us through it and how Ruth got involved in it. I do need to ask you one question though, that I should have asked you earlier.'

Dominic was on the edge of his seat, all his anxiety propelling him forward. 'What is it, Claudia?'

'There was a broken glass in your kitchen bin when we searched the house. What do you know about it?'

He rubbed at his head. 'I don't . . . I don't remember breaking a glass. Unless Ruth did at some point. I imagine it could have got in there at any time. It's been a few days since that bin was emptied.'

Claudia shook her head. 'Even if we fingerprint it, there's no evidential value if your prints come back on it. After all it's your house and it's your glass.'

'I'm telling you, I have no idea why it was in the bin. Accidents happen with glassware all the time.'

'Okay. Let's go back to the investigation, shall we?'

While she might have been willing to move on at that point, there was something about the broken glass that niggled at the back her mind.

CHAPTER 41

Dominic

Four months ago

Two months had passed and they were no further along in the investigation than they had been at the start. CCTV had drawn a blank on every single murder. House-to-house enquiries near the victims' homes had not given them a single lead. They had eventually identified the third victim, who was likely to be the first victim, as Molly Jessop, a forty-six-year-old photographer, thanks to the press release.

Molly lived alone, didn't engage with her neighbours and worked for herself, so had no workplace to report her missing. Her parents lived abroad in Spain, having moved there in retirement. She was an only child and her friends said they were used to not hearing from her for long periods as she liked to spend time alone. And as the only single woman of their age group the rest of the women had families they spent their time with, was the unsaid part of the statements. Molly had a daughter aged twenty-three who lived in Manchester and who didn't check in with her mother particularly regularly.

Her business was doing well and a whole list of clients were contacted and investigated. One was considered as a potential suspect for a couple of weeks but eventually he checked out and the lead went cold.

There was an ex-boyfriend but he was now married to another woman and his alibis checked out for the times of death for all three murders.

Dominic had looked at Alex Chapman but though he had no real alibi there was no evidence placing him at the scene of the crime either. Whoever they were looking for was forensically aware. Chapman was a highly intelligent man and perfectly capable of being the person they were looking for. The case frustrated Dominic.

Again Molly's mobile phone was missing but friends had said they were aware she was using a dating app on her phone. It was a fairly new thing. She liked her own company, but thought a couple of dates might be fun. It was the same app, Close to Me, that had been mentioned in the first two murders.

The American company had finally come through with the information they required. The account details of Madeleine and Julie. It had proved hopeless. Whoever they had been connected to had deleted themselves and deleted the chat messages through the account. The company did not save these messages. The team decided the dating app was what linked the women and was how the killer was connecting with them.

What they were unsure of was how he was choosing his victims. Julie had been a blonde white female, Madeleine was of mixed heritage and Molly was a brunette with dyed red tips. They were all very different women. Aesthetically speaking, he didn't seem to have a type.

Dominic was walking back into the incident room when he was met by Kapoor heading in the same direction. He didn't look happy.

'Just the person I need to speak with.'

Dominic didn't like the sound of this.

'Can you go to Rivelin Valley Park? We have another body.'

Dominic ran a hand through his hair. 'You're kidding me, boss. I thought he'd finished. We've another? You're sure it's the same guy?'

There was a pause. 'I'm sure, Dom. Nadira is on her way, if you could meet her there I'd appreciate it.'

Dominic walked to his desk and picked his keys up out of the top drawer. Kapoor trailed behind him.

'I'm on my way.' And with that he was out of the station and travelling to another crime scene. The fourth in the space of three months.

Nadira was climbing out of her car as he pulled up.

'I hear we have another one allocated to the Sheffield Strangler,' said Nadira when she saw him.

He grimaced. 'I'm sick of this guy.'

'You and me both. It's not a pleasant way for these women to go. They must have been terrified knowing what was coming.'

Nadira grabbed a Tyvek suit, dropped it to her feet, lifted a leg up and hopped her way into it one leg at a time, struggling as her feet got stuck in the crinkling material and nearly flying backwards onto the ground. It was always more difficult to get into the Tyvek suits in the winter when you were more wrapped up in thicker clothes underneath. You worked a long time in them, you needed to keep warm if you were outside. Eventually she was upright and in the white papery suit, zipping it up to her chin.

Behind them Paul, Krish and Hayley pulled up. A marked car was some way in front of them with an ambulance in front of that. The scene was getting busy.

A uniformed officer stood with someone in front of the marked car. Dominic walked over to them. It was a woman. She was sobbing. Her head in her hands, dark hair tumbling over the side of her face. Dominic recognised the officer from the station. He was an older guy with a girth that was straining over the top of his trousers. He couldn't have much longer left to serve. Dominic looked to the sobbing woman.

'This is Maura Brady. She found the body,' said the cop. 'It's upset her so I called the ambulance.' There was a paramedic standing off to one side waiting. The cop had his notepad and pen out. He'd be getting a quick first account before he let her go. It was difficult on witnesses and victims, but police often wanted to get the information at all costs. It was vital in investigations if they were to stand any chance of detecting a crime. This old-timer knew the ropes and Dominic was pleased to have him here.

Dominic waved the paramedic over; the uniformed cop could get his account while the paramedic took care of the witness. It was also important that she was taken care of. That way they would get the best possible evidence from her.

'What can you tell us?' the old-timer asked gently as the paramedic wrapped a blood pressure cuff around her arm. His shock of auburn hair was lit up by the lights of the vehicles around them.

Tears were pouring down the woman's face. She was ghostly white, her eyes shot through with red. She peered up at Dominic through a long fringe as more tears formed and fell.

'I've never seen a dead body,' she said. She was young. Maybe in her twenties.

'It's only early, what were you doing this morning?' he tried again.

She looked past him to where the crime scene tape was set up. 'I had a fight with my boyfriend as he was taking me to work so when he stopped the car at some traffic lights I climbed out. I was furious and needed to calm down so thought a bit of a walk would cool my mood. I'm on flexitime so it wouldn't really affect me if I was later than I usually am.' She started to sob some more. 'I'm a bit of a hothead, you see, and knew the fresh air would do me good. I didn't expect to stumble on a dead body as I cleared my head. It was . . .' The tears flowed freely. 'It was so horrific. I've never seen anything like it. I've never even seen a dead body of a relative.' The young woman was devastated at her early-morning find.

Dominic quietly thanked her and informed her that they would get her taken care of and then they'd need a statement. They'd do it later that day when she was feeling a little more up to it. The officer would take her details and arrange it with her. A detective would then be in touch.

She agreed with everything he said, to anything that would get her out of this situation. 'Why?' she asked.

Dominic waited for her.

'Why was she pulled out of the grave? Who did that to her?'

'It's the animals. They sense the body under the soil and tend to drag it free, I'm afraid.' It seemed their killer didn't like to bury the bodies particularly deep.

She nodded her understanding but grimaced at the thought. Her phone, Dominic noticed, was clamped tight in her hand.

'Can I ask,' he said before he moved away, 'that you not discuss the details of this with anyone. Obviously you can get support from a loved one and tell them you found a body, but the details of it, we'd rather them not get out if we can.'

She nodded. Words seeming to be stuck in her throat. She lifted an arm and with the back of her wrist swiped away at her eyes which were puffy and sore looking.

'Thank you,' Dominic said again.

He strode over to his team who were waiting at the vehicles.

'Nadira has gone up to the body,' Hayley said.

'Thanks. Can one of you give Maura a lift home please? She's in a bit of a state and I want to make sure she's okay.'

Krish said he'd do it.

Dominic grabbed a Tyvek suit and pulled it on. Once he was set up he walked to the crime scene where Nadira was crouched over the body.

Standing at the side of her he could see what had got Maura so upset. The brutality that had occurred to this woman was clear to see and she had only just been dumped. The bruising around the neck was vivid with the smear of red lipstick gave the woman a gruesome appearance. Her eyes were open and she looked terrified.

'How old would you put her at?' asked Nadira from her crouched position.

Dominic twisted his head to get a better look at the woman. 'I'd say she was late thirties early forties.'

Nadira sighed. 'I think you have your type there, don't you?'

'You think he goes for a woman of a certain age?'

'It looks that way to me, having had every single one of them on my table.'

'You could be right, Nadira. We've been considering their looks, their social circles, but you're right about their ages. We need to identify this woman and ascertain her age for definite. If she falls in the fortyish age bracket then we have our profile and we can work on that.'

'I think you probably had it before now,' she said taking fingernail clippings from the woman. 'You just hadn't officially named it. You're not stupid, Dom. Your team isn't stupid and Adyant Kapoor definitely isn't stupid.'

Dominic laughed. 'You're right there. He's one of the most intelligent people I know but he's under so much pressure and I think it's getting to him. Not being able to identify this guy, it's hard. The media will come down on us like a ton of bricks when we release the fact that we have another body and he'll get it in the neck from above because of that.'

'He's clever.'

'Our killer?'

She looked up. 'Unfortunately, yes. I hate to say that. I really do. But he's also an intelligent man, but with a violent streak and obviously a bit of a screw loose.'

'That's the official term I take it.'

'Absolutely.' She bagged the woman's hands and taped them up.

'He has a ritual, doesn't he? There has to be a reason behind it.'

'He's certainly sticking to the same MO with every murder. From what I can see of this one, he's not veering from anything he's done in the past at all. Like you say, it must have meaning for him. In every grave there has been the House of Maven lipstick and I imagine when we move this young woman that we'll find the same thing again.' Nadira pulled a large plastic bag out of her medical bag. She gently lifted the woman's head and placed the bag over, taping it into place just under her chin, making sure to avoid the cut to her throat.

'If people could see this they'd be horrified.' The sight of the dead woman with hands and head in clear bags was bizarre. Her lipstick-smeared face ghoulish through the plastic.

'I know. But we need to keep all evidence intact on the journey from here to the morgue. We don't want to lose particulates. It has to be done.'

'I know. It just doesn't look like we're taking care of her, does it? It looks like we're torturing her more.'

Nadira held the woman's plastic-sealed hand a moment. 'It's because we care about what happened to her that we have to do this. Her loved ones will need closure and she's the best way to try to find that.'

'You're preaching to the choir, Nadira.'

Nadira stood and stretched her arms over her head, straightening out the muscles that had started to seize up from crouching over the body. The CSI who had been at her side photographing her work stepped out of her way. 'This has to stop, Dom. We need to find a way to identify him. We need to find some trace evidence that links back to him in some way. We can't keep losing women like this.'

CHAPTER 42

Dominic

'There's a woman at the front counter waiting for you, Dom,' said Kapoor when Dominic walked back into the incident room.

First of all Dominic was surprised to see Kapoor in the incident room and secondly why was a woman waiting to speak to him? He'd only this minute walked back into the station. 'What's it about?'

'Word has already leaked that another body has been found and the woman walked in and asked to speak to the officer who had been to the crime scene. Her friend didn't turn up for work this morning.'

Dominic swallowed. 'You mean the woman hasn't even been reported missing yet?'

'Looks like this is it, the reporting of her being missing. I thought it best she talk to you because you'll be able to ID her from a photograph and know if we have our victim.'

Dominic wanted nothing more than to sit down for ten minutes. It had been a long morning and he needed time out to process it. Not long, a few minutes quiet was all he was asking for. 'Yeah, okay, I'll grab my notebook and a pen and get myself down there.'

'Want me to get you a coffee, Dom?' Hayley asked, her voice subdued, obviously aware of how tired he was.

She was sitting behind her desk, paperwork strewn all over the top of it. She was busy and yet she had managed to read his mind. 'I'd love a coffee. Thank you, Hayley.' He smiled and her eyes lit up.

'You're not going to keep her waiting though, are you?' worried Kapoor.

'No, boss. I'm not going to keep her. I'll grab a drink and take it down with me. I've just walked in. I need to recharge, if only for a second. That's okay, yes?'

Kapoor capitulated. 'Of course. I'm sure she's fine for another five minutes.' He patted Dominic on the shoulder as he walked past him and out of the incident room.

'How long's he been in here?' Dominic asked Hayley as she rose from her chair.

'He's been in and out as long as I've been back. I think he's been waiting for you to return and then the woman walked in and he realised he likely had his ID and he settled a bit more. Though he still looks like he's walking on hot coals. Must be what it's like being the boss.' She crossed the room, the same path Kapoor had just walked. 'I won't be a minute with that coffee.'

He thanked her and sagged into the chair at his desk. Civilians didn't realise the mental exhaustion this job took out of you. Seeing people desecrated the way this killer was working was soul destroying. No one should have to see another person hurt in such a way.

He was in a world of his own for a couple of minutes before Hayley returned with two mugs in her hands. She placed one down on his desk and kept hold of the other. Steam rose from the drink on his desk and he could smell the coffee. It pricked at his brain and the scent alone gradually woke him from his internal thoughts. He picked the coffee up. 'Thanks for this, Hayley. I suppose I should get downstairs and see if this woman is bringing news of our new victim.'

'Want me to come with you? You're looking tired, if you don't mind me saying.'

'Bit late if I do mind, isn't it?'

She laughed at him. 'You can take it. Tough as old boots.'

'You're full of compliments today, aren't you?' He stared at her and she chuckled to herself again. 'But no thanks, it's fine. I can manage this one. I'll give you a call if I need help. Though if it is a friend of our victim I'm going to need a statement so expect to hear from me.'

Hayley agreed and wandered back over to her desk.

Dominic made his way downstairs and through to the front waiting area. He stopped in at the front counter and asked for the details of the woman waiting for him. Kalisha Abebe was pointed out to him. He ushered her into a witness interview room and closed the door behind them. She was anxious, her hands intertwined in front of her, fingers twirling and fidgeting.

'How can I help today?' he asked as he sat in the chair opposite. The small window in the room was throwing light across the table between them, dust motes dancing above the wood.

'I heard another woman was found . . .' She struggled for words. 'And I work with my partner . . .' She'd been staring down at the table but looked up at Dominic now. 'My business partner, Victoria Ryan, and she didn't turn up for work this morning. She never fails to come in to work. We both love our floristry business. I thought she must have been really sick or something to not come in so I called her and her phone was dead. I tried the hospitals and she hasn't been in an accident that I can work out. Then I heard about the woman being found and it's the only thing I can think of. Please, can you tell me if it's Vicky or not?' Her words were rushed as though she were trying to get them all out at once.

'It's okay,' Dominic said, in an attempt to calm her. 'I'm sure she's fine. There are lots of reasons people don't turn up for work. It might be that she got involved with someone last night and has lost track of time? Is she married or single?' His stomach lurched when he asked this question. A single woman fitted the profile.

'You don't understand — nothing would stop her turning up for work. Our business is our life, we adore it. We've grown it from nothing and it's thriving. It's our baby. Something is really wrong for her to not turn up even if she did spend the night with someone. And yes, she's single.'

A cold chill swept through Dominic. 'Can I ask how old Victoria is?'

'She's forty-two.' Tears bubbled up in her eyes and burst their banks sliding down her cheeks. 'Please tell me it's not her.'

Dominic didn't know if he could do this for her. She was adamant that Vicky would turn up for work. This was unusual behaviour and she fitted the age range they had as a profile. He hoped it wasn't but she had to be someone's loved one. Someone would be grieving for her today. Someone would be stripped of everything they ever thought they knew of life. 'Do you have a photograph of Victoria?'

Kalisha looked scared. She shrank down in her chair. The answer to her question now imminent and she wasn't ready for it. 'I have one on my phone.' She picked up her bag and fished around inside pulling out a worn looking mobile. Her fingers shook as she tried to access the app that would show Dominic what he needed.

'It's okay,' he said. 'Take your time.'

She looked at him. Her bottom lip quivering. 'You think it's her.' It was a statement rather than a question.

'I think she's probably slept in at someone's house and her battery has died and you'll be hugging the life out of her later today.' And he was sure of his answer. It was the most likely reality. Phones ran out of charge all the time. God knows he'd let his run down time and again and had been given enough of an ear bashing for it by Ruth to try to keep it charged.

Kalisha's finger tapped her way through the phone until she got to a photo she was happy with. She wiped her tears away and turned the phone around. 'This is Vicky. Tell me this isn't the woman you found this morning.'

Dominic stared at the image on the phone. The woman smiling. Full of life. She was holding a bunch of flowers out to the camera, beautiful colours that brought out the blue in her eyes. Eyes that were sparkling, filled with fun and mischief.

He couldn't.

CHAPTER 43

Dominic

Kalisha broke in front of him. Dominic picked up his chair and carried it around to sit beside her. He held her hand and tried to comfort her but there was no comforting someone after a violent loss like this.

'We'll need to take a statement,' he said.

Snot and tears were falling from her face. A bunched-up tissue she had found at the bottom of her handbag, now screwed up in her hand, dabbed randomly at her face. 'Who would do something like this to her?'

'We're hoping to get as much information about Victoria from you as we can. It'll help us build up a picture of her. Of her life, her activities. And hopefully lead us in the right direction to find out.' His voice was quiet. The emotional energy this job took from him was immense.

As he sat there comforting Kalisha and talking to her he realised he needed to take stock himself and attempt to get himself on a more even keel. He was being sucked into the case more emotionally than usual. But then again, the cases never usually dragged on this way.

Kalisha sobbed and sobbed. Her heart was breaking. Her best friend was gone, and gone in the most brutal way possible.

'Do you know where she was last night?' Dominic asked.

Kalisha dabbed at her face some more but the tears she soaked up were quickly replaced by new ones. The tissue she clung to was disintegrating in her grasp. 'She mentioned something about a new guy. She hadn't had much luck in the love department, not since she and her ex split. She has a daughter.' She started to sob harder. 'Oh my God.' Her hand went up to her mouth. 'Amelia. If Victoria went out last night Amelia will have stopped at a friend's house. She'll be at school and will have no idea.' She sobbed hard. 'That poor . . .' More sobs wracked through her body. 'G-girl.'

Dominic's stomach twisted. This bastard definitely had a type. Women in their forties with children. What a sick twisted fuck. Someone was going to have to get this girl out of school and tell her the world as she knew it was over.

He desperately wanted to help this woman but felt helpless. Then he remembered a secret weapon he might be able to use. 'I have someone you might be able to talk to if you think you'd find it useful?' he said quietly. 'I think it's usually a resource for family members but the guy is someone I know so I can ask him to get in touch with you if you'd like?'

Kalisha blinked. 'I don't know. I'm sorry. I don't know what I'm supposed to say here . . .'

Dominic reached out and patted her hand. 'Take your time. I'll give you my contact details and if you decide you want to talk about this then give me a call. Samuel is a decent guy and has supported a lot of people. He'll be a good person to talk to.'

She blinked at the tears that filled her eyes. 'Thank you.'

He hoped Samuel would be okay with him offering his services. After all, Dominic had no idea how busy the man actually was. But he'd been positive about supporting the loved ones of those the Strangler had murdered.

Now Dominic needed to get the conversation turned back around to some investigative questions. 'How did she find the man she was dating?' he asked.

Kalisha swiped at her cheeks. Dominic could see she was physically trying to pull herself together, trying desperately to help. If this had happened to her friend then she would do everything she could to support the police in their effort to find her killer.

'She was on the Close to Me dating app.'

'And did you see the guy she was dating or get his name or any of his details?'

'He called himself Nathan Ward, said he was forty-six and was divorced.' She wiped away more tears as she remembered the man who may have been the last person to see her friend alive. 'They chatted for a bit on the app and then they agreed to go out and I think that was last night.'

'Did you see a photograph of him? Can you describe him?' Dominic had made a note of his name. This was his man, he was sure. He needed a better description of him though. Someone who had actually seen a decent photograph of him.

'I can do one better than that,' she said. 'I took a photograph of the photo Vicky showed me—' she looked up from her phone to Dominic — 'in case something happened to her.' More tears rolled down her cheeks. 'You say that, don't you, never usually expecting it to be the case that something happens and you need it.'

Excitement built up in Dominic. 'You have a photograph of him?'

'Yes.' She flicked through her phone again. 'It's not very clear though.'

'Anything is better than nothing,' Dominic reassured her. He leaned forward in his seat.

Kalisha spun the phone around towards him. He had the image of the Sheffield Strangler.

CHAPTER 44

Dominic

It was as everyone had previously described. The sun was behind his back and was blazing into the camera. You could clearly see what he was wearing, jeans and a pale blue shirt, open at the neck and tucked into his jeans, you could tell his hair was dark, but his face was completely obscured.

It was no help whatsoever.

It could be Alex Chapman. His hair was dark.

'Do you mind if I take a copy of this?' Dominic asked.

'Of course not, if you think it'll be helpful.' She handed Dominic the phone.

'It's not that we can make out who he is from this,' he said. 'But it's the first time we've seen this image and if we disseminate it we can at least prevent other women from going on dates with him.'

'Oh God, yes. Of course.'

Dominic thought about the best way to get the image from her phone. 'If you email it to me, I think that might be easiest. Then we can work from my email within the police systems.' He handed the phone back and reeled off his work email address as she thumbed the details into the phone.

'I'll get someone to come down and get a statement from you.' He rose from his chair. 'I'm so sorry for your loss, Kalisha.'

'And Amelia?' Tears started again.

'We'll get someone to pick her up, alert Social Care, and go from there. Does she have any family she can stay with?'

'There's her grandmother but she lives in Leicester. It's a huge upheaval for her. She can stay with me if she wants to. Vicky wouldn't have minded that.'

'How old is Amelia? Social Care will be involved in sorting that side of things. It's not our area, I'm afraid.'

Kalisha dropped the now soggy tissue in her bag and started fishing around for another, frustration obviously building inside her as it became clear there were no more.

'I'll get whoever comes down to take your statement to bring some tissues with them.'

'Thank you.'

He left her wiping her nose on her sleeve as she continued to sob for her lost friend.

Dominic's earlier despondent mood felt slightly lessened by the fact that they could potentially prevent further deaths by releasing the image he now had his hands on. What had started as a bad day had been lifted by this turn of events.

The incident room was buzzing with activity. Dominic went straight to his desk and turned on his computer. As he waited for it to wake he turned to Krish. 'Can you go and take the statement from the woman downstairs, please, Krish. You'll need tissues, she's devastated. They were best friends and ran a business together. A florists they started a couple of years ago that seemed to be doing well from what I can gather. Apparently our victim had a knack for it.'

Krish picked up statement paper and his pen. 'Absolutely.' He strode across the room and out the door.

The computer monitor was awake and Dominic went straight to his emails. The one from Kalisha was there. He opened it up and the image of the Sheffield Strangler was staring back at him. 'I've got the photograph of our killer,' he told the room. Silence fell and all eyes turned to him. 'I've also got an ID on the victim, she's Victoria Ryan aged forty-two. Picked up on the same dating app as the others. Only this time her best friend Kalisha Abebe took a photograph of the image he put on the app in case something happened to her friend.'

'Shit,' Hayley blurted out.

'Exactly,' he agreed.

'Any good?' asked Paul excited.

'Not for identifying him, but we can use it to warn other women off him. We'll get it out to the press immediately. We may be able to save someone's life this way. I've got the image on my email. I'll forward it on to our press department and they can disseminate it. I'll also forward it to the digital crime department, to see if they can clear the image any.'

'Is it the one with the sun glaring behind him that's been described to us?' Hayley asked.

'That's the one. Once he's aware the image is out there he could change it. But if he's currently charming someone using this photograph and we save one life because that woman sees it, then it's worth doing.'

Rhys shook his head. 'Clever bastard.'

'We're further ahead than we were this morning.' Dominic was determined they would look on the bright side of this. Their spirits needed lifting. His certainly did and he could only imagine his team's did as well.

'Saving a life is better than a kick in the teeth,' admitted Hayley.

'Now we need to catch the nasty little fucker,' muttered Paul.

Dominic stood. 'I need to go and tell Kapoor what we have. That this is going straight out to the press. He needs to be kept up to date.'

'This feels positive,' said Hayley. 'Even if we can't work from it, we're scuppering him and I like that.'

He placed a hand on her shoulder as he passed and squeezed. He was pretty buzzed himself.

CHAPTER 45

Claudia

Twenty-four hours since Ruth's attack

Claudia rubbed at her eyes. 'Talking of press conferences, I think I'm going to do one this evening.'

'Saying what?' Dominic asked.

'I'm going to appeal to the killer and ask him to release Ruth. I'm going to appeal to his better side and see if he'll let us have her back.'

Dominic scoffed. 'You think that'll work?'

'You think it'll hurt?' she countered.

He went quiet.

'No, I didn't think so. Why would you suggest we don't do it?'

Dominic stared at the floor. His mouth moved as if to speak but nothing came out.

'What is it?' Claudia asked. 'Why are you against a press conference?'

At last his mouth worked again. 'I'm not, it's just we have no evidence it's him, other than my gut feeling. Isn't putting it into the public domain, the fact that he's brave enough to take a cop, going to—' he waved a hand in the air as if trying to grab for a reason — 'upset the public. They won't feel safe at all.'

'Have you forgotten already that we have the lipstick from your garage he left behind? Though I do think it's odd he left it at the scene of the abduction rather than where he dumps the body.' Claudia clamped her mouth shut as she said the last sentence, gutted she herself was classing Ruth as a body rather than someone they were searching for as a missing person. Ruth was an attractive, vibrant, intelligent woman. They'd only been out for drinks the night before last. Ruth had been pushing Claudia to put in for her exams, to go for promotion again and Claudia was fighting her, telling her she was happy where she was for now. That she had plenty of time to progress. And here they now were, classing Ruth as a body, just two days later. Where was Ruth's time? Where was her opportunity to do what she wanted in the force and with her life? Claudia pushed her hair behind her ears.

'It's okay,' Dominic said. 'I know the facts of the case better than anyone on your team, I know how he works. No need to feel bad for talking facts with me. I'm clinging on to hope that she's still alive. We don't have a body so in my book she's still alive.'

Claudia brought herself back to the here and now and the job she was doing, pulled herself away from the night with Ruth. 'But the lipstick goes to show he's likely got her. It's enough to come to that conclusion, wouldn't you say?' Why was he so against this? Why was she having to encourage him that it was the right way to go?

'Not that I want to admit this, but you're right.' Dominic slouched down in his seat. 'But do you want to frighten the public this way?'

'You shouldn't be worrying about that. You should focus on Ruth and let us consider how we're going to play this. I'll obviously run it up the flagpole and speak to Sharpe, but I can't see her having an issue with an appeal. She's as concerned as the rest of us.' Why wasn't he? What was the issue?

'I'm sorry, it's a natural part of me, the job just kicks in.' His voice was quiet. 'But if you think it'll help get Ruth back I'm all for it.'

'Even if we don't reach him someone might've seen Ruth. They might have seen her being lifted into a vehicle or carried somewhere. It's as much about searching for witnesses as it is about reaching out to him.'

'You don't need to keep selling it, Claudia. You have me on side.'

It hadn't felt like it. She smiled at him. 'We'll find her, Dad. No matter what it takes, you have the full might of the force behind you on this. She's not alone. Wherever she is she'll know she has several thousand cops on her side who won't back down.' And that thought alone was something that had kept Claudia going all day. Knowing her colleagues were doing everything in their power, following every lead, every sign, turning everything upside down to search for her.

Dominic looked broken.

Claudia stood. 'I'm going to put you back in your cell while I sort this other stuff out. You okay with that? Keeping you here a little longer while I sort out the briefing?'

'If it'll help then yes, of course I am. I've only ever wanted to help find her, Claudia. It's been hard being locked up in here not able to get involved in anything.'

'You couldn't have anyway. There was no way anyone was going to allow you access to their incident room.'

He smiled at her.

'And that includes me.' She turned to Kane. 'Take him to his cell, will you, please, Russ?'

Kane stood and Dominic rose from his seat.

'Thank you for making this as easy as you could, Claudia.'

She dipped her head in acknowledgement and left the interview room.

An hour later the press had assembled. It was the quickest she had ever been able to get them gathered at headquarters.

There was a lot of noise from them as they tried to figure out what the urgent matter involved. Most of them decided the Sheffield Strangler had struck again. After six months of dealing with the case they were getting a little immune to the story. Awful as each murder was, each case was the same and they wanted something different to say.

'You're sure about this?' Sharpe flicked ash onto the floor of the smoking hut as she stood outside with Claudia before the press briefing. It was getting dusky. It had been a long day and it was far from over. 'Dominic was right when he said it's possibly going to frighten the public that a police officer has been taken by this sicko. They're scared as it is and if the police can't protect themselves then how are the public meant to do so?' She blew a smoke ring up in the air, blush-coloured lips pursing into a perfect circle.

'I think we need to talk to him and it's the only way we have of conversing. For all he likes to talk to Dominic, he never sent a burner phone. He sent Dom letters and we said what we needed through the media. From what I can gather he wanted the publicity. My judgement is that Ruth's safety is more important than whether or not we raise the level of public fear.'

Sharpe flicked her glowing stub into the air and watched it dive to the ground before she planted her pointed toe onto it and ground it out. 'What are your thoughts on our culpability?' she asked getting to the point.

'For Ruth being in the position she's in?'

Sharpe glared at Claudia.

'Okay. We haven't got that far yet. We haven't got to Ruth going undercover. But he definitely has a type. Women in their forties who have children at home. Ruth doesn't have any children so I'm presuming her profile was set up with at least one child.'

Sharpe agreed it was.

'Look, I can't say. My focus is on getting her back. Whatever state that may be in.' She paused as she considered this statement. Let it sink in that they were, again, talking about recovering Ruth's body. 'But Dominic definitely had a relationship with this guy, who's to say he didn't figure out Ruth was his wife and he targeted her because of that.'

'For what reason though?'

'I don't know. Like I said, I haven't finished interviewing him yet. I wanted to get this press conference done first. I thought it was the most important thing to do. Dominic was happy to wait. There's still plenty of time on his clock.'

Sharpe turned and looked at Claudia. 'What are you planning to say about Ruth?'

'I don't understand.'

'Don't play stupid with me, Claudia. I know you're not. Are you going to say a police officer is missing or are you going to name her? Thereby giving the killer the information that he does indeed have Dominic Harrison's wife if he wasn't already aware. If he thought he had taken someone from the dating app then he'd think she was single.'

'I think we can forget her meeting him on the app and being taken. The fact that she was taken from the home she shares with Dominic is enough to say he knew she was married to him. Whether he initially saw her through the dating app is another issue we don't yet know. But there are photographs of Dominic and Ruth together in the house.'

'So you're going to name her?'

'I don't see that it can hurt anything from here.'

'We'd better get in there,' said Sharpe, straightening up her jacket and brushing off an invisible piece of lint. 'The vultures are waiting.'

* * *

Claudia followed Sharpe into the press briefing room. She always felt a little bit dowdy in comparison to Sharpe who pretty much matched her name in all manner of ways: her speech, her conduct and her clothes.

They sat down behind the long table and peered out at the sea of faces staring back at them, eager to know why they had been called in so late in the day when they hadn't heard of a new body being found. Whispers were going around the room that maybe the police had someone in custody at last. This could be the reason they would call them in without it being another murder. That or someone at the top had finally lost their job because of it all. They had been talking about that one for a while. A six-month investigation without changes in staff, someone surely had to answer for the fact that they hadn't got anywhere. They were certainly making them answer in the pages of the press. Be that on paper or online.

'Thank you for coming in,' Sharpe started and the room fell quiet but for a couple of people who finished off the conversations they had started. Sharpe glared at them, and soon the whole room was silent and waiting for her to continue.

'As you can imagine, being called at such short notice like this, we have something we want to tell you that couldn't wait. It's important and we wanted to do a press conference rather than send out a note.'

Pens were being scribbled across notepads and cameras were on and aimed at the pair of women in front of the room.

A hand went up in the middle of the huddle of reporters.

'We'll take a couple of questions at the end of the briefing,' Sharpe cut them off.

'Where are Harrison and Kapoor?' the determined reporter persisted.

'Like I said—' her stare was hard, flinty — 'we will answer questions at the end and if you let us get on with the briefing you may find you have some questions answered.'

A rumble went around the room as people presumed someone had in fact lost their job over this case.

Sharpe was clearly not impressed with the behaviour. She was used to her subordinates listening to her when she was talking and waiting for her to continue. This rabble seemed to be pissing her off. Maybe this was why she rarely did press conferences.

Sharpe and Claudia waited for the noise to die down. Eventually it did.

'If you don't mind giving us your full attention for the next ten minutes we'd appreciate that,' Sharpe said. 'I'm going to hand you over to DI Claudia Nunn who will inform you why you're here and what's happening.' She inclined her head towards Claudia who smiled in response.

Claudia's nerves were getting the better of her. This was a huge gamble. She was making a lot of assumptions coming out here with the story she was about to tell. But it was information-based if not evidence-based. She swallowed and started.

'A woman has been reported missing and a thorough investigation has led us to believe that she has been taken by the Sheffield Strangler.'

There was silence from the room as they waited for more details.

She continued. 'This is the first time we've been in front of him this way, knowing he has someone before we find the body. But he's made it clear he has this woman. He wanted us to know. So we want to ask him to return her to us with no further harm caused. You'll see in your press packs on your chairs that there is a photofit of a male. We'd like you to circulate this image as we believe he may be able to help us with our enquiries.' This next part was the difficult section, the information that was going to cause uproar in the room. She took a deep breath in, held it and released. 'We can inform you that the woman who has been taken is DC Ruth Harrison of South Yorkshire Police. She is a serving officer and—'

The room exploded. Voices shouted out to her, arms flew up into the air, flashbulbs blurred her vision. She tried to battle through the wave of sound.

'We want no further harm to come to DC Harrison. All we ask is that she is returned immediately.'

It was no use. They had heard enough; they had heard the important information and wanted their questions answering. Claudia looked to Sharpe. Her fingers were clenched together under the table. Her knuckles white with the pressure. She looked out to the reporters. Arms still in the air. Phone calls were being made. This was news and they wanted to get it out as quickly as possible.

'We'll take a couple of questions,' Sharpe said, only loud enough for those who were still listening to hear her. Another couple of hands went up and she pointed to one of these. One of the reporters who hadn't been rude enough to interrupt before. Claudia liked her style.

'How do you know it's the Sheffield Strangler?'

Sharpe looked to Claudia to take the question. She'd said she would. This was her show.

'He left something behind that could only have come from the Sheffield Strangler,' Claudia answered as vaguely as she could, then pointed to another reporter.

'How long has DC Harrison been missing?'

Claudia sighed. 'She's been missing since yesterday evening.' It was too long. She didn't like how long it had been. They had no real concept of when she had been taken. She had left work at around five but Dominic said he hadn't got home until about nine thirty. It could be any time between.

'Her name is Harrison?' said another reporter — here it came. 'Is she any relation to DS Dominic Harrison?'

Of course she bloody was. 'Yes, it's his wife.'

Again the noise in the room erupted and Claudia's ears were assaulted by the ferocity of the sound.

Sharpe nodded towards the door. It was time for them to leave. Claudia placed her hands on the table, ready to rise from the chair. 'We are doing everything in our power to find Ruth Harrison, but again, if I can ask the person who has her to release her immediately, before any more harm can come to her, we would be really grateful.'

'What do you mean, any *more* harm?' someone shouted out from the rear of the room.

Claudia and Sharpe rose.

'Has she been hurt?' they shouted again.

'That's all in the way of questions for today.' Sharpe closed it down.

'What aren't you telling us?' from the left side of the room.

Claudia shuffled along behind the empty chairs that were pushed in behind the long table.

'Where was she abducted from?' this from the left side again.

'Thank you,' said Claudia as she disappeared from view.

Sharpe turned to her in the corridor. 'They're a pack of vultures. Why can't they sit quietly, take the information we have for them, ask the couple of questions we allow and write up their articles? Why does it have to turn into—' she waved her hand about in the air — 'that.' Her nose wrinkled in disdain.

'They're doing their job,' said Claudia as they moved away from the door towards the stairs, back up to the incident room and Sharpe's office.

'If they were doing their jobs properly they'd have listened to the briefing, not exploded the minute they heard something remotely interesting.'

She had a point. They'd been like a bunch of school children. It wasn't like them. But Ruth Harrison being abducted was big news. They had to get it out fast and they wanted as many facts for their articles as they could gather and quickly. Though behaving like a rabble wouldn't achieve that.

'You're going to bed Dominic down for the night and start again in the morning?' Sharpe asked.

Panic and fear gripped Claudia's chest like a vice. 'I was going to go back and continue.'

'You look tired.'

Claudia understood Sharpe was attempting to show compassion but it came across hard and cold. 'I can cope.'

'Don't get me wrong, Claudia.' Sharpe directed a piercing gaze at her. 'I'm not for one moment suspending the investigation for the night. It'll continue throughout. Ruth is out there and she's in trouble. You should know we don't leave one of our own out there like that. But . . .' She checked the corridor behind her. 'You need to rest or you'll not be able to take this all the way to the end.'

Whatever the end might be, thought Claudia darkly. Sharpe wanted Ruth back as much as she and her father did. It was the reason she had put Claudia on the job in the first place. This morning's talk in the smoking shed seemed like weeks ago, and yet it was only this morning. 'I can manage.'

'But if we don't allow Dominic to rest properly and he gets charged with anything—'

Claudia opened her mouth to interrupt, to remind Sharpe that her father was likely innocent of murdering Ruth, but Sharpe held up a finger.

'I said *if*, Claudia. See, your hearing is already going. That or your ability to analyse spoken sentences. Your emotions are heightened and as you're getting more tired the job is becoming more difficult. It really won't hurt for you both to get your heads down. And like I said, *if* your father should be charged with anything then we need to have done everything by the book and that means allowing him to have his eight hours sleep.'

'You know he won't be happy.' *She* wasn't happy. Ruth was missing and she was being ordered to go home and leave her father in the cells overnight.

It was as though Sharpe could read her mind. 'I'll be here for a long time yet. I'm not resting quite yet.'

That was the positive thing about Sharpe. She may be all flinty and blunt, but the job was important to her. She was loyal to her staff. If the wheel was about to come off you could rely on Sharpe to be there trying to hold it on.

'You'll keep me updated?' Claudia asked with reluctance.

'Isn't that my sentence?' Sharpe tried a smile on for size. It really didn't fit. 'Just go. And yes, I'll let you know if anything of significance occurs.'

With that Claudia walked away and headed back to the cells to inform her father he was staying for the night.

CHAPTER 46

Claudia

Her father hadn't taken the news well. In fact Claudia had never seen him so angry. He was all over the place. It was to be expected with what he was going through, she supposed. She had to reassure him that though the interview was postponed for the evening and an extension would be sought tomorrow, the investigation itself was not closing down. There were officers on the night shift who were still searching for Ruth. His wife was still the force's top priority and no one was backing down from finding her.

In the comfort of her own home Claudia allowed the mask she'd been wearing all day to slip away. The mask that enabled her to deal with the case that involved family. With one member desperately at risk and the other on the hook for her potential murder. Now, in the quiet of night, with the curtains drawn on the world, Claudia let the pain of the day wash over her as she couldn't hold back the tears that had been threatening to fall every hour.

Claudia stood in the shower and allowed the jets of water to cascade over her as she sobbed. Her heart breaking. Nothing in her life or her career could have prepared her for this. Where was Ruth now? Was she being kept alive somewhere? Was she cold and afraid? This thought nearly brought Claudia to her knees. Considering that Ruth was injured and cold and afraid while she stood here warm and safe. Claudia clutched at her stomach, physical pain tearing through her body.

Or were they already too late? Claudia howled out in protest. At the unfairness of it all. Her father locked in the small space in the custody block, terrified for his wife but unable to actively do anything to help. He was innocent but she followed orders and the logic behind them made sense. It had to be done this way. It would happen like this if it was anyone else, she couldn't deny that.

She towelled herself dry and padded to the bedroom. Sleep would be elusive but she'd make the pretence of trying.

Eventually in the early hours of the morning she slipped into a dark sleep where she found herself sitting with Ruth in a bar, both of them holding a glass of red wine. Ruth laughing at something she'd said. Then, as she sipped on her wine, blood started to pour from Ruth's mouth. Loud laughter carried on around them. Echoing and repeating. Ruth's eyes bulged in horror, her wine glass filling with blood, mixing with the red wine, swirling in a vortex. Claudia reached out to grab her but however far forward she leaned she was unable to reach her. She shouted out and found herself in the inky blackness of her bedroom once again.

After that she didn't sleep. Her fear tormented her. Her mind whirred.

As soon as was reasonable, she rose, grabbed a tea in a reusable carry mug, pushed her shoulders back, put her work mask back in place and left the house.

There had been no forward momentum during the night. It was always a difficult period where little could be progressed. They had no idea where to even start searching for Ruth. Not one witness had mentioned a vehicle they could trace. It was a matter of hoping someone recognised the image they put out yesterday and hoping the interview with her father gave them something useful. Thinking of her father, she really wanted to get back to him and start again.

Russ entered her office. 'How'd you sleep?'

She shook her head. 'What about you?'

He shrugged.

There really were no words for how shitty they were all feeling.

Russ slumped into the chair in front of her desk. 'You want to get back over to the custody block?'

She was about to answer him when her phone started to ring. She picked it up, tried to tell the caller she was tied up and then said she'd be there shortly.

Russ raised an eyebrow in question.

'Someone has come in and wants to talk to me.'

'You think it might be from the press conference yesterday?'

'He says he's family of one of the victims. I couldn't send him away.' She rose from her chair. 'I won't be long and then we'll get straight off.'

* * *

The man waiting for her stood with his hands behind his back, his shoulders straight, and where people usually appeared a little nervous in a police station he had an air of self-importance.

'How can I help you, Mr Chapman?'

They were in one of the witness interview rooms. In fact it was the very same room she'd spoken to her father, just yesterday morning.

'I saw the media appeal that went out yesterday. I believe it was you who ran it.'

'Have a seat.' Claudia waved at the chair opposite her as she slid into the one nearest her.

Alex Chapman let out a sigh of impatience and seated himself in the chair she'd pointed out.

'How can I help?' she asked again.

'My ex-wife, the mother of my child, was murdered by this animal. You've done nothing to catch him but now he's taken one of your own it's all systems go.'

Was he going to ask her a question or was he here to make a complaint? 'The team dealing with the case have been working hard for months. I understand it's been difficult—'

He waved his own hand at her. 'I don't want your platitudes. I want to know that you're going to catch this man. That I can tell my son he can sleep at night.'

That problem at night was familiar. 'Mr Chapman. I'm sorry it's taken so long. I can assure you the investigation team are dedicated to their task. But yes, while we have the opportunity to get one of the women back alive we're going to do everything within our power to find him.'

Apparently appeased by what she'd just said he rose from his chair. 'Please do let me know when you catch him, won't you.' That was it. He was done.

She promised to do so.

And on that point, it was time for her to organise the extension of her father's detention and get back to the custody suite to continue interviewing him. It was a good job the press hadn't got hold of that information last night, that DS Dominic Harrison had been arrested for the murder of his own wife.

* * *

There was a message waiting for her when she got to the custody suite. The custody sergeant waved her and Russ over and then rummaged under the desk where Claudia couldn't see what he was looking for.

'It's in here somewhere,' he said, face pasty and grey looking. You never saw the light of day when you permanently worked Custody. It was a grim place. Claudia had worked it for six months when she had first been promoted to sergeant and she had hated every second of it and had been glad to get out of there, back into the real world. Some cops loved it, the ability to go to work and hand their jobs over to the next sergeant on the following shift when it was time to leave. No worrying about cases at home. Everything was left at work.

'Ah-ha!' He waved his arm in the air, a piece of paper in his hand. He looked pleased with himself. 'So much crap down here.'

She smiled at him. Impatient to get started on the interview again, the expression tight on her face. If it was Sharpe she was surprised she hadn't called on her mobile.

The custody sergeant looked at the note in his hand. 'We took a call for you.' He turned to her. 'We're not a bloody answering service though.'

She side-eyed Russ, they were known to be a little on the grumpy side in Custody. Probably due to the fact they never saw daylight.

'Sorry about that,' she said, for the sake of saying something.

He nodded, appeased, then looked back down at his note. 'He said, he doesn't have Ruth and you have your facts all wrong. Please don't attribute all your shit—' the custody sergeant looked back up at her — 'yes, he said shit and it was written down. God knows why. We don't take that shit on the street.'

Claudia smiled. He didn't notice the irony of what he'd said.

'Anyway . . .' He went back to the note. 'All your shit that you can't detect onto him.'

Claudia was puzzled. She was sure she hadn't heard him correctly. 'I'm sorry, can you read that again?'

He rolled his eyes and read from the sheet again. 'He doesn't have Ruth and you have your facts all wrong. Please don't attribute all your shit that you can't detect onto him.'

They both looked at each other simultaneously.

'He doesn't mean . . . he's not . . .' The custody sergeant stammered, looking at the custody record in front of him. Seeing who Claudia had in custody and for what offence. The note wafting in his hand in front of him. 'Oh shit.'

Claudia held out her own hand. 'Can I read that, please?'

He handed it over. 'Ruth is Ruth Harrison?'

She was reading the message again, with Russ peering over her shoulder. She nodded as her eyes skimmed the paper.

'He's the Sheffield Strangler?' His voice was quiet, not to alert the rest of the custody suite what they had in front of them.

Claudia read the note a second time and then a third, trying to get the words to sink in and allow their meaning to gain some understanding in her head. 'What time did you take this message?' she asked, her voice brittle.

'Not fifteen minutes ago. He was put through from the switchboard who had tried to locate you and someone had identified you were on your way here so he was put through.'

'And it was you?'

He had managed to pale even more. 'Yes, it was me.' He bit at his lower lip. 'When he said Ruth I didn't think of Ruth Harrison. It didn't cross my mind that the killer would phone up and talk like that.'

'What did he sound like?' Claudia didn't have time to make the sergeant feel better for not taking any action sooner.

'He didn't have an accent I could place. Maybe a local lad? Not a strong Yorkshire accent though. Nothing about him stood out.' He picked up the phone and dialled. 'Hello, switchboard. A phone call was put through to this custody suite less than fifteen minutes ago, I want to know from what number it came from. Yes. Yes. It's urgent. Thank you.' He listened and waited.

'Okay, that's great, thank you.' He scribbled onto a notepad and when he placed the receiver down he tore the sheet out of the pad and waved it at Claudia. 'I have the number he dialled in from.' He was pleased with himself.

Claudia was less happy. She didn't expect it to be this easy. 'Can I use your phone please?'

He handed her the phone from behind the desk and she dialled the number. The line was dead.

'You think he used a burner?'

'I do. This is time sensitive. Can I ask that you find me someone to submit the number, see who it belongs to? We need to get in to interview.'

If he hadn't have missed such a big issue as talking to the killer and sitting on it for fifteen minutes, Claudia knew he'd have told her it wasn't his job and to sort it out herself, but as it was, he'd be feeling pretty bad about that so agreed to get someone to sort it out for her and straight away.

Claudia turned to Russ — her stomach churned with the betrayal of what she was about to say. 'We need to speak to Dominic. If the Sheffield Strangler is saying he doesn't have Ruth then we need to break Dominic down and find out which parts of his story aren't true, because I don't believe he's telling us the whole truth.'

CHAPTER 47

Claudia

With the custody keys in her hand Claudia unlocked Dominic's cell and looked in. He was on the solid bed in the right-hand corner, back against the wall, feet up on the edge, knees bent in front of him.

'About time,' he said. 'Who knows what's happened to Ruth in the time you've been having a nap.'

He didn't mean to hurt her, he was angry and hurting himself, but his snide comment sliced through her, cutting deep. She didn't respond, merely gave him a look that told him he was out of order. He raised his hands, palms forward, and shrugged. It was the most she was going to get from him.

Eventually he asked, 'How did it go?' Letting his legs drop and shuffling to the front of the concrete slab. He was talking about the press conference last night.

'Come on.' She twitched her head sideways. 'We need to talk.'

He stood. 'But how did it go?'

'We put it out there. We shared the photofit image and we directly asked that she be returned. Now it's back to you.

Come on.' She was short with him. She had no time for these games. Ruth had no time for these games.

Dominic looked at her, puzzled. 'I don't understand. What's happened?'

'We need to get you back into interview. Get a move on, will you, or do I need to get Russ to pull you out of there?' She meant it as well. She didn't care that this was her father. Sharpe had given her this job to do and she'd bloody well do it. If he was lying to her about something then she wanted to know what it was.

He raised his hands again in surrender.

In the interview room the recording device was switched on and the interview started, Russ going through the introductions and official dialogue.

'You're lying to us about something, Dominic, and we want to know what it is.' Claudia jumped straight in.

His eyes widened. 'I don't know what you mean.'

'We can go round in circles for as long as you want, but we'll get there eventually. Or you can simply tell us what we want to know straight off the bat.'

'Where is this coming from? I thought everything was okay when you left?' He looked from Claudia to Russ and back again. Waiting for an answer from one of them.

They stared back in stony silence, giving him nothing.

The silence stretched on. Eventually Claudia broke it. Silence was seen as oppressive in the courts and Dominic knew this. She was aware he could sit in a silence as well as they could because he was trained the way they were. Your average interviewee hated silences and tended to fill them, but Dominic could sit and wait it out.

'We've had contact from the killer, Dominic.'

His jaw slackened and his face paled. 'What the fuck? Already?'

She waited again.

'What does that have to do with me? What did he say? Please, Claudia, tell me what's going on.' There was a slight whine to his voice.

'He doesn't have Ruth—'

'No. No. I don't believe that.' He was on his feet before they knew what was happening. Backing away from the table, from them. 'What does that mean for Ruth? If he says he doesn't have her? I don't believe him, I don't believe he doesn't have her. He does. He's hiding the fact. He's biding his time. He's going to wait until you find her body. He's going to make us, me, find her body in the ground, desecrated like the others.' He was shouting now.

Claudia and Kane both rose from their chairs. Claudia had expected him to be upset but this was extreme. He was panicked. Kane put his hands up. 'Hey, Dom, calm it down. We're telling you what he's said. We're still working on the assumption he has her. We're still out there searching for her. We haven't abandoned her.'

Dominic was backed up against the wall. The room wasn't very large.

'Please don't lean back hard,' Claudia said. 'You're up against the panic bar and if you lean on it you're going to have half of the custody suite barging in here with their asps raised.'

Dominic took a step forward. 'I'm sorry.' He looked his daughter in the eye. 'I'm sorry, Claudia. I'm just afraid.'

'I know you are. Please come and sit back down.'

He took another step forward. Kane and Claudia hadn't moved. They were standing in front of their chairs.

'I don't want to lose her.'

Claudia seated herself again. Kane followed suit and leaned back in his chair showing Dominic the situation was calm and there was no need for this.

Dominic took another step forward and he was nearly back at the table.

'He made contact quickly,' Dominic said.

Kane crossed his legs. 'He did.'

Dominic sat down opposite them, scraping the chair on the ground as he folded himself into position.

Claudia tapped a finger on the table. 'We still believe you're lying to us about something, Dominic.' She had referred to him by his name again, rather than calling him Dad. She was back in investigative mode. 'We want to know what that is. It might not be big, it might not even be relevant, but something feels off and we want to know what it is so we can move on from it and focus on what's important. If you don't tell us what it is you're hiding we're going to think it's bigger than it is and lay more prominence at its feet than we might otherwise.' She stared hard at him and tapped a pen on the pad in front of her.

Dominic rubbed at his forehead.

'Do you want us to go down that rabbit hole?'

He shook his head. His eyebrows furrowing deep down over his nose. 'There's something but it's not relevant at all. It's not even worth mentioning, but now you've put it like that you're not leaving me with any choice.'

Kane tapped his foot in the air. 'It's best to let it out.'

Claudia looked at Kane, concerned. There was a minute shake of his head as he tried to reassure her this would not be what she was afraid of. Did Kane know something about this? Why hadn't he told her?

She had no idea what was coming but fear ran the gauntlet inside of her. 'Tell us what it is you're hiding.' It took all her strength to keep her voice on an even keel.

'I lied to you.' He paused, putting off the moment of truth. 'More an omission than a lie.'

Claudia didn't care about semantics. She just wanted him to spit it out. Her patience was wearing thin. If whatever he was hiding could help with their investigation into Ruth's disappearance, then he needed to speak.

'What is it?'

'It's about Ruth.'

Claudia's blood ran cold. Her mind began to spiral. She gripped the edge of the table, her fingers turning white.

'I've been seeing Hayley behind Ruth's back.'

CHAPTER 48

Claudia

The silence stretched out between them. She didn't care about how it would be perceived this time. That silence on an interview recording is seen as oppressive, but it didn't bother her. Claudia didn't speak and allowed the silence to play out. She would not be the first person to speak. The fact was that at this time she didn't have the words. She was so let down by him. She'd been through this situation with him before. She thought that was the one and only time he would tear a family, her family, apart.

Now he was doing it again.

She had grown to love Ruth. At first it had been uncomfortable — she'd been the other woman, after all — but Ruth had taken her time with Claudia and had not pushed or asked for anything from her. She'd accepted the cold shoulders Claudia had doled out until eventually she had thawed and they started to talk.

Claudia had come to realise what it was her dad saw in Ruth, how well matched they were. It was much easier once her mum was okay and settled but Ruth had made the transition something that Claudia controlled and Claudia had never been more grateful to her. She could see how much Ruth loved her dad and now here he was telling her this.

She stared at him.

He started to twitch.

'I didn't mean it to happen.' Eventually he broke. As she knew he would. They all did. They couldn't sit there when they were guilty and had words to say if the room was filled with silence. It was one of the reasons silence was seen as oppression. It really did make an interviewee talk.

'You're a grown man. How can you not mean it to happen?' Claudia hissed at him. 'Did you lose control of your faculties? Did you get some kind of virus where you lost your mind? Do we need to go through your jobs in that case to check you haven't screwed them up?'

'Don't be like that, Claudia.' He talked to her like a father to a daughter who was reprimanding a child. Short and sharp.

Impatient.

She glared at him. 'Do not speak to me like that. It is you who is under caution and is being interviewed for murder here. You have absolutely no right to talk to me like I'm a child.'

He bent his head.

'This is a professional interview. I don't care how you see me. You will answer the questions properly. Do you understand?'

'I'm sorry.'

'So how did you not mean for it to happen?'

'We were working late all the time. We went for the occasional drink after work together. A relationship built up. It doesn't mean anything. It should never have happened. I was exhausted with the case, it started to mean more to me than anything else, being at work was more important than being at home with Ruth. The job consumed me and Hayley understood that, we leaned on each other. But I can see that it's nothing, that it was just easy and that's why it happened.'

'You're unbelievable, do you know that?'

He hadn't yet looked up. His shame obvious.

Kane stayed out of it. This was now something between Claudia and Dominic. It was too personal for him to ask questions about.

'This was exactly the same thing you did to Mum with Ruth. You cheated on Mum with Ruth, who by the way was far too young for you. It was as though you were going through a mid-life crisis. But you were adamant she was the love of your life and you had found your soulmate. Because you stayed with her and married her I accepted her into my life and grew to know and love her and now you're doing exactly the same goddamn thing to her?' Her voice was rising a little and she had to rein it in. This was still an interview and not a family argument.

Dominic looked beaten. 'I'm sorry, Claudia. This thing with Hayley, it's been a mistake. I promise. It's Ruth I love. Can you imagine how I feel knowing that sick fuck has her and what she's going through? It's tearing me apart. I've made a huge mistake. I want Ruth back and when I get her back I'll never let her out of my sight again. You'll need to tear us apart with a crowbar.' He leaned forward. 'I promise you. I want her back.'

Kane was making notes in his pad as he had been doing throughout the whole of the interview process. Claudia looked at it, hated that her personal life, that of her parents, was recorded this way. But there was nothing she could do about it. This had happened to Ruth and her dad and she had to deal with what was in front of her. Ruth was banking on her.

'Does Ruth know?' Claudia asked.

Dominic shook his head, confused. 'I don't understand, what does that have to do with anything? It's me who has lied to you. It's that bastard who has her. What do her feelings have to do with this?'

Claudia tapped her own pen on the table. A sign of her impatience with him. 'It has everything to do with this. You know how an interview works, we cover all the bases and go over all the ground. You never know what might be important so better to cover it than realise you've missed something.'

Dominic waited a beat. 'No, she didn't know.' He hung his head again. 'I was too good at being deceptive. She had no idea. I'm glad that she didn't know and wasn't hurt. I'm ashamed of myself and my behaviour. When she's home I'll make it up to her. I'll show her how much I love her. She'll need so much love and care and I can give it to her.'

'Okay,' she said. 'I can't believe you did it again, but our focus has to be on finding Ruth.' She was still furious with him, for doing it again, but they had bigger issues to be dealing with. She would talk to him about his behaviour later when they weren't being recorded in a custody suite.

'I've been completely honest with you. You can't believe what that bastard says to you. He has her. You know that from the lipstick we found in the garage. I don't know how he dare deny it after leaving that behind. I don't know what game he's playing but don't let him screw with you, Claudia. I've given you everything. Now please hunt the bastard down.'

Claudia regarded him closely. Never had she been through anything so difficult in her life. Only further examination of the Strangler case would help her sort through this. They had to keep going with the interview. Difficult as it was.

CHAPTER 49

Dominic

Three weeks ago

Nearly six months had passed and the Sheffield Strangler had managed to evade detection and arrest. He had also managed to kill a further three women. These women fitted the same profile. They were in their forties, they had one or more children and were using the Close to Me dating app.

'We've liaised with the undercover team,' Kapoor said in the morning briefing. The mood was heavy. It had been a long haul and they'd trudged in day after day and pulled their weight for all that time. Putting in the hours and the emotional energy, in an attempt to bring this killer to justice, with no break in the case. The team had expanded. More staff had been brought in to give it fresh eyes and an injection of new blood. 'We're going to see how they can help us with this. We can't let him keep killing this way. It seems that he's changed his photograph on the dating site, but one that still makes sure he can't be identified. The app has noted a decline in use but women are still lonely and still using the app, believing it won't happen to them. But, unfortunately, it has to happen to someone.'

That night was the night Ruth came home and told Dominic she had been assigned the case. She was to be the lone single woman who would start using the site, with a profile that said she was a single mother. This meant she had to go out on several dates as men asked to meet her, because they never knew which men were genuine and which were the killer. This caused tension in the house as she readied herself for her dates. Dominic stressed that she was either on a date with an eligible bachelor or a crazed killer and the tension within the house grew. They were barely speaking to each other by this point. Dominic didn't know how to talk to her. He was so consumed by the case that life outside of work was meaningless to him.

As far as the investigation went, Ruth was an attractive woman so she had quite a lot of hits on the app. It was a busy time for her. The team were with her every step of the way and she said she was never afraid at any point. If it looked to be a genuine date and not the killer one of the team would text her that there was a problem with her 'son' and she would make her escape. The undercover team were prepared to be in it for as long as was needed. They were sure he would connect with Ruth at some point. The way the app worked was you could have conversations through the app for as long as you wanted before you set yourself up on a date. At all times Ruth had multiple conversations going as well as arranging dates. She made it clear on her profile she had a young son and reiterated this in the conversations. Because it was in her profile, she only got hits from men who were okay with this. It seemed it was the expected thing of a woman of her age to have already had their children. It wasn't as shocking as it might have been had she been dating when she was in her twenties.

Two weeks in and the team thought they might have started chatting to the right man as the image on his profile photo was blurry and his face was hard to make out.

Dominic's instinct to forbid Ruth from meeting him fought with his desire to catch this monster.

CHAPTER 50

Claudia

Forty hours since Ruth's attack

'You're being bailed.' Claudia stared at her father across the interview-room table.

'What's happened?' he asked.

'We want time to get a better picture. You'll have conditions, of course. I want your passport. You're not to leave the country. But the evidence so far is circumstantial. You know that, you're a cop. The evidence is in your home. Any prints or DNA found is likely to have a genuine reason for being there. We got the results back on the lipstick, your prints aren't on it.'

'You think I'm the Sheffield Strangler?' He sounded incredulous.

Claudia ran a hand through her hair. 'Of course not, he contacted us while you were in custody, which is the main reason you're being bailed.' A strand fell back down in front of her eyes.

'And if he hadn't?'

She shook her head.

'You're not sure, are you?'

'Of course I am. You're my father.' The reality was that she was confused by the whole situation and needed solid evidence one way or another. What they had now was neither here nor there. 'Do you want this bail or not?'

Dominic stared at her. 'I didn't do this, Claudia. I promise you. Once you find her, you'll know that.'

She stared at him.

'You know I want bail. I want to do something more proactive to find Ruth than sitting in here like I have for the past two days.'

'It's late now, there's not a lot you can do. We don't have a body.' She bit her lip. 'I'm sorry, Dad, but you know the score, it's how we work. If she hasn't survived we don't have as much evidence of the offence until we have her body.'

'I want her back, Claudia, in one way, shape or form. Be she alive or dead. I would rather have my wife back but if you have a body then you have a body.' He stopped talking and stared down at the table.

'It's been so long and she's lost a lot of blood,' Claudia said. 'The odds aren't in her favour. I'm so sorry, Dad.' She stood. 'Let's get you out of here so you can go home.'

'It's safe to go to the house? CSU have finished?'

'Yes, they finished last night. I'd take you but I've got some stuff to do. Will you be okay?' She was tired and just wanted him gone for the day.

'I'll be fine. I drove into work yesterday morning. I just need a lift back to HQ.'

She messed with her hair again. 'Dad, we seized your car.'

There was silence. They stared at each other. Knowing it had to be done. It was the right thing to do once he was arrested for Ruth's murder but that fact was a sore between them now. One they were to worry at or avoid at all costs for the pain it might cause.

'I'll see what I—' Claudia started.

'Don't worry. I'll get one of the lads from the station to take me home.' He spoke over her.

Her cheeks coloured. 'I'm sorry, Dad.'

He shook his head. 'Don't be. You were only doing your job.'

She opened the door to the interview room. 'I'm sorry they decided I had to lead this investigation and interview you.'

He shook his head again. 'It's fine, honestly. You were the best person they could think of and if that's what they thought then I'm good with that. All I'm interested in is getting Ruth back.'

Claudia went to speak to the custody sergeant. 'Any word on the telephone number yet?'

'It's a pay-as-you-go.' His mood was sombre.

Claudia rolled her eyes. 'Pretty much as expected.'

'Paid for in cash and the store doesn't have CCTV. It's only a small corner shop.'

'So it's going nowhere.' She was sick of this job. People watched far too many crime dramas and knew how the police investigated crime and therefore knew how to avoid detection. It frustrated the hell out of her.

'If I'd realised, I could have kept him talking,' the sergeant complained.

She'd been annoyed with him earlier but there really wasn't anything to be done and she told him as much. 'He wouldn't have talked to you. It's not likely he would have let slip something that would have helped us. He's too smart for that. He's proved too smart all the way through this. That's why the investigation has been running so long.' She could see her words were not having much effect on the sergeant. He was berating himself for his earlier slip. 'Thank you for running the number though.'

'The least I could do. I've had the results emailed to you for reference.'

She thanked him, completed the necessary work to release Dominic then unlocked his cell and let him out.

He looked smaller than she remembered him being before this started. More shrivelled and, if possible, more grey. His skin pallor and his hair.

'Let's get you back,' she urged him into the sunlight out of the building.

Back at HQ Dominic walked into the corridors of the station, looking for a friend, a colleague who could run him home. Kane walked to the incident room and Claudia went to her office. There was a pile of paperwork she needed to do to make sure what had occurred over the last couple of days was above board. For all Sharpe's promises of there being nothing untoward, Claudia didn't want to risk it and would write up her own account.

Several hours later her eyes were crossing and she could no longer think straight. As far as she could see, everything had been covered as far as her involvement in her dad's case went. It was time to go and see Sharpe and catch up with her.

Sharpe was in her office, head bent over some paperwork on her desk. 'Ah, Claudia, you've finished up for the day?' Sharpe looked pristine. As though she had only just walked into her office, not that she'd been there for a very long day.

'Dominic's been bailed,' Claudia said sitting in the chair opposite Sharpe without waiting for an invitation. She was too tired for politeness.

'And your thoughts after spending two days with him?'

'He's my dad . . .' She paused, attempting to parse out her thoughts.

Sharpe waited her out.

'The bottom line is I need evidence. You know me, the way I work. There isn't a rule book I don't like.' She bit her lower lip. 'They don't have the perfect marriage. He admitted to an affair with Hayley Loftus who's on his team, but said it's over or it's going to be over.' She rubbed at her eyes. 'I'm not sure which it is to be honest.'

'Could be motive.' Sharpe shuffled the papers in front of her and tidied them into a neat pile, tapping the edges on the desk to align them.

'He'd been caught lying to us, he had to be honest about it. I don't think it's anything more than a work fling that has probably run its course. We have the lipstick in the same make and colour the Sheffield Strangler uses, at the scene where Ruth was taken.'

'Mmm.' Sharpe was thoughtful. 'You heard from him this morning.'

'Yeah, said he doesn't have Ruth.'

'What do you think of that?'

'Dominic seems to think he's waiting to dump her so we can find her body. Says he likes the ritual of the burial, and the strangulation. It's his thing. It's what gets him off. Dominic thinks the Strangler wants us to find her like that. I think Dominic has a point. He's worked the case for six months. He knows the guy pretty well.'

'You're right. And there was nothing on the lipstick?'

'No. There never has been in any of the cases. It's not unusual.'

'What about Ruth's cells on the lipstick, has he used it on her yet?'

'I didn't want to tell Dominic this but yes, he had smeared the lipstick on Ruth.' Claudia let out a long sigh. The last two days had been difficult.

'Go home, Claudia. It's a new day tomorrow. We have a late shift on tonight, they'll keep making enquiries and will be available should anything come in overnight, but for now, you need some sleep or you'll be no use to anyone and I want you fresh for tomorrow.'

Claudia stretched her arms over her head and yawned, only now realising how tired she was, though it was doubtful she would actually sleep.

'You look like shit,' Sharpe said.

Claudia didn't comment. But how was it she looked like shit and Sharpe looked immaculate? She rose from the chair. 'I'll see you tomorrow.'

'Bright and early, Claudia.'

* * *

It felt like she'd only been away from her desk a couple of hours when Claudia found herself sitting back at her desk the next morning. She immediately started to type up the interview from the previous day. She had an hour or so before the rest of the team was due in. It should give her enough time to catch up on deskwork. She needed to go through her emails. Two days of not going near them meant they would be stacking up.

Staff started to trickle in. Then it was time to do a team briefing and see where everyone was up to with their enquiries. She looked at the clock, eight a.m. They should be ready for her now.

Claudia's office was two doors away from the incident room. She liked that she was close to her team. It meant she was accessible and she liked that they came to her if they had a problem. She strode the short distance to the morning briefing.

'Sorry I didn't get to see much of you yesterday. It was a tough day all round and I want to thank you for your dedication and professionalism as well as your generosity in dealing with such a sensitive job. I'm sure you've already collared Russ and if I know him, he's been discreet and not given anything away.'

Kane inclined his head in agreement.

'We've no leads on Ruth and it looks like the Sheffield Strangler has her, but we don't count her out until we have her body. Do I make myself clear?'

There was a quiet round of agreement in the room.

'So, let's get on and work through what we have.'

Graham went first, updating the room about the forensics on the lipstick and that it was clean other than having Ruth's DNA on the actual lipstick itself. Though it didn't fit with the usual scenes of being left with the body, the make and colour did match that of the Sheffield Strangler and that was a part of the MO that hadn't been made public.

Claudia looked at Harry. 'You were tasked with liaising with the source handling team to see if anyone on the streets had heard anything about the missing woman or the Sheffield Strangler. How did you get on?'

Harry leaned back in his chair. 'No one is reporting having heard anything. It seems that the killer is pretty much keeping to himself.'

It was as she expected.

'Have we had any results from the photofit we put out?'

Harry again. 'There have been a few phone calls from people who think they recognise him, but we've followed through on them and the majority have alibis for the time period Ruth went missing — it was the easiest period to check. You know what people are like, they want to be involved in a high-profile murder investigation so are nominating their neighbours. Poor guys are gobsmacked.'

'Someone does know him though.' She was exasperated they were no closer.

Harry kept quiet. There was nothing to add. Claudia took a deep breath. 'Russ and I interviewed Dominic Harrison and, for anyone who doesn't know, he's my dad.' Silence smothered the room. 'He was distraught as you'd expect him to be. He was adamant the Sheffield Strangler has done this as he's been chasing him for the last six months and thinks the killer wants him off his tail. If it is the Sheffield Strangler, and the lipstick goes some way to prove that it is, then this is as good a way as any to get the detective you see as bothersome off your back. His focus is going to be directed elsewhere. Little does our killer realise there's a huge team involved in tracking him and not just the one who he's been liaising with.'

She let the information sink in. 'Today we continue to work with the Sheffield Strangler investigation team. It's going to be another long day, I'm afraid.'

Claudia thanked them and walked back to her office. There was a small pile of mail waiting for her. She picked up the top envelope as she seated herself behind her desk. It was hand-delivered as it had no stamp or postmark. She opened it and stared as she read the note. Then dropped it on the desk, picked up her phone and photographed the paper in front of her as she re-read it.

> *DI Nunn,*
>
> *It's unusual for me to make a phone call. Letters are my usual mode of communication. I wanted to make sure you believe I do not have your missing officer. Because taking a cop is a step too far and I need you to believe this. I want to meet with you, so I can prove I do not have her. Come alone and I'll tell you where I was and what I was doing at the time she was taken. But you must come alone. I do not trust anyone else. If I see signs of any other police presence I will not show up. Trust that I will know if they're there. To find out the truth, meet with me at the graveyard at Cemetery Avenue at 11 a.m. in front of the Nonconformist chapel. Don't be late or risk your investigation being stuck in the wrong place and your cop running out of time.*

A sudden coldness filled her chest and her skin prickled. This was direct contact from the Sheffield Strangler and he wanted to meet with her. She had no idea what she was going to do. It was a chance to finally capture him, but he'd said she had to be alone and he'd know if other cops were present. She had no idea what he had put in place to detect the other cops, but she was wary of scaring him off if she could get into a real dialogue with him while Ruth was still missing. Ruth was the priority here. She didn't want to do anything to jeopardise her safe return. If going to speak to him, under whatever pretence he was setting up, was a way to get Ruth back safely then she would do whatever was needed. And that included going to meet him.

But without backup?

It just wasn't something she was capable of doing. It went against everything she stood for. She was a rule-follower.

But what about Ruth? What if involving the troops got Ruth killed?

277

This guy said he didn't have her and if he didn't have her then what was the risk? Though the whole point for Claudia was to find Ruth. There was a chance he was lying to her and this made her wonder what game he was playing.

Claudia looked at her watch. She didn't have much time. The Sheffield Strangler, as the press dubbed him, had obviously planned it so that the police couldn't easily set up any kind of surveillance or anything where they were to meet. She couldn't do this on her own though, no matter what his instructions were, it wasn't how she was built.

She had to get moving if she was to do everything she needed: to update Sharpe and also to appraise herself of where the location of the meet was. She wanted to make sure she arrived in plenty of time, calm and organised. Quickly she dialled the Crime Scene Unit and informed them there was a letter on her desk that needed processing.

The next stop was Sharpe. Claudia printed out the photographed letter and with hot paper in hand she ran up the stairs to Sharpe's office. Her head was spinning with fear and anticipation of what the next hour was going to look like. The apprehension of how this would go down with the Sheffield Strangler, and of locating Ruth wherever she may be and whatever state she may be in.

Maxine, Sharpe's PA, was at her desk and Claudia could see beyond her into Sharpe's office. It was empty. Claudia's veins ran cold.

'Where is she? I need to see her, urgently,' she said as Maxine looked up.

'She's on her way back from a meeting with Connelly and the PCC. She shouldn't be long.'

Claudia paced backwards and forwards in front of Maxine's desk. 'How long do you think she's going to be?'

Maxine looked at the clock on her computer monitor then shook her head. 'I really couldn't say. She sent me a text when she was leaving to say she was on her way back. That was about twenty minutes ago.'

Claudia, desperate to get to the cemetery on time and not miss the Strangler, shifted impatiently in front of Maxine's desk. It was urgent that she had backup. She needed to let Sharpe know about the meeting. Yes, she could organise the backup herself in normal circumstances, but these weren't normal circumstances, she was on the clock. She needed to be doing other things and allowing someone else, someone higher up, to be organising the support. Plus, Sharpe really needed to be in the know.

She looked into the room again. Nothing had changed. The chair behind Sharpe's desk was still sitting empty.

'Do you want to leave a message?' Maxine asked as Claudia paced past her desk once more.

Claudia scrubbed a hand through her hair. She needed to identify the meeting place and she also had to put a call in to her dad. He deserved to know what was happening after what he'd gone through yesterday. She checked her watch, looked to the empty office and then to Maxine.

'No, I'll call her. It's too important.'

Maxine went back to her work and Claudia dialled Sharpe's number.

As soon as the phone started to ring, Claudia realised she was holding her breath. Her chest was tight and the air around her suddenly seemed far too hot. Slowly she let it out as she paced in front of Maxine's desk waiting for Sharpe to pick up.

The ringtone cut off sharply with no answer, not even voicemail. She tried again, and again there was no response.

Maxine looked up at her a question in her eyes.

'I think she's on another call,' said Claudia. 'She's not picking up.'

Claudia tried again. Where the hell was she? Again the call ended with no connection.

She had no choice. She had to move on this, regardless of the difficulties with Sharpe. It went against everything she was but it had to be this way.

Claudia wanted to pull her hair out.

'Maxine, I have to go but I need you to pass on a message the second Sharpe steps foot through that door.' Claudia urgently needed the backup organising, but if she didn't leave now then she'd miss him. 'Don't let her start issuing orders on anything else. Interrupt her if you have to.'

Maxine frowned.

'You'll understand why when I tell you.'

Maxine picked up her pen and readied herself to take dictation. A minute later Claudia was reading back the note. Then she handed over the photocopy of the letter to go with it, thanked the woman and ran back down the stairs to her office.

The next thing to do was find out where she was going and plan her route. Her mind jittered as she waited for the computer to chug through the screens as she searched for her destination. Eventually she had another printout in hand. Placing it on her desk she pulled her phone out of her pocket. This call was going to be difficult.

She dialled the number and he picked up straight away.

'Have you heard anything?'

'No, I'm sorry, Dad, not yet.'

The line went quiet.

'Did you manage to get any sleep?' she asked. Knowing he would have had very little if her night was anything to go by.

'I had some.' He was trying to make her feel okay. She wasn't going to call him out on it. 'What is it?' he asked. 'Are you okay?'

'I'm fine,' she lied. 'It's just something has come up I thought you should know about. It's a little . . .' She paused, the fact that this really was not in the rulebook needling at her. More silence played out along the network line as she tried to figure out how to phrase it and how much to tell him. She had called him too quickly before she had thought it through.

'What is it?' Dominic asked.

Claudia read the letter on her phone again, scared by the implications it held. Scared for Ruth and scared for what she was about to do.

'You're worrying me,' Dominic said.

'Don't worry. It's just that something came up this morning and it's a little out of the usual lines of policing, but it might help us to locate Ruth.'

'You're going to do it?'

'Of course I am. If it will help get Ruth back, then I'm all in.'

'What is it? How far outside of the lines are you colouring, Claudia? Is it dangerous?' He'd asked the most pertinent question last of all. How was she supposed to answer? She didn't believe she was in danger. The man wanted to prove a point, have a discussion with her. He was obviously getting agitated about a cop being involved, it was doubtful he was going to involve another cop in his evil games. These were things she was telling herself.

'I can't give you the details. I don't want to involve you. Look at yesterday, you're already too far involved in this as it is. It's pretty far outside the lines but it's worth it if it pays off, wouldn't you say?'

'I want Ruth back, Claudia, but not at the expense of you. Whatever it is, don't do it.'

'I'm sorry, Dad. Take care of yourself today, okay. And I'll call you later and let you know if I have anything.' She hung up the call.

She hadn't meant to scare him the way she just had, but she figured he deserved to know what was happening, especially with what he went through yesterday.

Now she was ready, it was time to leave and meet the Sheffield Strangler in person. This was their chance to catch him and to find Ruth.

As she travelled her nerves started to get the better of her. So many things could go wrong: he could fail to turn up; this could be a trap of some description that she couldn't figure out because they didn't have enough time; he could spot the cops in their hiding places and make a run for it and they lose their chance to not only arrest the Strangler but lose their chance to locate Ruth, and that was all Claudia was really interested in today.

Police operations took a huge amount of effort and planning. Usually days. This was set up ridiculously quickly. A message for Sharpe and rushing out the door hoping the backup could get there in time. If anyone was capable of doing it Sharpe was that person.

She drove out to Cemetery Avenue, parked up and left her vehicle, checking her phone as she walked to see if Sharpe had given her any specific operational directions. Claudia's main objective was to locate Ruth but if Sharpe had pushed this up the chain and Connelly had got involved then just making the arrest of the killer who had been terrorising the city for the last six months might be their main concern. Her nerves were getting the better of her. Her heart thundered in her chest and her mouth was like a desert.

There was nothing on her phone.

This didn't feel right but she had to trust that Sharpe wouldn't leave her out here alone.

Was the Sheffield Strangler really going to meet her and allow her to see his face? He would be known, and she would be able to identify him for the other murders. Unless of course this was a hoax, someone else not the killer, who was wasting her time. Wanting to be involved in the police investigation. She hadn't considered this. Though the public didn't know how he communicated with them so that was something on his side. But without direct communication there was no way she could prove one way or the other until he got here. And hopefully, face or not, they were going to be able to make an arrest anyway.

Nerves ran through her veins. Itching like a clutter of spiders running rampant as she walked through the Egyptian Gate into the cemetery, the richly ornamented gate bearing snakes with tails in their mouths did little to ease her nerves. She had to get herself under control.

Claudia followed his instructions, taking a dirt track that would lead to the chapel. The sun was breaking through the clouds, making Claudia feel unreasonably warm and uncomfortable. She took several turns until she was in a part of the cemetery that didn't look as cared for and was more discreet. She looked at her watch. It was two minutes past eleven. There was no sign of anyone around. Had she missed him? Was he so punctual that her tardiness had prevented her helping Ruth? Sweat beaded at the base of her neck and slipped down her spine. She'd wait and rely on the fact he said he was coming.

Claudia hoped her backup was silently stashed away where no one could see them — including her. She didn't like the idea of standing out here alone waiting for a killer.

CHAPTER 51

Claudia

Claudia checked her watch again — seven minutes past. How long would she wait? She was prepared to wait as long as it took if it would get her to the truth about Ruth. But how long exactly was 'as long as it took'?

And although she was hopeful, she couldn't spot any sign of her support team hiding out behind overgrown tombs or leaning headstones, waiting to pounce at the earliest opportunity.

Claudia pulled her phone out of her pocket and dialled Sharpe. She picked up on the first ring.

'Ma'am, it's Claudia.' She kept her voice low in case she should be interrupted, in case he was listening, waiting to see if they had prepared this.

'Why are you whispering, Claudia?'

'I'm at the cemetery.'

'The cemetery? Why? Is this something I should be aware of?'

A stone-cold brick landed in Claudia's stomach. 'Where's Maxine?'

'Oh, she had to dash off, her daughter fell off some bars or something in gym class at school. Broken her arm and banged her head pretty badly. Apparently the poor girl was unconscious for a while. Maxine was in floods of tears when I arrived back from my meeting. She'd only just found out. I had to get someone to take her, she was in no state to drive herself.'

Claudia looked around at the cold grey stones littering the ground — the silent empty grounds of the cemetery.

She was alone.

It was then she heard the heavy footsteps. She froze. The blood rushing through her veins turning to ice as the sun shone down on her. It was only now she realised what a dangerous move this was. How stupid she'd been not to have organised this herself. Was she about to become the next victim? Was she about to meet Ruth trussed up in a warehouse somewhere, where no one would hear her screams?

Her breath caught in her chest and she ended the call and placed the phone back in her pocket and, as she did, she checked for the CS cannister she'd placed there before leaving the station. The cold solidity of the metal cannister in her hand provided security and some resolve.

She could do this. She had to do this.

'DI Nunn, I presume.' The voice was close and behind her. She could almost feel the warmth of his breath against her neck, the small hairs rose in response and she shuddered. She was alone with him.

There was no support team. Maxine hadn't passed on her message. Sharpe was unaware where she was or what she was doing. If this went wrong, then she was gone. She had no one to rely on but herself so she had to pull herself together because this was now life or death.

Her life.

Her death.

She spun around, dirt kicking up from below her boots.

The male was about six feet tall, dressed in jeans and a light jumper with a plain white plastic mask over his face. It looked out of place in the middle of the day and in a cemetery like this, and though his face was obscured, he nevertheless managed to make her skin crawl. His hair, she could see over the top of it, was short and dark, peppered with silver at the sides.

In his gloved hand was a large bladed knife. The silver-coloured blade currently pointing down following the line of his leg. His grip seemed relaxed.

Her stomach twisted and her legs started to shake as they held her upright. This had been a stupid move. She would not let him take her. Had he brought her here so he could have two cops and not just the one?

Had she really been that stupid?

He saw her eyes find the knife. 'It's insurance. I'm not here to hurt you, but I'm not here to be taken in, you understand.' His eyes flicked around the grounds. Happy they were still alone, he focused back on Claudia.

'I thought you weren't coming.' It was all she could do to make her voice level and calm when inside she was shaking and struggling to hold it together.

'I had to make sure you followed instructions and didn't bring anyone with you. I'm glad to see you listened to me.'

It hadn't been on purpose. How angry she was with herself. 'How do I know you're really him?' She had little doubt but it needed clarifying.

'Because you haven't released the significant part of my MO to the public. I leave a very specific lipstick at the scene.'

A shiver travelled down her spine. Her already unstable legs made even more unusable. She was standing in front of the Sheffield Strangler. She could hear the rumble of traffic on the road in the distance and it reminded her how fragile she was here right now.

She shoved her hands into her pockets, gripped the CS cannister, inhaled, tried to get a tight hold of herself. She was a cop not some innocent woman who hadn't known what was coming. She wouldn't be easy to take.

But neither, she imagined, had Ruth been.

The blade on the knife looked lethal. Long, sleek, sharp. 'Why did you want to see me?'

'I don't like being blamed for work I haven't done. I haven't taken your cop. You need to look elsewhere.' He sounded serious. This was not something he wanted laying at his door.

'But there are signs it is you, how can you prove it's not?' She wanted answers and he was here, prepared to give her them. The shaking in her legs started to quiet down. It was a unique opportunity even if she was unable to take him in on her own. She certainly had no intention of getting into a knife fight with him when no one knew she was here. Again she kicked herself for how wrong this had gone. All she could do was make the most of the situation in front of her.

'Your cop is married to the officer hunting me, is she not?'

'You know she is.'

'Then I also know she has no children.'

Claudia frowned. 'What does that have to do with anything?' The interview with Dominic came back to her, the profile for the Sheffield Strangler. The women had children.

'I'm doing it for the children. So they don't suffer like I did.'

'CLAUDIA!' There was a sudden shout from the distance. Panic and fear in the sound.

Claudia turned to look. Someone was running towards her. Too far away to make out who it was. She hadn't told anyone about the meeting. Someone could have been in her drawer and found the letter . . .

The knife suddenly shot out towards her. 'You said you came alone!'

Claudia's hands flew out of her pockets in submission, raised to her shoulders, the cannister gripped in her hand, the lid popped and ready to emit its violent spray. 'I did. I don't know how he's here. I didn't bring him, you have to believe me.' This couldn't be happening. She nearly had answers. It was falling apart. How could she stop this? She'd wanted support but now she wanted answers about Ruth.

He took a step toward her, the blade of the knife twisting in his hand as it edged closer.

Claudia automatically took a step back. 'Tell me how I can know you don't have her!' She had to salvage something from this meeting.

The man was nearly on them, his footsteps echoing loud on the compact ground in the quiet space. His shouts of 'Claudia' ringing out around them.

The man in the mask turned away, ready to run.

'Tell me!' Claudia begged, desperation tearing at the edges of her voice.

He turned back to her briefly. 'Ruth doesn't have children. Haven't you noticed that all the victims have had one or more children? There's a reason for that and if there's ever a day that you catch me you may very well find out what that reason is. But for now, you have to trust that I wouldn't kill unless the woman had a child.' And with that he was running in the opposite direction to the man who had appeared.

Then he was there on top of her. He grabbed Claudia by her arms. Gripped her tightly, fingers squeezing and digging into flesh. 'Claudia, what the hell!'

She rounded on him, all fear gone the way of the man she had been talking with. It had been replaced with fury. Red-hot rage. 'Dad, what the fuck? What are you doing here? You just blew it. He's gone. He was talking to me and now he's gone.' She screamed at him, frustration driving her forward. She pulled her arms out of his grasp. He had no claim on her. And why was he so panicked about her doing her job?

Dominic stepped back. 'You were talking to . . .' He paused. Searched for a word. 'A maniac.' Then he went with it. 'It wasn't safe, Claudia. It's a good job I followed you from the nick. You could've been the next person he took and I don't think I could've lived with that. I've already lost Ruth to him; I couldn't lose you as well.'

'You followed me?' She was furious. Blood pounded in her head. He was playing on her emotions, but it wasn't enough. She had been so close and he was responsible for screwing it all up. She had to get herself under control.

'Of course I fucking followed you after that phone call. I sensed you were going to do something stupid and look at what you did? Don't you think Ruth could have done something like this and this was how he took her? How stupid can you be? Did you not tell anyone?'

She turned away from him not wanting him to see the anger raging inside her. He was obviously afraid for her, but he had jeopardised the whole investigation because he had got too close.

'Did you tell anyone, Claudia?'

He was treating her like a child. Not like a detective inspector. A cop of higher rank than he was. 'Of course I told someone,' she said eventually knowing she had in fact been alone out there. 'I also told you.'

'Jesus Christ.' He ran his hands through his hair. 'Anything could have happened to you, Claudia. You barely told me anything. What the hell were you thinking?'

She turned back to him, finding it difficult to hold back the fury she was feeling. 'I was thinking I could obtain a lead on Ruth. After what you went through the last two days, I thought I could get him to tell me where she was and get her home for you.'

Dominic's own anger subsided a little. He took her by her arms again and looked her up and down, saw she was okay and backed away from her. 'Okay, okay. What did you find out?'

She barked out a laugh. 'How did you expect me to find anything out when you come stampeding into the meeting like John Wayne trying to protect the poor little woman.' She couldn't help herself. The anger was still simmering. 'I'm sorry,' she said. 'It's just he was right here with me. Talking to me. Who knows what he would have told me if you hadn't turned up.'

Dominic shook his head. 'I can't apologise for turning up, for following you, Claudia. You're my daughter. You're all I have left. I'm not going to risk losing you.' He paused, then in a much quieter voice, he added, 'I saw the knife he was holding.'

She would never admit to her own fear. Instead she defended him. 'He said it was in case I tried to take him in.'

'He had to give you an excuse, right up until the moment he forced you to go with him because he'd got it stuck into your side and you couldn't say no.'

Claudia exhaled. She would never win this argument with him. He had been scared for her and would never back down that he didn't need to be. In his eyes he had protected his daughter. 'Shall we go and grab a drink?' she asked. 'We both need to calm down somewhat before I head back to work and you go back home.'

CHAPTER 52

Claudia

They entered the coffee shop and Dominic went to the till to pay for the drinks while Claudia found a table. As she was sitting her phone rang. It was Sharpe.

'Ma'am?'

'Have I caught you at a bad time? You ended the last call quite abruptly.' There was something in her voice Claudia couldn't place.

'No, ma'am. I'm getting a drink with my father. Making sure he's okay and bringing him up to speed with where we are so far today.' Sharpe didn't need to know what had just happened right now; she'd update her in person.

She heard the exhale and something inside her fractured and went cold.

'I was going to ask you to come to my office, but bearing in mind what you've told me I think I should inform you now.'

The cold ball in the pit of her stomach started to spread out.

'I'm sorry to have to tell you this, Claudia, but Ruth's body has been found.'

The coffee shop closed in around her. In her peripheral vision, tilted at the side, she could see her father carrying two steaming mugs towards her.

'Claudia?' Sharpe's voice broke through the grey fuzz that had become Claudia's world.

'Yes, sorry, I'm here.'

'I'm sorry, Claudia. Do you want me to send someone to bring you both in? So you don't have to drive.' It was unusual for Sharpe to show this level of concern.

'How did she . . . how?'

'Initial findings at the scene would indicate that it's the work of the Sheffield Strangler.' Her voice was quiet. Respectful.

Claudia thought back to the conversation not twenty minutes ago — *I wouldn't kill unless the woman had a child.*

'Anything different?' she asked as Dominic placed the mugs down on the table sitting himself opposite her. Her skin prickled in fear at what she had to tell him. It could be a copycat. The man she met had been right about the women.

'To the MO?'

'Yes.'

'Not that I'm being told at this point.' *I wouldn't kill unless the woman had a child.* 'You'll make your way in?'

'Yes. I'll see you soon.'

'Okay. Again, I'm sorry, Claudia.' And the phone went dead.

Claudia looked across at her dad. The words lodged in her throat.

Dominic pushed the drink towards her. 'You've had a bit of a fright this morning, but if you drink this you'll start to feel better. You look dreadful. In fact I'd say you look as bad I think I look.' He forced a smile.

This wasn't the place to tell him, but she couldn't put it off. She couldn't make small talk for half an hour, knowing what she knew and then tell him later. He was trying to take care of her and she knew his wife was dead. She had to tell him. 'Dad, we need to go.' She stood. Picked up her car keys from the table. 'I'll take you into work if you want. You can speak to whomever you want about the investigation.' She needed to get him into the car.

'I've brought my own car, Claudia, well, a hire car, bearing in mind you have mine. I don't need you to take me into work. How do you think I followed you this morning?'

Of course he had.

'Sit, finish your drink.' He looked up at her. 'What is it, Claudia?'

She was immobile.

'Claudia?'

She had delivered so many death messages. But never one to her own family. How do you deliver one to someone you loved? 'Dad . . .'

He stood, comprehension dawning. 'No.'

How was it people knew before the words were uttered what the news was? He had to have been half-expecting it. 'I'm so sorry, Dad.'

He shook his head. 'Where?'

'I don't have the details. Sharpe has asked us to go in.'

'She knows we're together?'

'She does.'

Dominic shuffled around the table to her side.

'I'm sorry, Dad.'

He took her hand like a small child and they walked out of the coffee shop. Their drinks completely untouched.

CHAPTER 53

Claudia

Sharpe wasn't in her office. The large room was empty.

'I know where she'll be if she's not in here,' Claudia said and led her dad back downstairs and outside.

'She's outside?' Dominic queried.

Claudia quietly led him to the smoking shed where Sharpe was puffing away on a cig. In the far corner desperately trying to be unseen by her was a uniformed cop. As soon as Claudia and her dad turned up he paled even more, stubbed out what was left of his cigarette and left.

'Oh, Dom, I'm so sorry.' Sharpe flicked ash off her cig as she spoke to him. Her eyes holding genuine sympathy.

'Thank you.'

Sharpe took two steps forward and placed her arms around Dominic. Claudia stared at her, shocked by the public show of empathy that her boss was exhibiting.

Dominic was stiff in her arms. She held the hug for a couple of seconds, cigarette smoke winding its way up from her fingers, then stepped away.

'What can you tell us?' asked Claudia getting straight down to business.

Sharpe looked grateful to be heading back into familiar territory. 'At first look it seems to be the Sheffield Strangler. We'll know more after the PM but first impressions are pretty strong, so I'm told.'

'And my dad?'

Sharpe inhaled on her cigarette and waited a beat as it hit her lungs. Then she looked at Dominic. 'Pending the results of the PM, your bail will be cancelled and we'll be focusing on catching the Strangler.'

Claudia gave Dominic a weak smile. It wasn't worth much. They would both much rather have Ruth back than any resolution to Dominic's predicament. But as it stood it was good to know he was in the clear.

'As I'm no longer a suspect, what can you tell me about the investigation?' Dominic asked.

Claudia wished he would break down and go home. Grieve for his wife, but she also kind of understood his need to have something to focus on after the last couple of days. It had been traumatic for him being arrested for her murder when he'd been innocent all along. Only to find she'd been killed by the Strangler when he'd been saying that during the entire time he'd been in custody. Could they have done anything differently? Could they have found her before she died? Claudia didn't think so.

It was then she remembered the folded piece of paper she'd shoved in her bag. She hadn't shown it to her father. She heard Sharpe updating him on what actions the team who were investigating Ruth's murder — it was no longer Claudia's team now she'd been found — were taking, as she rummaged through the glut of rubbish she had in her handbag.

Then she found it and produced it with a bit of a flurry. 'Dad, I haven't shown you this.' She waved it in front of him. Still folded.

His brow wrinkled. 'What is it?'

'It's the photofit of the man the witness your team identified managed to create.'

He snatched the paper out of her hands. 'What results have you had from it?'

Claudia frowned. 'Not much I'm afraid. We had some calls but we seem to have knocked the majority of them out. I think there are still a few to follow up on.'

Dominic opened the paper up and stared down at it. A slight breeze blew through them and rippled the paper in his hands. Dominic's eyes narrowed.

'Dad?'

'I know this man.' He sounded confused.

Sharpe stepped closer. 'You do?'

'Yeah. I can't place him, but I know him.' He squinted at the image. 'Why do I know him?'

'Someone you've already talked to in the investigation?' Sharpe offered. 'A witness?' She threw down her cigarette and placed her pointed toe on the stub crushing it out. Again disregarding the bins at the side of the shed.

Dominic shook his head. 'I don't know. I don't think so.' He rubbed a hand along his jawline. 'It's certainly not Alex Chapman who I had a thing for.' He looked up at Claudia. 'What did this witness see?'

She was shocked that her dad recognised the image. If she'd only shown it to him earlier they may have been able to make a move and find Ruth.

'Claudia.' Dominic gave her a nudge.

'Sorry.' She shook herself. 'The witness said this guy was holding the woman up and herding her along the road. He had control of her.'

'So drugs were involved?'

'Looks that way, but probably ones that leave the system pretty quickly because, as you're aware, there were never any drugs found during post-mortems.'

Dominic looked down at the image again. 'Where do I know you from?' His voice was quiet.

Sharpe looked to Claudia then inclined her head towards the building. They moved away from the smoking shed. Dominic was glued to the spot, staring at the image in front of him.

'Let it percolate,' said Sharpe. 'If you try to force it, you'll end up pushing the answer away. Lessen your grip on the answer.' She stepped further away.

Dominic looked up, realised they were leaving him and pushed the paper into his back pocket and caught them both up.

'You'll get there, Dad.' Claudia wrapped her arm through his. 'It's in there somewhere. It'll dislodge at some point and we can act on it then.'

In Sharpe's office they were met by Kapoor. He offered his condolences. A hand placed on Dominic's shoulder. He could take as much time off as he needed. They'd keep him updated.

Kapoor coughed lightly. 'We're not going to insert a FLO into your life. I'll liaise with you directly. But would you like Victim Support to get in touch?'

It was like a match had touched a badly-made firework. Dominic exploded out of his seat.

'Jesus fucking Christ. How could I not see it?'

The room stared at him.

Dominic yanked the paper from his back pocket, waved it at them. 'I said I recognised him. I TOLD you I recognised him. The guy, the one with the woman, he works from here. He's got access to the nick.'

Mouths were open.

Dominic ran from the room. Claudia, Sharpe and Kapoor chased after him. He ran down the corridor, turned left and came to the stairs, ran down one flight and turned onto the first corridor. He pushed through the door, his arms out, ready to . . . what? Claudia wondered as she tried to keep up with him, what was it exactly he was going to do should he find the person he was looking for. She looked at the sign on the door they'd run to. Victim Support.

Inside the office a young woman, no older than twenty-five, was sitting at a desk, her mouth hung open at the sudden and violent entry.

'Where's Samuel?' screamed Dominic.

The girl couldn't speak.

'Where is he?' Dominic was losing his mind. Claudia grabbed hold of his arm. He shrugged her off.

'DS Harrison.' Sharpe's clipped tone sliced through the room.

The girl recognised Sharpe and her eyes widened even further.

'Samuel?' Sharpe asked in a kinder tone.

'He . . . he's . . . It's his day off today. I think he's at home.'

Dominic spun on his heel and left the room.

CHAPTER 54

Claudia

Claudia sat in the unmarked police car with Kapoor who was standing in for Dominic, who was allowed nowhere near this case at this point in time. A marked van was parked behind them. They were around the corner from Samuel Tyler's home address.

Further discussion with Dominic had revealed that the photofit image was of a clean-shaven male, but the man he knew had a beard. Not difficult for someone to grow and they were popular in the current climate. This is what had made it so difficult for Dominic to place him initially. It was the mention of Victim Support that had triggered his memory.

A deep dive into Tyler had, unsurprisingly, considering his role, found him to have no criminal record. Which, bearing in mind he had jumped straight to violent murder, was the surprising factor. But a search of Social Care records revealed the truth of Tyler's anger at women in their forties. His mother had left him, as a child, unattended, to go out on dates. And on one occasion he had badly burned his whole hand while attempting to feed himself. She had forgotten to feed him in her excitement to go out. Tyler had been placed in the foster care system after that and life hadn't treated him well.

'So, he blames it all on his mother?' Kapoor unclipped his seatbelt.

'It appears that way.'

'And the lipstick?'

'I imagine it was one his mother wore.' Claudia was numb. The man they were after had been under their noses the entire time. She had probably run into him herself at some point. If she'd picked up on something then they wouldn't have lost Ruth. She pushed the car door open. 'Shall we go and do this?'

They climbed out and headed towards his address. Behind her the police van door squealed and boots hit the ground.

They didn't wait for him to answer. With three hits of the ram the front door caved and they piled in, screaming 'Police' as loud as they could. It was dim. The curtains were closed. Samuel Tyler half rose from his position in front of the television. His features sculpting themselves into a mask of shock and horror. The flickering light of the programme in front of him giving the room an eerie glow.

Claudia flicked on a switch and bathed the space in bright light. She strode up to him. He was a little over six feet tall. The man who'd met her at the cemetery. 'Samuel Tyler, I'm arresting you on suspicion of the murder of Ruth Harrison—'

Before she could name the other victims, Tyler started to protest.

'I didn't kill her. I didn't take her. You have this all wrong.' His hands were pulled behind his back. He winced. 'But I didn't do it.'

Claudia named the rest of the victims and cautioned him. Eventually he fell into an uneasy silence.

'I'll take him to the car.' This was no longer Claudia's case. She'd been allowed on the arrest out of courtesy. But once Tyler was in the car and away to the police station it was all out of her hands. The top brass had got what they wanted out of her and now she was being discarded. She'd be angry about the situation if she wasn't so obsessed with Samuel Tyler. He was like a small splinter that was stuck in her thumb that she couldn't get out but kept needling at, the sting a reminder of its presence.

Tyler was the splinter and the sting. Every second she had with him was now precious to her.

The uniformed officer who had Tyler by the arm looked at DI Kapoor who now had control. He gave a short nod and Claudia took Tyler's arm and manoeuvred him out of the room. She knew better than to make a scene about who was in control here. All she cared about was Tyler and Ruth.

Once they were close to the front door and out of earshot of most of the cops in the house Claudia spoke quietly into his ear. 'Why Ruth?' She needed answers. She'd lost her friend. Family.

His head shot up and his eyes bored into hers. 'I didn't take her. I didn't kill her. I told you that.'

She opened what was left of the front door. 'The others?'

He looked back to the floor. A silent agreement without incriminating himself. Then he was looking at her again. 'I told you, she didn't have kids.'

How could she believe a violent killer? Claudia pushed him down the single step and he stumbled, righting himself and scowling at her. 'I didn't kill your cop. That's far too much heat coming down on me.'

They were nearly at the marked police vehicle now. A couple of uniformed cops stood by the side of it waiting to transport Tyler to the police station.

Claudia handed him over. He hadn't given her the answers she wanted. There was a block of stone sitting in the pit of her stomach.

'I didn't do this,' he hissed as one of the cops pushed him into the rear seat with a little too much force.

* * *

301

Claudia's involvement was over. As agreed, she left the scene to be searched by the other officers in attendance and climbed into her own car and drove steadily back to the station. Her mind was a jumble of thoughts. The last three days replayed in varying snippets. She lost focus and ran a red light causing an angry motorist to press his hand to his horn for an inordinate amount of time. Guilt flooded through her but she couldn't correct her error. She continued on.

Once in her office she closed the door to the world and sat silently, looking at her computer occasionally as though she might be prepared to do some work, but she never moved.

A few hours later there was a knock at her door and Sharpe pushed her way in.

'Good God, Claudia, open a window, would you.'

Claudia blinked. How long had she been sitting in here? 'Ma'am.' She rose and unlatched the window, cracking it open, feeling the breeze float across her skin.

Sharpe took the chair across from Claudia's. 'The search team from Tyler's address have updated me.'

Claudia waited.

'They've found several phones they believe to belong to the victims. A couple have blood on. We expect DNA testing to identify it as belonging to the victims. Fingerprints have already been done and Tyler's prints are on them so he can't claim they were placed there by someone else. And by fingerprints I mean his right hand. Did you notice his burnt-up left hand?'

Claudia couldn't remember if she'd seen it. If she had wouldn't it be something that would stick in her mind? 'I'm not sure . . .'

'Dominic said it was something to do with him cooking alone when he was a child. His whole left hand is stripped of flesh and is just angry scar tissue. Anyway, there are even prints from those fingers, which though they can't be identified the same way as typical fingerprints they add to the weight of the evidence against him. He might have been careful at crime scenes, but I don't think he expected us to come through his door. He also had a couple of brand-new House of Maven lipsticks in Velvet Berry. He wasn't planning on stopping. This was a good collar, Claudia.' She paused. 'You've worked hard. We asked a lot of you. I think you need to take a little time off along with your father—'

Claudia opened her mouth to object.

Sharpe held up a well-manicured hand. 'At least for a few days. You need it.'

'Has he gone into interview yet?' Claudia asked.

Sharpe shook her head. 'He's about to. They were waiting to see what the search yielded. It doesn't matter what he says, they have him sown up. He's going down for a very long time. Now forget about Tyler. Go and spend some time with your father. It's not every day we ask you to arrest a parent for murder. We accept this hasn't been ideal, but we are grateful for the hard work you've done.'

Claudia was exhausted. They'd been through so much and now she had to say goodbye to Ruth.

* * *

Two weeks later they gathered for Ruth's memorial.

She couldn't be buried yet as Tyler was fighting the charge of murder for Ruth. He was entitled to a second post-mortem on her body.

The space was heaving with cops in dress uniform. So many people attended that there was standing room outside. She had been a popular officer and friend within the service. Claudia was proud to have known and loved her. Tears welled up in her eyes and she fought to retain a level of professional dignity even though there was nothing undignified about giving in to grief. She wanted to hold it together for her dad who had been a tower of strength these past two weeks. Now he walked up to the front to give his speech.

Dominic stood tall and proud and looked out at the hundreds of mourners that had turned out for his wife. He pushed his shoulders back.

303

'Thank you all for coming today. Ruth would have loved to have seen you all. I'm sorry she has to miss you.'

A tear slipped down Claudia's cheek.

'I know many of you loved Ruth. She was that kind of woman. She was kind and generous and funny and she gave everything to the job and, when she came home in the evening, she gave everything to me. She didn't do anything by halves. It's why I fell for her. She was a whirlwind and she scooped me up and never put me down again. Now the whirlwind is gone and I'm not sure where I'm going to land. I'm lost without her.' His voice cracked and he paused to gather himself.

Claudia swallowed. It was difficult to watch her father struggle this way. She looked down at her feet in an attempt to stop herself falling apart. He needed her now. He didn't need her to be the one going under as he was.

Dominic looked to the photograph of Ruth that stood at the front with him instead of a casket. 'She was taken from us far too soon. She will have put up a fight, she will not have gone willingly. She had too much to live for. Too many people she loved and who loved her in return. Now it's our turn to fight for her. This will not go unpunished. Our love will rise up and we will finish this for her.' His voice dropped. 'I love you, baby.'

Claudia didn't think it was the right place to talk about the killer. This was Ruth's time, but her dad was so caught up in it all she had to let him say what he needed to.

He wiped at his face before he walked over to Claudia. She smiled at him quietly telling him he did good and he sat beside her as the service continued and people paid their respects to his wife.

CHAPTER 55

Dominic

The night of Ruth's attack

It didn't take long to get home. Ruth's car was on the drive. He couldn't remember whether she had driven to work or if she had been picked up by a colleague that morning. He was hard pressed to recall who had left first that day because the mornings were all so alike they blended into each other. It was just a matter of getting ready for work. The usual family morning stuff.

Dominic entered the house — Ruth was home, she'd finished before him. The argument started practically straight away, she'd had enough, she wasn't going to be taken for a fool any longer. This time she had evidence that he'd been seeing that slut Hayley from the office.

His blood froze as she said this. He thought they'd kept it well hidden. They'd been careful. Ruth laughed in his face. Showed him a photograph on her phone of him kissing Hayley in a car park one night before he'd come home to her. She'd followed him. Had enough of his lies. She talked about divorce, about the fact she should have known he would do it again. He'd cheated on his first wife with her. Why on earth wouldn't he do it again?

This time though there would be no happy ending. This time she would shame him for his behaviour. It wasn't a one off. It wasn't a love conquers all. He was a disgrace and all his work colleagues would know. His bosses. His friends and co-workers.

As a woman, Hayley would come out of this worse. She'd be the force slut. Women are never given an easy ride when they slept with men on the job. Her life would be hell. And Ruth laughed.

Dominic refused to engage with her and walked away and closed the curtains, blocking the outside world away.

The fury built up inside him. Like a monster waking from a deep sleep, it rumbled and unfurled as he paced around the house. The words of the argument going around and around in his head, each sentence, each phrase winding him up more and more until he could bear it no longer. Who was she to talk to him this way? How could she do this to him with all he was going through. He'd given his all, he was tired and she was about to tear his world apart.

He entered the kitchen again. Standing behind her as she stood at the sink washing some glasses. He waited quietly, the monster within him watching. Then he heard it.

She exhaled.

He exhaled. It was time. The argument over Hayley had been the last straw. He wouldn't have her divorce him and take him for everything he had, his home, his police pension and with it his reputation. She had her own fucking pension, there was no way she was taking his as well. He wouldn't be made to look like a fool as she wiped him out. And he treasured his reputation. She would destroy it. He couldn't allow that.

She spun around with the glass still in her hand.

She had a weapon in her hands. She wouldn't go down quietly, but he had a plan. He'd been building on the plan for weeks as his relationship with Hayley had blossomed. He hadn't realised that was what he'd been doing, but now it came down to it he realised it was perfect for him. It would sort out all his problems and no one would even look at him. No matter what happened with Hayley he couldn't live with the fact that Ruth had found out.

His face was impassive.

He took a step towards her, his hand outstretched and open, she turned to her right and ran, a scream about to leave her lips as his hand closed on her hair at the back of her head, jerking her back, pulling her feet up from under her. The glass in her hand flying up into the air as she landed with a thud on the floor at his feet. The glass shattered at the side of her head, shards splintering off and embedding themselves into her arm and face.

His hand was tight in her hair. He twisted, increasing his grip, the strands digging into his skin. She cried out, a low complaint in the circumstances. He turned his body so he was bent over her, straddling her. Face to face. There was no coming back from this. If he let her go there would be a nasty domestic assault charge. How could he deal with that in his position?

It was as though she knew.

She reared up, fists and feet flying. She caught him between his legs. He sank down onto her. Knees buckling, a small grunt of air leaving his mouth as the pain in his groin caught him off guard and made his eyes water.

She punched out again and pulled her knees up with as much force as she could muster. Her breath coming strong and ragged. He leaned down close onto her to protect and gather himself. She continued to punch out and kick and squirm.

And then he did it.

A blinding blow to the side of her head from a fist she didn't see coming.

'Stop fighting,' he grunted.

His weight was on her.

He raised himself up above her, pushing his elbow into her shoulder. 'Stop fighting,' he growled again.

'Never,' she breathed out.

He punched her hard again and her eyes fluttered in her head until they were still and she was silent.

He had to put his plan into action. He had to make it look like this was the Sheffield Strangler. If he killed her here and left the blood in the garage he risked being arrested, but once her body was found he would be exonerated. No one would expect him to kill and leave the blood in his own house. It would be easier to leave the blood than try to clear it up because everyone knew the CSU could find the smallest amount and he would never be able to clear up every single drop. Better to leave it all and claim someone is setting you up than try to hide it and be made to look like a liar at a later date. He'd never get out of that one.

She'd made this easier the minute she'd come home and told him the team thought they had connected with the Sheffield Strangler on the app. The killer took it slow on the app, really got to know the women and reeled them in. Gave him time for this plan to percolate in his head. Not that he thought it would ever come to fruition, but if he needed it then it was there.

He dragged her to the garage looking at her face as he did so, regret fleetingly passing through him. He'd loved her once. She was his wife. He'd left his first wife for her. But it seemed that he was not meant for a life with only one woman. Now she had figured it out she said she would take him for everything. She already knew which divorce lawyer she would speak with. He would be left with nothing by the time she was finished with him, she'd said, and he couldn't allow that to happen. Not after he'd worked all these years and been put through one divorce already. A second one that was messy and brutal would destroy him. No, he would never let that happen.

She should have known better and walked away quietly.

In the garage he copied the slash mark he'd seen so many other times over the past six months. Her eyes flew open and her arms punched out as he made the initial incision, but he'd expected it and he was swift. He didn't want her to suffer for all he wanted her gone. The life ebbed out of her as her heart pumped the life blood through her neck. Soon she was a lifeless corpse and he just had to bury her and copy the MO of the Sheffield Strangler, making sure she was in a place she'd be found easily enough. He didn't want to be on trial for her murder. The husband, after all, is always suspected at first.

He laid a sheet of plastic in the boot of his car and drove to the location he'd decided on, burying her in a shallow grave by the moonlight that shone from above.

Then he went home, cleared up the glass on the kitchen floor, looked in the garage at the blood and decided to leave it. He called Ruth's phone again as a worried husband would do and then he showered quickly, paying particular attention to his hands, fingernails and hair and then used Ruth's hairdryer so when the cops came round they didn't note damp hair and wonder why he'd had time to shower before calling the cops out on his missing wife.

It was time to call the police. Dominic took a deep breath. He was going to have to act the next period of his life like he'd never acted before. If he managed to get through it he would be free and clear to live the rest of his life the way he wanted to. He'd made a huge mistake marrying her. She should have remained a fling. The fact that he'd been distracted with Hayley the way he had, proved this to him.

The dial tone in his ear made his stomach twist. He wouldn't need to put on a show. He would be genuinely anxious.

The call was answered. He stumbled over his words, 'Hello . . . hi . . . I'm DS Dominic Harrison. I want to report my wife's not here, she's . . . I think she's missing. I mean, she hasn't come home.' Perspiration slipped down the side of his face and he wiped it away with the back of his hand. 'She's also a cop. She'd know better than to let me worry this way.'

'What is your wife's name, Sergeant?' There was tapping down the line as the call-taker input the details Dominic was passing him.

'She's Ruth Harrison. My wife is Ruth Harrison. Please help us. Please send someone round and get an investigation started.'

CHAPTER 56

Claudia

Three weeks after Ruth's memorial

Claudia knocked on Sharpe's closed door and waited to hear her call to enter. From inside there was the sound of hushed conversation. She hadn't expected that. She'd been called to Sharpe's office and thought it was a one-on-one talk but there was definitely someone else in there.

'Come.' Sharpe's voice was clipped and to the point.

Claudia entered the room and was surprised to see her father sitting in one of the chairs opposite Sharpe. He looked up at Claudia and appeared just as surprised to see her.

'Morning.' She gave a general greeting to the room.

'Claudia.' Her father welcomed her.

'Sit, sit.' Sharpe waved at the empty chair next to Dominic.

This was the first time Dominic had been in the police station, that Claudia was aware of, since Ruth's death. He'd told her he was returning to work today. It had been three weeks. He'd had extended leave due to the circumstances surrounding her death. No one blamed him. In fact they were surprised he was returning so soon.

Sharpe waved to the chair again, a tut forming on her lips.

Claudia sat next to her father and smiled at him, trying for encouraging, then turned to Sharpe who as always looked immaculate.

'You'll both be wondering why I've brought you here,' she said leaning back in her chair.

Claudia and Dominic looked from each other to Sharpe.

'It had crossed my mind,' admitted Claudia.

'First things first I wanted to update you both on the outcome of the Samuel Tyler arrest. I'm aware you were updated on the charging decision, that he's been charged with all murders—' she looked to Dominic — 'including Ruth's.'

Dominic inclined his head but stayed silent. Claudia wrapped her hands together to keep herself quiet.

'I wanted to let you know how the interviews had panned out,' Sharpe continued.

They both waited her out.

'While he forcefully denied Ruth's murder—' her voice was unusually quiet — 'there was enough evidence to charge him anyway. But he fully admitted the other murders. I'm under the impression he probably thinks sentencing will be worse if there is a cop involved.' She leaned forward in her chair. 'Believe me when I say the evidence is there. He will not get away with this.'

They knew this. Claudia didn't understand why they had been brought together for this meeting.

Sharpe took a beat and leaned back a little. 'Like I said, I wanted to let you know how the interviews went. What he said. Why he did what he did.'

This was interesting.

'You may have noticed his left hand was scarred. It was caused when his mother went out and left him alone in the house. He had an accident frying something in a pan. Bacon, I believe.'

Dominic nodded as though he was aware of this fact.

'His mother had left him to go on a date. Samuel never forgave her for the pain caused that evening. From what I can gather, burns are one of the most painful experiences you can go through. The pain was seared into his brain and he carried it with him. When his mother returned she smothered his face in kisses apologising for abandoning him and the lipstick she was wearing stuck to his face, which he saw when glanced his reflection in a mirror. That lipstick was, as you can now imagine, Velvet Berry by House of Maven. And that's why he selected older women with children, because they reflected his own mother who was of a similar age when she had him. She was a very neglectful mother who caused him much pain and the scarring from the accident with the hot oil, all his mother's fault in his eyes.'

'Where's his mother now?' asked Claudia.

'She was his first victim but she had no one to report her missing. He was her only family. He refuses to disclose where her body is.'

There was a loud tut from the chair at the side of her. She couldn't imagine how her father was feeling. The savagery this man had used, he'd terrified women across the city. All because he was hurt as a child. Though childhood pain, Claudia knew, was processed very differently to adult pain and suffering.

'You think it'll affect his sentencing?' she asked.

Sharpe looked up to the ceiling as though the answer was hiding up there, then back at Claudia. 'I don't know. I doubt it. He's still murdered a lot of women which he's going to have to pay for. He's certainly not going to get away with it if that's what you're asking. The trigger for him was working in Victim Support and seeing children harmed. It reminded him of his own childhood. He really was quite chatty once he got going.'

Dominic rose from his chair. 'Thank you for letting us—'

'Sit down a moment, DS Harrison.' Sharpe stopped him.

Dominic paused mid-rise then slowly sunk back into his chair watching Sharpe as he did so.

'That's not the only reason I brought you both in here. We've had a little time to think and assess the situation over the last few weeks while you've been off, Dominic, and we've decided that we're going to set up a new task force to focus on more complex crimes. For instance, ones like the Strangler case.'

At the mention of his media-allocated name a violent silence fell over the room. No one moved.

They waited.

'People have not been happy with how long it took to bring this guy in.'

Dominic bristled.

Sharpe folded her hands on the desk in front of her. 'Look, we're not apportioning blame here and even if we were, there's plenty to go around, let me assure you.' The way she said it Claudia got the impression Sharpe had been on the pointy end of a ticking-off herself.

Sharpe looked to Claudia. 'You're going to lead this task force, Claudia.'

There was a quick intake of air from Dominic.

Sharpe ignored it but turned to him. 'We also want you on the team, Dominic. You have a wealth of experience hunting a serial killer like Tyler. He connected with you for some reason.' She paused. 'I don't know how you're feeling about the job after everything that's happened. Maybe you want to step back and take a more sedate role? We'd fully understand that and be supportive of it.'

Dominic looked to Claudia, whose eyes were like saucers. She hadn't expected this. She hadn't expected the new task force, to be the DI leading it and she certainly hadn't expected to have her father as a DS on the team under her. Especially after everything he had gone through. What she did expect was for him to turn this down and for Sharpe to accept that decision.

Dominic cleared his throat. 'I can manage the position.'

'You know you'll be answering to Claudia?' Sharpe said.

He looked at Claudia. 'Of course. I'll do anything to be a part of this team.'

'Okay, good. I know it's unconventional. Having father and daughter working together this way, but there's nothing in the regulations that prevents it, so Connelly has signed off on it. I've already outlined why we want both of you on the team. And as well as yourselves, we'll be bringing people together from various incident room teams, particularly the Strangler team as they know that specific case inside out. But we're starting afresh. You two are going to work together and stop complex crimes in their tracks before they manage to take hold the way this last one did.'

Claudia smiled, accepting her new position. She was to lead her father, newly grieving, into complex crimes. She only hoped he was not a broken man after what he'd been through. Things were about to get serious and she needed to be able to trust him.

THE END

ACKNOWLEDGEMENTS

It is my name is on this book cover, but many people have provided their precious time, expertise and enthusiasm to bring *Blood Stained* to life and I couldn't have done this without them.

Huge thanks to my editor, Emma Grundy Haigh, for her encouragement, enthusiasm and insight throughout the editorial process. Thanks also to Laurel Sills for editorial input and Anna Harrisson for doing such a great job with the copyedit; Annie Rose for marketing and Jill Burkinshaw for the blog tour; and to all at Joffe Books for such a seamless process, getting this story from rough draft to polished and published book.

I couldn't have done this without my amazing agent, Hannah Weatherill; so many, many thanks to her. With calm and determination, she brought this book to life. I am thankful for both her editorial vision before submitting to publishers, and in keeping me calm when stress crept in. I am extremely lucky to have her by my side. Thanks also go to Sophie Burdge, marketing assistant, and the rest of the fabulous team at Northbank Talent Management for the support and tireless work they do.

I have to thank Clare Mackintosh for giving me the push to write this story when she confirmed my own recollections on police policy — that there are no specific rules in place to stop you interviewing your own family. Even if it is slightly unusual. The police do not follow the same rules as doctors, which is where some confusion might come from.

Thanks to Graham Bartlett, my police advisor, for answering my questions. Time away from the job has made my memory a little hazy on some subjects.

Thanks to subscribers of my Facebook page, Rebecca Bradley Crime, for helping me create the make and colour of the lipstick used by the Sheffield Strangler. They really were an inventive bunch when I needed them.

To the crime-writing friends (who know who they are) who have kept me sane and on an even keel when book-writing wobbles hit. Because trust me, book-writing wobbles is a real thing.

To Jane Isaac for chocolate when it was needed most. I can't wait for lockdown to end!

Thanks to all the early readers who provided quotes and enthusiasm for the book prior to publication. To all the book bloggers who took time and energy to support *Blood Stained*. And to you, the reader of this book, who has taken a punt on a new series, thank you.

And, finally, thanks have to go to my family, for their never-ending support. I love you dearly.

Thank you for reading this book.

If you enjoyed it please leave feedback on Amazon or Goodreads, and if there is anything we missed or you have a question about, then please get in touch. We appreciate you choosing our book.

Founded in 2014 in Shoreditch, London, we at Joffe Books pride ourselves on our history of innovative publishing. We were thrilled to be shortlisted for Independent Publisher of the Year at the British Book Awards.

www.joffebooks.com

We're very grateful to eagle-eyed readers who take the time to contact us. Please send any errors you find to corrections@joffebooks.com. We'll get them fixed ASAP.

Made in the USA
Las Vegas, NV
07 April 2021